GOING
to the
WATER

Ann Hite

FIREFLY
SOUTHERN FICTION
Imprint of Iron Stream Media

Firefly Southern Fiction is an imprint of LPCBooks
a division of Iron Stream Media
100 Missionary Ridge, Birmingham, AL 35242
ShopLPC.com

Cover design by Elaina Lee

Library of Congress Control Number: 2021942986

ISBN-13: 978-1-64526-287-9
Ebook ISBN: 978-1-64526-288-6

Praise for *Going to The Water*

Ann Hite knows how to wrangle a heart and heal it again. Her beautiful words transport us across time and space, once again proving her worth as a storyteller. Readers will enjoy this complex tale that examines both the darkness and the light. And in the end, they'll want to fight the good fight.

~ **Julie Cantrell**
New York Times and USA TODAY bestselling author of *Perennials*

Ann Hite's masterful storytelling is on full display in this vivid whirlwind of a read. She had me in the palm of her hand through all the twists and turns. Compelling and atmospheric.

~ **Lynn Cullen**
Bestselling author of *Mrs. Poe* and *The Sisters of Summit Avenue*

A vivid, captivating novel that unfolds with intrigue and nuance, *Going to the Water* has all the elements you'd hope for in a multi-layered, Southern-set story: complicated family ties, misunderstanding and secrets, a mysterious past that haunts, spunky characters with pitch-perfect vernacular and their own agendas, and a pithy, unpredictable plot in a lush setting that delightfully exemplifies the South as place.

~ **Claire Fullerton**
Multiple award-winning author of *Mourning Dove* and *Little Tea*

ACKNOWLEDGMENTS

I must thank my husband and daughter, Jack and Ella Hite, who lived in the same house with me while I wrote and rewrote *Going to the Water*.

Without my awesome editor, Eva Marie Everson, this novel would not exist in this form. Her artful attention to detail helped me see where the story needed to grow.

Thank you to Karen Lynn Nolan for making me aware of Firefly Southern Fiction. The experience with this publisher has been as awesome as she suggested.

To my Fiction Writing Master Class for encouraging me to step out of my comfort zone of writing historical fiction. Teachers do learn from their students.

To my daughters and stepson and grandkids, who all grew six years older through this process. It is hard to have a writer in the family sometimes.

A personal nod to a friend from way back in junior high, my own personal Dar. She's had a rough road to travel of late, but one wouldn't know it by talking with her. Reading is in her blood.

And most of all I want to say a hearty thanks to my readers who have stuck with me through every book I've published. I wouldn't be in this business without you.

Ann Hite

DEDICATION

To those of us who believe rivers are God's gift
to heal and nurture this awesome earth,
and the souls that wander its lands.

CHAPTER 1

Isla

The night I began to live my own ghost story—only I had no idea I had stepped into the Neverland between reality and fantasy, the scary place of oily smoke and found treasure, family legend and factual history—I sat in the large pristine house, planning the herb garden I would put in the next week. I never thought I would face my worst fear and break a promise I had kept for seventeen years.

Mama always said our lives were ghost stories, metaphors to hide the truth behind. I was nearly thirty-two—well that's a lie; I was almost thirty-six—when I finally came to understand what Mama meant. That she wasn't talking about real ghosts at all, even though we had our share of those. Mama meant something much deeper, less tangible, more spiritual. I think she was talking about our souls. The essence that makes us who we are, the spark of life, the real truth.

In a matter of five minutes a woman's whole world can spin on its axis and begin rotating in a different direction. It was nine o'clock on an unseasonably hot Friday night in late April when the phone rang and caused me to jump and drop my cup of Russian tea, breaking my favorite mug.

"Shoot."

The number on caller ID wasn't familiar. Scott was out drinking like he did most nights. We had a deal: I pretended not to notice his faults, drinking being one of them, and he pretended I didn't exist on most days, allowing me to do whatever I felt like with his money. Yes, I was that shallow. Settling for a life that helped me fit in and turned me into this new person. Leaving my family legacy behind. The arrangement was very satisfactory.

There was no telling what Scott had gotten himself into. Probably jail or some disgruntled husband had murdered him. "Hello." The brown liquid spread across the white tile floor in the sunroom, and I hurried to the kitchen for a towel.

"Izzie, is that you?" A recognition of the man's voice slid through my memory, but no one called me Izzie anymore, except Scott.

"This is Isla Weehunt."

A pause, then a breath, as if the man was put out with my answer. A siren wailed to a stop on his end of the line, causing me to pull the phone from my ear.

"Izzie, are you there?"

"Yes."

"This is Stuart Collins from Nantahala. We went to school together. I'm the fire chief and arson investigator here now. You do remember your hometown?"

I stood in the kitchen with a dish towel in my hand. Well, sissy, little Stuart had grown up and got a mouth on him. "There's no need to take that tone. I go by Isla, have for most of my adult life."

It had been exactly seventeen years since I had been in Nantahala. A woman doesn't forget the day she decides never to go home again. The tea edged its way to the pure white baseboards. Lord, cleaning up white tile would take forever. The stuff would stick to the bottom of my shoes, no matter how many times I cleaned the spot. "What is this call about?" I sounded testy, but who cared. I threw the towel on the floor to soak up the tea.

"We have a problem here."

"We? What do you mean?" This had to be about my family. I loved Mama. That deep-down kind of love that's not a bit healthy for any of the parties involved. I couldn't shake her no matter how I tried to convince myself of her faults; even sixty miles didn't make a difference. I also hated her. The two feelings were downright confusing at times. Hate and love went together even if I didn't want to admit they did. I clung to the hate. See, the monster part of Mama was much easier to deal with than compassion and fragile vulnerability. And after all I had been through with her, choosing to hate came natural.

"Your mama's house ..." Stuart grew quiet for a minute.

My promise to stay away from Nantahala had held fast, even when Mama had to be placed in assisted living a few years before because she tried to shoot the tax assessor as he walked her property, taking photos. That's when the law decided they couldn't look the other way any longer. Mama had done many odd things in her life, but the county finally sat up and took notice.

When Stuart spoke again, it was with a softer tone. "Velvet is dead." His words sat in the air like a fragile bubble ready to pop and disappear.

As a kid, I would submerge my whole body under the hot water in our cast-iron, claw-foot tub. The world would turn into a muffled roar. At the moment Stuart spoke, the same sound began at the base of my skull and worked its way over the top of my head. I had to get off the phone.

"Izzie? Izzie, are you still there?"

Hanging up would be as simple as pushing the button on the portable phone. "How?" I whispered.

"The house is still burning, but I'm pretty sure Velvet is in there. Her car, what's left of it, is parked right out front. She has to be in there."

Silence. Long strung-out silence. The fallout of the nuclear bomb that had waited far too long to detonate. Mama—when she was younger—said a woman on the run ought to keep a lookout over her shoulder. She also said a girl shouldn't get so big for her pants that she outgrew her history. But some ancestral memories deserved to be abandoned. My running had been so intense my breath caught in my ribs as a permanent sharp pain on most days. The Leech legacy was left in the dust. And there were losses. Lots of them. To leave for good, I had to drown my dreams in the Nantahala River that snaked through the gorge. This meant, especially, my writing. Lord only knew what would go on paper if I started. Talk about World War III. I had been a good writer back then. Real good. Mama said—always with a sharp edge to her words—I got my talent from Iris Harris, my grandmother, a famous writer when women of means were nothing but a shiny trinket on their husbands' pocket-watch chains.

"I'm sorry I told you like that." Stuart took a breath.

If I remembered correctly, he had been a real pain in the butt, following me around school like I would ever pay attention to him. And hadn't he begun hanging around Velvet while I was at college? She was four years younger. Of course, guys of all ages flocked around Velvet. Always had. It was her pitfall, attracting attention from the wrong men.

"I'm not good at this stuff, Izzie. Being kind, breaking news. I need a next of kin out here."

"What about the boy? Was he in the house too?" The words were pieces of bitter chocolate in my mouth.

"The boy, your nephew, is a minor. I'm not sure if he's in there or not. There is no way to tell until I can get closer. Policy says I need an adult. You're the only reliable next of kin. I know Velvet and you weren't close."

A hard laugh bubbled out of my chest like the burning fizz in a can of soda. "I would say you got that right, Stuart. You got that one fact dead right. I haven't spoken to my sister since I left Nantahala."

"Izzie, will you come?" Stuart asked with the patience of Job.

The word no swirled through my fast-moving thoughts. No. No. No. I can't go back to that place. The girl I had been died long ago. No.

"Yes, but against my better judgment. I'll see you as soon as I can." And there it was, a betrayal against myself.

The smell of rosemary caught in the wind and wrapped around me as I climbed into my SUV. Rosemary, an herb, represented memories. And the Lord only knew all the memories banging around in my head. The last time I saw Velvet was in Nantahala, and the boy, my nephew, had been born on the living room floor of Mama's small five-room house. I was there to tell Mama I was marrying Scott, that I was leaving the gorge for good. Mama was all set to talk me out of becoming part of the Weehunts. This baffled me because the Weehunts were from old money from Georgia.

"I have to tell you a story, and you will not want to marry Scott Weehunt when you hear it. You will wait for better."

But I never got the chance to hear her elaborate tale because Velvet busted through the door, screaming like she was dying. She had hidden her condition for the whole nine months. Her water broke before emergency could even be called. I got caught up in the drama of childbirth, and before I knew what had happened a baby boy was in my hands. He was quiet and limp. My heart pounded so loud I was sure Mama could hear it.

"Do something, Izzie," Mama had cried.

I slapped the baby on the bottom like I'd seen on some television show. A loud cry came from his little lungs as he breathed in air. His fists balled, ready for a fight, as if he knew what life held for him. Velvet had given Mama a boy, the only grandchild she would ever know. Not that I didn't want children, but life ended up throwing me a sideways curve. I couldn't have children with Scott. This was probably a good thing, seeing the road he walked down. Mama cut the cord with her sewing scissors, tied it off with thread, and cradled the boy close to her, singing to him. No reason to tell me a story. No need to care whether I stayed or left. A crack had formed inside my heart. Because deep down I knew the story she wanted to pass to me. I knew she had been telling it to me for a while. I decided right there, with my hands covered in blood and birthing fluids, I had to save my life and walk away, never looking back. That minute. There was no time to wait for some big wedding. I calmly washed my hands in the kitchen sink and slid out the door without anyone noticing or caring.

CHAPTER 2

An hour after leaving Mountain City, I turned into the gravel and dirt (mostly dirt) drive of my childhood home. The ruts had remained deep, and out of instinct, I kept to the far right so as not to get stuck, trees scrubbing my paint job. I stopped the SUV and stared at the smoking ground where the house had been. Only one skeleton wall stood. Hoses snaked and twisted along the ground from the fire trucks. I opened the driver's side door and entered the chaos. The thick smell of burned wood filled the air. Red and blue lights bounced off titanic puddles. My whole body tensed.

"Izzie." The man stood close to the smoking rubble. "Over here. That didn't take as long as I thought. My God, you look the same." Stuart still had his long, lanky legs, but now sported a receding hairline. He was now a man instead of a boy.

My focus on Mama's property was sideways, off kilter, reminding me of the time I went to the fun house with slanting floors at the county fair. Scott had laughed at me because I had such a hard time walking straight.

Firefighters and police officers stood around the burn site. The silhouette of the small mountain, Grassy Bald, showed off and on as the lights flashed.

"I'm sorry." Stuart closed his fingers over my arm. Heat seared my already sweaty skin. "Velvet didn't go to work like she was supposed to. She normally worked the second shift at the casino." He looked at me. "Her boss, Rudy, came out to check on her because she hadn't shown up, and her phone went straight to voice mail, so he was worried. He found the house engulfed. The neighbors up the road called it in. They saw the flames above the treetops." Stuart released my arm and looked away. "I think the fire was set on purpose, Izzie." He ran his fingers through his blond hair. "I'll have to investigate tomorrow. This is only the beginning."

"That doesn't surprise me." A mean laugh moved through the words. "My sister has always been over the top. I would think you'd remembered that. She never did anything small. Of course it is arson."

"What happened between Velvet and you?"

A tremor shook my insides, but my hand remained steady. "I think that's a bit personal, and frankly none of your business. I'm sure you heard the talk back then. But the truth is I left the gorge to save my own life." I looked at him. "Have you ever had to save your own life?"

He gave me a strange look and paused a minute longer than was comfortable. "I shouldn't have butted in where I didn't belong, but yes, I know all about saving myself."

"There's nothing to tell, Stuart, that the world outside of Nantahala would acknowledge as important. I left here. It's that simple. I began a new life." The glowing embers put off smothering heat that wrapped around us. "Velvet and I didn't even talk when I arranged for Mama to go into assisted living." Judgment thick and dark hung in the air, threatening to choke me. Folks in the gorge looked after their old people. They most certainly didn't haul them off to homes. "How will you find Velvet's body? What if the boy is in there? Maybe they are both out with friends. If I remember correctly, my sister was a very sociable girl." Before I could catch it, a silent prayer that Velvet still lived pushed into the air.

"Oh, she'll be there, and I will find plenty of evidence. The fire was hot, but it takes a lot to destroy a human body completely. Velvet had no friends that I know of and her son, that's another story, not so different from his mom's." He measured me with his stare. "I insert my foot in my mouth all the time. That hasn't changed since school. This is my job. I don't think beyond the facts. Can't. It would eat me alive." He looked away. "I'm guessing your nephew is down at the fishing camp. That boy loves the river. But I'm not sure why he hasn't come up here to see what is going on. I hope he wasn't already in the house tonight." He gave me a funny expression. "Do you even know his name?"

Shame squeezed my heart. Maybe I regretted one thing, just one thing, about my leaving. I didn't want the boy hurt or dead. "Daddy's old fishing camp is still standing?" The last time I saw the place it had been crumbling into the river.

He accepted the change of subject. "Actually, it's your nephew who is renovating the old place. He spends all his spare time there." Stuart frowned and lines formed around his mouth. There was something solid about the man he had become. He shrugged. "It's a small place. I fish on the river and have seen him breaking a sweat. He reminds me of a much younger you. Always working on some project that set you apart from the other kids." This time, his eyes found mine. "We both worked at surviving this place."

"But you stayed, Stuart. You didn't have to live here."

"My family has been here forever. It's home for better or worse. Do you still garden?"

My childhood wall had been covered with 4-H ribbons won for my herbs and flowers. The large garden in the side yard of Grassy Bald, my grandmother's old place, had been my solace, my quiet place. "Yes. I do."

"Good. You were the envy of all the girls. Most were so jealous they hated you. Did you do anything with your writing? You were the best on the school paper. Didn't you go to college for something you wrote?"

Again, I sidestepped his question. "What will happen to my nephew?"

"First we have to make sure he wasn't in the house. But you're his only family, Izzie."

A fair amount of smoke shrouded us. Coming back to the gorge was a reckless knee-jerk reaction to the news of Velvet's death. It wasn't like the two of us loved each other. Some feelings couldn't be altered. If I allowed the door to my emotions to swing open, I would lose the ground I gained by leaving this place. No attachments and no telling my real feelings were my mottos.

"Will you take him?"

"No." The red and blue lights flashed. Water still rushed over the hot remains. The skeleton wall stood, as if refusing to give up. But the crumbling of my family had been occurring for years, a slow eroding of the souls that began their lives within the walls. The gravestones faded in and out of view.

"He'll go into foster care until he ages out next year. That's no place for any half-grown young man, but especially him. He'll end up in a group home. The other boys will have him for dinner."

A knife twisted in my brain. "No."

"Don't decide now. He's smart. He needs someone, has since your mama went downhill."

I never stopped to ask why Stuart knew so much about this boy, about Velvet. Instead, my mouth went dry. "I can't. I'm not the person."

Stuart shook his head, clearly disappointed. "You're his chance. You said yourself you needed a chance when you were his age."

"This is not about me. It can't be. You don't know anything about the situation."

"This is about you. He's your blood family. He needs a get-out-of-jail-free card. Take him away from here. He didn't choose what the adults around him decided to do. There he is."

The red light from the fire truck illuminated a tall, slender figure emerging from the edge of the woods.

Stuart took a sudden step away from me and cupped his hands around his mouth. "Randal," he shouted.

The boy, man really, moved toward us.

A wave of sorrow swept over me. My knees shook, and I thought I was going down. Some emotion outside of me, yearning, twisting, took over, owned my movements. I pulled my feet from the designer heels—mired in mud—and ran across the yard as if I were sixteen again and sticks and rocks wouldn't hurt my now sissy, tender feet. I gripped the boy's wrist, the touch searing my skin. My head spun. My fingers went numb. The fuzzy, buzzy feeling of an electric shock ran through my hand and into my arm. I couldn't let go.

"What are you doing, lady?" He pulled hard against my hold. "My mom's in there."

"She's dead." My horrible numbing tone delivered the worst news he would ever hear. A frantic scream worked in my chest as I looked at him. God, it was like I had known him forever, lost him, and found him again.

"Let me go." But he no longer struggled. "Velvet," he yelled.

I kept my hold on him. The boy I touched when he was born, held against me for only a minute. I wasn't myself, or maybe I was more myself than I could ever be again. Maybe my life was about that very minute. The lights from one of the police cars hit the boy's face. There she was, Velvet. Her nose, her angry expression chiseled into his features. My sister I left behind and hated. My sister in a tall, lanky male figure, looking like a panther about to pounce.

"She's not dead. She was taking us away from this place. We fought about it this morning." He turned his face toward the house. "*Velvet.*"

"Randal, we'll figure this out, buddy. We'll get the whole mess sorted." Stuart's kind voice startled me.

Still, I held on to the boy. Like he mattered. Somewhere an owl called and further away his companion answered; they spoke back and forth over the rush of noises. The forest listened to us humans making a muck of our lives.

"This is your aunt," Stuart spoke again.

My bones ached. I wanted to pull this boy to me, whisper to him that he was my only regret. I had worked so hard in Mountain City to become someone who was noticed, appreciated for her class. A person who could hold her head high. All that could come tumbling down by taking some teenage boy home with me. But if word got out that I turned my back on family, my better life would go down the toilet faster. Hadn't I spent the last seventeen years looking over my shoulder, waiting to be caught in a skin that wasn't mine?

The boy turned a wild look on me. "I don't have an aunt. Velvet was an only child."

And there we stood with the lie as our close companion, one more thing we had in common besides blood. Velvet and Mama had written me right out of their lives with no problem just like I did them. We finally agreed on something. The boy's teeth began to chatter like he had a horrible fever. The vibration moved through my arm.

"Go get in my car. The white SUV over there. You don't have another choice. Neither of us does."

Randal looked at my fingers. "Why haven't you come around if you're my aunt? Granny got put in the home. Where were you?"

Still Velvet hadn't outed me. "I have my reasons for not being here."

He stared out into the black night. "I guess Velvet ticked you off like she's done most people."

"My leaving is complex. Velvet was my younger sister by four years." And in that moment, I knew my exit would have happened no matter what Velvet did or did not do. It was something larger. The reasons were so much bigger than the lying and disloyalty that took place between my sister and me. My actions were tangled and knotted with beliefs and judgments. Memories moved through me, fluid, a raging current. No one memory but instead, a group, screaming, accusing. The easiest thing to do was to walk away and never speak to the boy again. Randal. Randal Leech.

"Go get into your aunt's car. I need to talk to her for a minute." Stuart touched my fingers, and I released my hold, a trigger on a gun.

Randal shouldered a tattered backpack, stared one more time at the place where he was born, and walked to the SUV.

"Don't say a word, Stuart, or I'll change my mind. I might anyway."

"You don't fool me for a minute. You've always done what you wanted, when you wanted. No one bosses you. You're doing this because you want to do it."

Heat moved through my hand. "Why do you think you know me that well? School is a whole world, universe, from here, this minute."

"I know you even if I haven't seen you in years."

"Velvet is a stranger to me. She was a stupid kid when I left. I can't help you find who killed her, if anyone did. And why would they?"

Stuart shoved his hands in his pockets. "This property is your mama's and now, like it or not, you're in charge. Rumor has it that developers were talking to Velvet. Especially about your grandmother's place."

"Grassy Bald is tied up in a will until Mama dies. That makes selling it impossible. She'll probably outlive all of us." I bit the inside of my lip, a nasty nervous habit of mine.

A jeep pulled in. Out stepped a young woman. Something about her irritated me to death.

Stuart smiled. "I was beginning to wonder if she would show up." He nodded. "You remember Emily Greene?"

That was all I needed. "I thought you left here?"

"I missed you too, Isla." Emily was the one person in school who called me by my full name. "I did leave for a while, but I'm back. I have an art gallery and a loft apartment above it. I work part time for the Nantahala News. That's why I'm here tonight."

I stood in my dirty white two-hundred-dollar slacks, without shoes, and Emily was gorgeous in a t-shirt and jeans, looking like she was twenty-five. "I have to go. It's a long drive. Stuart, you have my landline number. And we do have to talk about how you got it. Keep me updated. I need to know when to make burial arrangements." I sounded like a cold-hearted soul.

"I'll be sifting through the debris at daybreak."

The cold finger of realization ran through me.

A woman stood just inside the headlights of the fire trucks. She wore a red party dress from her junior year of high school. Velvet. She stood close to one of the firefighters, but he didn't see her. Only I saw her.

My sister had come to welcome me home.

CHAPTER 3

Randal

Two weeks before the fire—the day was calm and still—there came a popping, a rash of what sounded like gunfire. Randal ran to his bedroom window just in time to see the tree nearest his room come crashing down, barely missing the corner of the house, shaking the earth as if it might crack open and swallow him. Had it hit his room he could have died. The next morning, right before school, a chickadee came to the kitchen window screen, holding on with its claws for dear life, looking in at him as he buttered toast. He pushed at the bird's grip to make it go away, but it wouldn't move. Nothing was normal about a chickadee wanting inside. Later, when he opened the door to leave for the bus, the bird darted into the house and flew straight to Velvet's room. He grabbed the broom and tried to shoo the chickadee back to the open door. The tiny thing would have no part of his plan. Instead, it circled around, bumping into the ceiling and walls. "Come on, bird, I have to go to the bus."

He tried closing the door to the bedroom and removed the screen from the open window. The spruce trees moved in the breeze, giving off a ghostly whistle, and the air smelled of freshly turned fields. Again, he gently tried to guide the chickadee out with the broom. Nothing worked. When the bus driver blew the horn, Randal thought of leaving, just giving up, but what if the bird died from flying into the wall? He let the bus pull away.

After a good forty-five minutes, Randal gave up and sat on Velvet's bed. "Go ahead. Do what you want, stupid bird. You're a real pain in the butt." And the chickadee flew over to the window, perched there for a second, and then took off, flying to the cemetery at the edge of the spruce trees, landing on the tall, slender headstone of his grandfather, Kenneth Leech. The bird watched him for a second and then flew toward the river.

That afternoon when Randal visited Granny in assisted living, he told her about the chickadee.

She turned a fragile expression on him. "Oh, that means somebody's going to die."

"Why would you say that?" Randal should have kept his mouth closed.

"Don't you know what it means when a bird comes in the house? A death is on the way." Her voice was a high pitch.

He couldn't help but long for the woman who taught him how to read at four, even if she had always been a little odd, plunging into a dark sadness. She called them her black moods. Randal had been twelve when Granny began to see the world through her own filter, events that manifested only in her mind. That was how advanced Alzheimer's worked. "Don't worry, Granny. No one is going to die."

"You're one dumb boy if you believe that, son."

She twisted the hem of her dress in her fingers.

CHAPTER 4

Randal Dar Leech harbored a deep-seated rage, a roiling mess of emotions, that had festered since he was a child of twelve and began to understand he wasn't anything like most of the boys his age. He was a freak, weird, a complete sissy. These feelings of his ate at him over the years, and by the time he was seventeen could have driven him to do a lot of things, even set a fire, if he let his worst side flap like a flag on the Fourth of July. His middle name, Dar—after his grandmother, Darlene Vivian Leech—alone had been enough to mark his fate, write his history in stone. But surely he didn't, or wouldn't, destroy the little house where Velvet lived her whole life. Shoot, she was the only person in the gorge who accepted him for the man he was turning out to be. No judgment. She taught him to believe people were good at heart. She always had his back. Yes, she was a cynic and irresponsible in more ways than he could count, but Velvet was soft, and she loved Granny deeply. Always had. Living with the two of them had been like living with children most of the time. He was the balance but also the adult, no matter his age.

And thanks to whatever Velvet did to get herself burned up, he had landed in the hands of Isla Weehunt, his aunt, proving his mother and Granny to be liars. All through his childhood, he believed Velvet was an only child, like him. And maybe if Granny had the presence of mind, she would have finally told him the whole story, how his aunt came to run out on her family.

Aunt Isla brought Randal and what little he owned—amounting to a backpack of hair magazines and a blue tin full of letters that stayed with him all the time—to her house.

"I'd rather no one knew you were my nephew. I haven't told

anyone in town about my family in Nantahala. It'll just be much easier if we keep our relationship quiet, don't you think? People in these parts hold onto stories, twisting and turning them. A person can't outrun some stupid gossip that probably wasn't even true anyway." She didn't bother to look Randal in the face. The humid night air flowed through the open windows of the fully loaded SUV: surround sound, two DVD players in the back, foldout food trays, key fob. He bet she even had Bluetooth and heated seats. How many kids did this lady have?

"You can help in the chicken houses, removing the dead ones and catching the live ones when they're picked up. It's a nasty job, but Scott will pay you. You'll have to change to a new high school. Education has to be the most important thing. You may not want to amount to anything, but I've worked hard to escape the gorge and its mentality. I will not have the life I've built be jeopardized. Do we understand each other?"

"What about Granny?" He didn't give a dern about the gorge, but Granny could not be left alone to die. "I can't just leave her in assisted living home alone. She is used to me visiting at least three times a week."

Aunt Isla was quiet for a moment.

"I can't leave her."

"I'm not sure what we'll do. Maybe we could move her closer."

"No." Deep in his gut he knew Granny couldn't leave what was now her home. She would die. "She needs everything to be the same. If you take her from the river she will die."

"We can't run over to Nantahala all the time, and besides, the mother I know hated the water."

He ignored the comment about the river, knowing that part was true, but still, he felt sure Granny was connected to the place, even the water. To move her would be deadly. To leave her behind would bring the same conclusion. "She needs me to visit like usual. Everything has to stay the same. I'll find a way."

"Does she even know who you are?" Aunt Isla kept her gaze on the dark road ahead.

"That doesn't matter. Alzheimer's patients need a routine. The nurses at the home told me this when I first began to visit."

"Listen," she interrupted, "I'll have to give it some thought." She slowed the SUV. "How can a person hate and love a place at the same time?" She looked out the window. "Do you hear the frogs? They are singing tonight. This is the perfect place to hear the river."

He rode through the foggy moonlight, sprinkled here and there on the dark highway, into some new life he'd never wanted. What would happen when this woman decided he was too much trouble?

CHAPTER 5

Aunt Isla's house looked like something from *Gone With The Wind,* complete with four white columns and a wide two-story front porch. Wooden rockers moved in the wind that kicked up as she whipped the SUV into the drive. Spotlights lit the house and yard. Around in the back was a four-car garage. Yep, she had made a good life outside of Nantahala, especially the gorge. He counted ten long chicken houses—the lights casting narrow shadows through the field. Chickens. God help him.

"Here we are." She parked near the back door and gave Randal a long look. "The new chickens will arrive any day now. That's a big deal here. Come on." She nodded to a single French door. Her heels made a clicking sound as she walked up the steps, leaving small clots of mud behind. "I like my home clean. *Clean.* We'll go over the rules tomorrow. We've both had enough for one night. I have a guest room upstairs that can be yours." The door swung open with the turn of the key. A floral scent hung in the air. The gleaming modern kitchen sparkled in the overhead track lighting. The whole thing seemed surreal. He should have been home in his bed. Velvet coming in after her second shift, tossing the car keys on the table with a clink.

Aunt Isla slid off her shoes and pointed to a closed door off the eating area. "There's a little TV in there with a sofa, chair, and a good reading light. That can be your very own place to keep occupied when you're not working. And you can study there. You have to finish school. It would be really good if you got some kind of scholarship to a big college. You know? It would show the junior league ladies and the church how much I've influenced you. What are your grades? Do you think you can manage this by the end of your senior year? That's next year, right?"

Not one single word came to Randal. Of course his grades were good, but who was she to ask? And what did she know? He had to begin the scholarship and college hunt by the beginning of next semester. This woman was a nut.

Aunt Isla waved her hand in the air. "We'll get the plans nailed down as we go. I'm moving too fast, but you can never be too prepared." She began to climb the stairs. "Remember not to bother Scott. That's my husband." She stopped and looked off into space a few seconds. "I guess you have to call him your uncle, but just not in front of anyone else. He's very busy. I'll show you the room. Do you happen to have any clothes in that backpack you're hugging so close?"

"No," Randal answered.

Aunt Isla's shoulders slumped. "I suppose not. Why would you? We have our work cut out for us."

Randal stared at her back as they stepped into the upstairs hall. "Yes, I guess we do." Sarcasm laced the tone of his voice.

She turned to face him. "It's 'yes, ma'am.' You haven't learned one manner from that sister of mine. You're not going to be living in a five-room house now, sweetie." Her voice was syrup dripping off of pancakes. "So shape up."

Oh yes, he understood this woman all too well. She was more worried about how she looked to all her fancy friends than losing her sister to a fire. "Why in the world would I call you ma'am? I didn't even know you existed before tonight. What is there to respect right now?"

She threw open the door to the room. The bed comforter, skirt ruffle, pillows, walls, and even the curtains were covered with gargantuan and small yellow, pink, and twenty shades of red roses. *Roses.* He thought he might throw up.

"This is my rose garden room. I always wanted to grow roses, but I just don't have the knack."

A horrible laugh built in his gut, a hysterical, wild energy, a cackle that should have been tears and chest-rattling sobs. He swallowed it by thinking of Velvet and what she would have said about the whole situation.

"You can use the dresser and the closest when we get you something to wear." She wrinkled her nose. "There's a consignment shop not far from here. You do know what a consignment shop is?"

He didn't bother answering.

She clicked her tongue in a way that made him think of Velvet. "It's a secondhand clothes store."

"You mean like Goodwill?" A piece of a mean laugh escaped him.

Her cheeks turned pink. "No. I wouldn't be caught dead in a Goodwill. This store has designer brands, nicer clothes. You'll need a decent suit for church too."

"I won't be going to church," he said.

She took two steps closer to him. Heat radiated from her. "Young man, you can lose your haughty attitude. I understand you lost your mother tonight, but it gives you no right to be rude or disrespectful. Where will you go if I turn you out? Do you have friends who will take you in?" She frowned. "Just as I suspected. I do not want to hear you speak to me that way again." She reached out to touch the backpack.

He pulled it away out of pure instinct.

"What's in there? Nothing illegal, I hope." Her face was stern, older.

He unzipped the bag and dumped the contents of hair magazines and paperbacks on the bed. The tin was safe in a zipped pocket.

"What on earth is all this?" She studied him. "You will be going to church with me, no choice. And styling hair isn't going to make you a good living. I hope you know that. You have to make me look good by going to a real college."

This collection was his life, his hopes, his dreams. And she was tapdancing all over them.

Aunt Isla reached for one of the paperbacks, examining the torn, delicate cover. A shadow passed over her face, and for a moment her plastic mask of the proper woman fell. Her expression turned soft. "Your mother always took this book everywhere she went. Lord, she read it over and over. We'd walk to the river. Sometimes we'd take out the johnboat and paddle downstream." She had a faraway look. "Mama would throw a fit if she found out. Velvet was the bravest and strongest even though she was younger. When it was my turn to paddle, she would lean back and read this book as if she'd never read it before." She gave a faint smile. "I liked her then." She nodded at the cover. "Flannery O'Connor grew up in Savannah. Maybe I'll take you there. Velvet always wanted to go. I don't know if she ever went or not. She read everything the woman wrote. So did I. Velvet took her babysitting money and spent it on books."

Velvet buying books. Didn't sound like the mother he knew.

Aunt Isla tossed the book on the bed. "It's a keepsake of your mother. Don't lose it. Next weekend I have to pick up the new pastor for our church. It's so important I make a good impression and get the house spotless. You have to help me."

Randal didn't answer.

"I can't find a soul to come cook for me. Apparently, I'm difficult to work for."

He took a deep breath. "I'm a much better cook than a farmhand. Granny taught me everything I know."

Aunt Isla held up her hand. "No, I don't want to know those stories of Mama and you. They'll make me sad, and I'll feel guilty. The Bible says guilt is of the devil." A satisfied look washed over the woman's face. "You know Mama had issues her whole life?"

This woman was going to kill him with the crap that came out of her mouth.

"I'll see you for breakfast. Maybe we'll try out your skills. And who knows . . . maybe Scott will come home early." She stepped out the door but turned back to him. "We shouldn't mention the pastor coming. It will put Scott in a bad mood. Tomorrow we will go to buy clothes."

Lord, Aunt Isla was a true piece of work.

Randal met his uncle late Sunday evening. Aunt Isla's chicken pasta hung heavy in the air like poison. The counters were cluttered with pots, pans, dishes, as if twelve people had eaten. Randal worked at loading the dishwasher when Uncle Scott threw open the back door.

"Chickens coming tomorrow morning." His expression resembled a storm way off in the distance, working its way across the sky.

"Scott, we have someone living with us now." Aunt Isla nodded to Randal.

He looked Randal over. "The chickens will be here at five sharp in the morning." He opened the stainless steel refrigerator and grabbed a beer from a drawer.

"This is Velvet's son, Randal. You remember Velvet, don't you?" Her voice was sweet, syrupy, coy with an edge of meanness. Or was it hatred?

His uncle stared at Randal. A grin spread across his face and he swore.

Aunt Isla's smooth lips drew up like an old lady sucking on lemons. "Language."

Uncle Scott nudged her. "Geez, woman, lighten up before you have a stroke." His words had sharp edges. He stepped close to Randal. "Velvet's kid. Wow, I haven't seen your mama in a long time. Years."

"And you won't," his aunt continued. "She died Friday night. In a fire, Scott. She burned to death. Of course you were gone when I left for Nantahala. The gorge looks the same in case you were wondering."

"You went to the gorge?" Bewilderment flashed across his face for only a second before the guarded look returned.

She took a deep breath. "There is no need to tell everyone, especially your parents, that he is my nephew."

Uncle Scott threw his head back in a hard laugh. "Don't worry, son." He straightened and gave his full attention to Randal. "You don't want to claim us anyway. We have way too many problems. Don't take it personal. Your aunt and uncle make Velvet and Dar look like the most normal people in these mountains." He guzzled his beer. "I liked your mama." And his sarcastic expression changed to a small smile.

"Randal will help in the chicken houses tomorrow." Aunt Isla's tone pulled at the air like a too-taut guitar string about to snap.

This man who was supposed to be Randal's uncle lifted his eyebrows. "Really. Excuse me for saying you don't look much like an outside worker."

Heat flushed Randal's face. "I don't know a lot about chicken houses, but I can handle my own on the river. I'm redoing an old fishing camp there. And Granny had ten laying hens and one mean rooster. My job was to get around him to the eggs each morning. The rooster ended up dead. I was twelve."

Uncle Scott hooted. "You sound like your mama. Be in the kitchen at four thirty. We'll see what you're made of. Where are you sleeping?"

"He's in the rose garden room." Aunt Isla said stiffly.

"Oh God, that's enough to turn the boy sissified."

Randal tried not to flinch at the name, even though it had been hurled at him too many times in the past years.

One too many.

CHAPTER 6

A hot wind blew in the opened window. Where was he? His heart raced. He opened his mouth to call Velvet when he remembered she had died. Dead. Why wasn't he a big mess of emotions? Maybe her death didn't bother him. Maybe he had seen it coming for a while. The company she kept, her moodiness. The way she would disappear for days without him knowing where she was. Maybe he was fighting off a bitter anger directed toward her.

He sat up on the side of the bed. The rose garden room. God help. Now he was going to work in these stupid chicken houses, and he was stuck with a snooty aunt. How could Aunt Isla and Velvet have been sisters? A deep yearning for the fishing camp and the river caught him off guard. This was where his grief resided.

He pulled on the pair of jeans Aunt Isla had bought him. The tattered backpack was a lump on the floor. Maybe he should just grab it and slip out of the house, run. Maybe to New Orleans or New York, even Atlanta, where he could blend in and be part of a community. Get his cosmetology license. But he had to finish school. Velvet taught him this. She hadn't finished. After he was born, Granny wouldn't let her go back and finish her senior year. Instead she went to night classes and took her GED. She never felt good enough to go to college, to seek out a better life. The casino job was it. But he always wondered what would have happened if Velvet had been happy.

The most wonderful smell pushed from the kitchen. Coffee. Good coffee. He looked at the time and ran down the stairs.

"You interested?" Uncle Scott held up his Georgia Bulldog mug.

"Yes, sir." Randal took an empty mug and filled it.

"None of that sir stuff, son. That's your aunt's mess, not mine. I'm just a working man, a businessman. Chickens and a little side deal here and there." He held up a flask. "I don't suppose you care to have a tad in your coffee this morning?" He poured a splash into his.

Randal gave him a half smile. He couldn't help it. Here was this man admitting exactly who he was with no shame. There was something to be said about that kind of honesty. "No, thank you."

"You can't be Velvet's son in that respect. She loved a drink."

"Yes, she did."

His laugh was joyous and carefree. "It's not against the law to make moonshine in the state of Georgia."

"I know." When Uncle Scott looked at him, Randal explained. "Velvet had a boyfriend a long time ago who made shine on our property. I had to keep it a secret from Granny."

"Sounds like Velvet was still Velvet. It's against the law to sell the stuff. So, I can make all I want, but I can only give it away." He winked. "At least I don't grow weed. *That's* against the law. I've tried to rationalize with Izzie, but she won't have it. She sees me as a sinner through and through." He shrugged. "Hope you don't mind getting your hands dirty. It's a lot easier when they get here than when they leave."

Randal gave himself a mental shake. For a minute he had no idea what Uncle Scott was talking about. "I can handle whatever you throw my way," he bragged. "This is a good cup of coffee."

"I do make a mean pot. If you haven't figured out how bad of a cook your aunt is after that meal last night, I'll tell you not to ask her to do anything in the kitchen. It's all poison."

Randal laughed but he looked around to see if she heard.

A rumble began in the distance, growing louder, as if the earth might be rolling open. The glass in the windows rattled. "Trucks are here. Let's go." He slapped Randal on the back. For one strange minute, Randal thought he might just fit in with this man. He could only hope.

Uncle Scott climbed on a large four-wheeler. "Don't be afraid to hold on tight, boy." He pressed the gas and nearly threw Randal off the back. He wrapped his arms around his new uncle so he might survive the ride.

The long tin buildings were farther from the house than they had seemed the night before. He imagined on a hot day, a good wind would push the smell in any open windows and a soul would have to go into hiding. There wasn't nothing worse than the smell of chicken poop caught in the air. Each building had long fluorescent bulbs spaced at close intervals, allowing for plenty of light. The floors were covered in sawdust and that horrible smell was covered by a cleaning chemical, maybe bleach. Several men gathered at the first truck stacked with hard, plastic crates like the ones used to deliver sodas to a grocery store.

Uncle Scott hooked the four-wheeler up to a long flatbed trailer. "This is my nephew, Randal." He nodded at Randal. "You watch so you get what we're doing." Lively peeps filled the air. The crates were piled chest-high in rows on the platform of the trailer, leaving just enough room for two men to stand and walk around the edges. Uncle Scott began to creep the four-wheeler up the middle of the long hot building.

One of the men yelled, "Ready?"

The other guy, more a boy, answered. "One." He flung the chicks inside the top crate to his left and grabbed another crate. Yellow and white fluffy balls flew into the air as if they knew how to use their wings. They landed in clumps that remained still, stunned, for a minute before they scattered, peeping even louder.

In the next house Randal got the job of throwing the chicks. For a minute, he stood still with a crate handle hooked in his fingers. Small sharp cries filled his thoughts. The other guy gave him a look—the same expression boys at school gave him before they bullied him. "One," Randal yelled. He flung the chicks with his anger. The birds flew into the air much higher than he intended. One caught its leg in a sliver chain that hung from the ceiling. The chick's leg separated from its body and the tiny creature fell into the huddle of crying birds. Randal took another crate and flung it so hard it flew out of his hands, landing on the ground, where the chicks scurried to safety.

"Randal," Uncle Scott yelled. "A little less muscle, son."

Randal's heart raced in his chest. Velvet's face floated through his mind. She was alive and now she was dead. He killed a chicken. Who cared? They were just chickens being raised for slaughter. They would be in a store packaged for dinner before a few months passed. Farmers raised animals and poultry for food. There was nothing wrong with what was taking place. It was an honest living. He grabbed another crate and continued dumping chicks until there were no more left.

When the trucks had been unloaded, Uncle Scott patted him on the back. "You proved your point. Good job, Randal. Now go get cleaned up and don't walk in the house with those boots. Your aunt will have a hissy." He tossed Randal some keys. "Take the four-wheeler."

Chicks scurried around Randal's feet. Sweat rolled down his back. He thought of how he always wanted a father. How it might have made a difference in how he felt about himself. Maybe a father would have understood who he was as a man. But that was probably a dream. It had been his experience that adults were just as flawed, maybe more so, than kids. And putting any measure of trust in them was opening himself up to disappointing pain. He would keep his backpack close in case he needed to leave.

〜〜〜

"Randal, I need you to cook the new preacher's dinner next Saturday. Am I smart giving you the job?" Aunt Isla gave a little frown.

Uncle Scott stood in the door. "Lord, don't make the boy cook, Izzie. Let him be a man."

Aunt Isla gave her husband a hard look. "So, he's not a man if he cooks, Scott? What about all the best chefs? Are they not men? Just because you live in the Stone Age doesn't mean everyone else does. You grew up trying to prove you were a man by drinking and driving fast cars and making lots of shady choices. We see where that got you. Have you looked at your old buddies? They are settled with families, kids going off to college. They have real lives." Aunt Isla's voice cracked. "But not Scott Weehunt. No, he's still living in the past. He's still the bad boy, the outlaw." A hateful look transformed her face into an old woman's. "Scott is still the king of petty crime."

Uncle Scott shook his head and walked through the kitchen without saying another word.

"Make me a list of what you will need, Randal. Keep it simple." She wrinkled her nose. "This house is enough to put anyone off. I don't want to be flashy."

Randal could have told her she was known for Uncle Scott's name, his family's money, but he kept his mouth closed and went upstairs.

After a shower, Randal collapsed on his bed and pulled the blue tin out of his backpack. He had found the letters, written by Velvet, on the top shelf of the linen closet when he was twelve. The dates on the earliest were written shortly after he was born but there was no mention of him as a newborn, which led him to believe maybe Velvet had written them to his father—whoever he was—but never mailed them. He knew, even at twelve, he should return them to the shelf, but he didn't. Now, he chose the letter on top. August 18, 2003, only a few of months after his birth.

Dear Deeply Missed:

I really screwed up and forgiveness is a slippery slope I can't entertain. I think of you all the time, but you wouldn't believe that. The river is my heart tonight, but I'm too tired, sleep-deprived, to walk to the water's edge. I love the Nantahala better than I've ever loved anything or anyone. I'm truer to her. I can depend on her in ways that I can't with people. I have a lot of regrets, but my solace is knowing I could change. Always. Mama told me a story when I was young, how the Cherokee have a sacred belief called "going to the water." They believe moving water like a river is holy and purifies. They go to be healed and renewed. I'd rather spend the day easing through the water, the trees hanging over like a protective shelter, the birds chattering. When I see the wingspread of a blue heron, my breath catches in my chest, my heart slows, and my shoulders relax. The Nantahala River is alive, a person, a queen, but she hasn't cured me no matter how many times I dip myself. Maybe my soul is black. Mama says I am like her; that asking for forgiveness is futile at this point in my deeds. And I fear she is right. But what I would give for just one slice of peace. I miss you.

Randal chose one more letter. It was the last one she had written.

May 10, 2016

Deeply Missed:

Mama thought I was Grandmother Iris today. I tried to tell her Grandmother died when the tornado came through before I was even born. She threw her mug of coffee at me and called me a liar. Something is bad wrong with her mind. If I could walk away from this place, I would, but I love her too much. She needs me. I met someone a year ago. He is different. I wanted you to know that this man loves me. I know it. We are together a lot and one day maybe soon we will be together forever. But forever is an awful long time. I'm faithful, no more sleeping around, and so is he. Can you imagine me being faithful? I know you can't. This will be the last letter I write. I can't do this to myself anymore. I'm letting go of the terrible guilt and following my true love. I have a deep want to fix what happened, make everything okay again. I'm incapable of doing this. I accept it.

Mama's need for me to make things right is as thick as the smoke from leaves burning in the ditch out front. I can't make her better either. So I go into the future and face what is to come. But when I look into Mama's eyes, I see love. Our love, you and me, was far from perfect but love all the same.

Have a happy life.

Good-bye,

Velvet

Randal knew Velvet's letters by heart but still, he read them over and over, trying to find the reasons she was so different from others, and why she couldn't be accepted for who she was. Yes, she had more than a few lovers in her lifetime and people looked down on her for this. What did it matter whom a person loved as long as the person loved? Randal believed all the strict rules and judgments he heard about from the church-going crowd were written by people who were afraid of what they might become or who they already were deep inside. God loved all people. All of them. At least that's what Randal understood from reading the stories in the Bible Granny had given him.

CHAPTER 7

Just like she said, Aunt Isla left early the next Saturday to pick up the new preacher. The space of a week had given the two, aunt and nephew, a sparse ease that allowed them to laugh together, sometimes, in guarded ways. Not close, or even slightly friends, just familiar. They didn't tiptoe around so much. Randal wanted to ask about his mother's funeral. When would it happen? What had Mr. Collins found out about the fire? He knew Aunt Isla had talked with him because he had listened in as much as he could. The one-sided conversation told him the fire had not been an accident. Velvet had been murdered. His mother had been murdered. This fact sat on his chest like the foot of an elephant, and Aunt Isla hadn't bothered to share the information with him. He didn't like Mr. Collins for his own reasons, so he sure didn't trust him to tell the whole truth. But still he kept his mouth closed so as not to flip Aunt Isla's canoe over and make her have a fit. Granny said opening a can of worms gave a person too much trouble. It was oftentimes better to just keep quiet.

"Remember, the house has to be perfect, Randal. Boil the water on the stove, add some bleach, and scrub the countertops. Scott refuses to clean his coffee spills. Make sure the dinner isn't overcooked."

"Don't worry." Part of Randal saw Velvet in Aunt Isla. The way she bossed him was the spitting image of his mother, but he didn't dare say this aloud.

She nodded. "Good."

"What about Uncle Scott? What if he comes home?" Randal had since learned his uncle could be in any condition, but most of the time he was drinking.

Aunt Isla backed up a step, as if this never occurred to her. "Good

Lord, don't say such a thing. Let's pray he stays away. He never comes home on Saturdays. He's too busy. If he shows up, just give him some food, and tell him to leave. Tell him the pastor is on his way. That normally gets him on the road quickly." Her laugh had a bitter edge. "I have to show that Cathy Belk I'm the better host. She's always rubbing her dinner parties in my face, not to mention she's become treasurer for the women's group at church."

"I don't think Uncle Scott would take too kindly to me asking him to leave his own house."

A wrinkle formed on her forehead when she frowned. "Just ignore him if he comes home."

That would be easier said than done. "You look real nice, Aunt Isla." He smiled. "You should let me give you a cut and some highlights. You would knock the whole church dead."

She studied him. "And what do you know about cutting hair and giving highlights? You need to be something besides a . . . a *hairdresser*."

"Not all of us have to be rich." He knew this was below the belt. "I want to be *happy*. I've spent most of my life around people who weren't. So, I'm moving to Atlanta as soon as I graduate. There's a good school there. "

"You don't graduate for well over a year. I have time to make you see things my way. I'll be back around two for your fabulous dinner." Her heels tapped down the hall. "I hate Atlanta, sweetie. I spent four years going to college there and thought I would kill myself. Trust me on this." She closed the big front door before he could open his mouth with a comeback.

~~~~~~

Randal did not set out to make things bad for Aunt Isla that Saturday or to get on her wrong side. Nothing of the kind was even on his mind as he worked at cleaning a house that was already spotless. It seemed a pure shame to redo Aunt Isla's hard work but sweeping the floor and vacuuming the carpets kept his mind busy. Still, the thought of Velvet dying in their little house alone came to him. Or maybe she hadn't been alone. If someone killed her, the murderer would have been there, too. Probably she had been terrified.

Randal got lost in preparing the meal, and the morning flew by. He was working in the kitchen when Guess Who came stumbling in the back door, a premonition come true.

"What you doing, Randal boy?"

Randal did his best to ignore his uncle by filling the sink with boiling water. It wasn't like he was new to drunks and their ways.

Uncle Scott leaned on the island. Muddy footprints tracked the floor. "Boys don't do girl chores."

Randal measured three cups of bleach and poured them in the water. He'd have to use the solution on the floor now. "I didn't know there were certain chores for girls."

Uncle Scott chose a spoon from the drawer, scooped some of the scalding bleach water, blew on the liquid, licked his lips, and slurped it down. He gave himself a shake. "That's a soup with some kick, Randal boy. You're a good cook, little man. You got all of Izzie's attention. That sure helps me out, son," he laughed.

"You're drunk. This floor has to be cleaned now. Go somewhere else," Randal complained.

Uncle Scott laughed and slapped his knee, nearly falling over. "I like you, Randal boy. You're a little on the sissy side, but honest. You're not afraid. You got your mama's gumption. I'd rather be around you than some Bible-thumping preacher. At least you're honest. Now take your aunt. Lord, she ain't nothing but one big lie, boy. Don't forget it." He winked. "Shoot, she used to be different. Ran rings around Velvet. Now she's only good for kissing up to some preacher or a junior league member. She's done turned into my mama, Mrs. Kathleen Weehunt." He stood still for a minute. "Izzie should have married a pastor. But most of them don't make enough money to keep her happy." He pointed a finger toward Randal. "Your mama used to fuss about how wild her big sister was. Izzie was the prettier of the two. Velvet was book smart, the safe one. Izzie didn't have time for a lot of learning until she came here and pretended to know a whole lot more than she knew. Seems she spends most of her time looking over her shoulder and making sure she measures up." He leaned on the island with both elbows, his head hanging low like an old dog's. "I never blamed Dar one bit for what she did. She was only trying to save her daughter, give her something better, but things got ruined. That's why Izzie can't ever really accept you. That's for sure. The past always messes things up."

A tug of anger heated Randal's chest. "You got to go somewhere else. Aunt Isla is bringing the new preacher here." He tugged on Uncle Scott's arm.

"You got a grip." Uncle Scott pulled away and rubbed the place Randal had grabbed him. "Your mama probably hated Izzie. Did you know that it was Izzie who put your granny in the nursing home?" He stumbled to the front room.

"Aunt Isla doesn't want anyone in there until the preacher comes."

"Really? You don't say?" Uncle Scott aimed himself at one of the big chairs but missed, hitting the wood floor instead.

Randal poked at him with the toe of his sneaker. "She's going to be madder than a wet hen when she sees you laid out here."

"Izzie is a pain in the butt. Go back to that soup. It smells like it might be burning." He rolled on his side.

The roast. Randal ran into the kitchen and caught the main dish just in time. Maybe a tad overcooked but Aunt Isla would never notice. And bad luck, being Randal's dear old friend from way on back, picked that minute to send Aunt Isla speeding into the driveway. Randal took one last look at the muddy footprints and went to throw open the front door.

Aunt Isla and Randal exchanged looks as she got out of the car. That woman wasn't one bit dumb. She knew something was up. She hurried around the car as the passenger opened his door. "I've got to run in here, Pastor Williams. Randal, show the pastor in." She whispered as she passed me. "He is here drunk, isn't he?"

"Yes."

"Not now," she hissed under her breath.

The preacher, dressed in black, unfolded from the car.

Something next to him caught his attention and he glanced to the front flower bed. A long chicken snake slithered through the flower bed. Randal was afraid of a lot of things but not snakes. And it did seem the preacher's God was sending Randal the perfect prank to play on the houseful of dumb adults. He waited for the good pastor to get in the door and then he scooped up the snake, holding its head, and dropped it on the front porch. Mr. Snake slid over the threshold.

"Pastor Williams, you must excuse my husband. He's turned quite ill and has stretched out on the living room floor." Aunt Isla's voice was high-pitched. "Let's go to the kitchen. We can sit in the sunroom. Randal has cooked a wonderful meal."

"Would your husband mind if we had a word of prayer for his healing?" This man of God was slick. Randal had crossed paths with too many of his type who thought they could change people, cleanse them of their natural selves, when what needed cleaning was the church and the congregation.

"Oh, he's too out of it for that. Besides, I don't want you to catch anything." Aunt Isla looked at Randal with a wild-eyed stare that pleaded for help.

"Nonsense. A good pastor prays for the sick, Sister, and doesn't worry about his own health."

Aunt Isla's hands fluttered as if she could still ward him off. "Well, I guess."

That's when Mister Snake slithered across the wooden floor like he owned the place.

The living room reeked of whiskey, but Pastor Williams never missed a step, never seemed to notice as he knelt down close to Uncle Scott's head. "Come, Sister Weehunt, let's pray for this unfortunate soul." He gave Aunt Isla a soft, kind look. "And for you. This must surely be a burden."

Tears welled in Aunt Isla's eyes. Lord help; that man was good. She looked like she might confess all her sins right then and there.

Mister Snake scooted across the floor, under the pure-white sofa, and settled on the tail of Aunt Isla's blue skirt. One of those full, church-lady kind, nice and long. Pure happiness filled Randal's chest, and that was his worst sin, enjoying his benefactor's demise.

"Heal this man, O God." Pastor Williams had his head bowed and eyes closed.

Randal watched from the door. No way was he leaving now.

"Yes, Lord," Aunt Isla breathed and an angry frown formed on her face. Her eyes fluttered open and caught sight of the five-foot snake. "Oh *God*!" She pushed to her feet. Mister Snake latched his fangs in the hem of the skirt and twisted in the air as Aunt Isla two-stepped, attempting to get free. "Oh, help me." She looked at Randal again. "You have to help me."

But Randal shook with a good belly laugh. He didn't have a thing against Aunt Isla, not really, but she looked like a comic-book character as she grabbed the shoulders of Pastor William's jacket and revealed who she really was. "Help me, you stupid fool!"

Uncle Scott opened his eyes and struggled to sit up. "What in God's green earth is going on?"

"*Help.*" Aunt Isla danced like some horrible ballerina.

Pastor Williams stood, grabbed the snake, and gave it a good yank. The fabric made a ripping sound. "Get away from her, devil."

Uncle Scott laughed. "By God, Isla, I don't think I've seen you dance like that since you and Velvet used to tear up the floor at Dale's Bar. You remember that?" He laughed so hard tears ran down his face. "I think we all could use a good stiff drink. What you say, preacher man?"

Pastor Williams pushed past Randal, holding the snake by the head. "He's not poisonous." The preacher tossed the snake out of the front door and it slid away in the direction of the chicken houses, where it could do a lot of damage.

Randal couldn't help but laugh. "We used to get them in the house where I lived. My granny had a chicken coop. Those snakes dearly love eggs . . . and chicks, of course."

Aunt Isla stood in the middle of her fancy living room. "I don't believe this."

"Well, my dear, it's good your new preacher found out up front the troubles you are saddled with." Uncle Scott walked to stand by Randal. "A drunken husband and an orphaned nephew. We make a nice family. Pleasure to meet you, pastor sir." He almost fell when he bowed. "I got some chickens to save." He stumbled out the front door.

"Shouldn't you go after him?" Pastor Williams asked.

"I don't care what happens to my husband. Maybe he'll fall down a well." Aunt Isla looked more alive since Randal had met her. Maybe it was the naked emotion of rage on her face. "This will ruin me at church," she said under her breath.

Pastor Williams smiled. "It's between us, Sister Weehunt."

Maybe the good pastor was after more than saving souls.

"Young man, do you read the Good Book?" The pastor's blue-eyed stare bored into Randal.

"I love Flannery O'Connor's collection of short stories, *A Good Man Is Hard To Find*. I've read it over and over. It's really good."

Aunt Isla let out a long sob.

Pastor Williams crossed the room and took her hand in his. "Sister Weehunt, you have your hands too full. We have to schedule a regular prayer time together. Don't you think that will help?"

She gave Randal a hard glare. "Let's just try to salvage this dinner."

If Velvet had been there, she would have kicked the preacher right out on his behind. And for the hundredth time that week, Randal reckoned on how he was going to manage without his mother.

CHAPTER 8

Isla

Our small group stood by the gaping six-foot deep hole in the little cemetery on Mama's property. Thunder rumbled in the distance and black clouds thickened in the west. Grass swayed in the wind, brushing at the older headstones, touching the edge of the forest that seemed to have moved closer over the years. I had lived away from the river for so long, my memory of the ebb and flow wasn't what it should have been. But then, I had never planned to return either.

In her right mind, Mama would have thrown a hissy fit about the overgrown graves that she had kept in pristine condition. In the right world, she would have insisted Velvet be buried in the First Methodist cemetery, and I wouldn't have been there anyway. The thought of not being at Velvet's funeral chilled my blood. This was who I had become, someone who had to be forced into coming to her own sister's funeral. I bent down to where Mama sat in the wheelchair. "Remember when you would make Velvet and me wash the headstones before we could go hang out with our friends?" We both had despised the job.

She looked at me with a cloudy expression. "I don't know you, young lady." And she turned to listen to Pastor Watkins, a family friend and the preacher at the First Methodist Church. So what if Mama didn't know me? Why would she? After all, I was only her oldest daughter, the one she didn't like too much. But our shared DNA wouldn't be preserved in her memory.

Funerals weren't about the dead. They were about those left behind. When Daddy died, the whole insurance company in Nantahala attended, but it was the river men, his fellow travelers, who circled the same cemetery as if to bring his spirit closer, keep him linked to them.

They mourned a man who loved the Nantahala River and lived as much of his life on the water as he could. That hot day in late April, we were burying this man's youngest daughter. The one he never saw because he died seven months before she was born.

From the low-hanging cypress tree limb, a dark-green birdhouse twisted on a silver chain. The delicate sound of baby birds punctuated the air as Pastor Watkins closed his Bible. "Let us bow our heads in prayer for the soul who moved on to a much better place." Tears glistened in his eyes.

Without even thinking, I rested my hand on Mama's bony shoulder. One would have thought we had only seen each other the day before, that we were close.

Mama looked up and met my stare. "I hope this will be over with soon. I'm going to miss lunch, and this is sub sandwich day. There's nothing I can do to save this lost girl. Never was." She paused. "Why am I here again?"

I held my finger to my lips. "We're going to pray."

Mama grunted. "I quit praying the day they came bringing Kenneth from the river. I begged him not to go, to stay with me and talk." She looked at her father's white headstone.

"Shh, now," I whispered.

Randal squatted in front of his grandmother. "Granny, we have to pray over Velvet. She died. We're burying her close to Great-Grandmother Iris. I think she would have liked that."

Mama looked at Randal. A light of recognition went off in her eyes. "For a minute I thought you were Kenneth. That's crazy thinking. I'm muddled today. But I got to confess, young man, there are days I miss my husband a lot."

Randal stood and bowed his head. My heart turned inside out. I couldn't think about any of that. Instead, I listened to the peeps of the baby birds and closed my eyes. If a person just looked at Mama, they would see a beautiful woman in her early seventies, wouldn't even think she was that old. How could a mind leave a person in a shell that fooled the world?

"Amen," said Pastor Watkins.

"Amen!" Mama shouted. "Let's get out of here."

I began to pull the wheelchair through the soft grass. Mama looked at me. "I respected my mother and because of that we were close as we could be." She frowned. "Not like you and me, chewing everything we said to each other three or four times before we swallowed. If my mother told me to do something, I listened."

I had no idea the woman could still shame me. What was worse? Her knowing exactly who we were together or the blank look on her face when she saw me? "Is Grandmother Iris's desk still in the writing studio?" I tugged at the wheelchair.

"I had Velvet lock up that studio for good when the other daughter left. She's the one that used that place. It was her that did all that writing stuff. Of course, if you ask me, telling stories ain't nothing but trouble. A girl just has to hold in what she thinks. Nobody's going to care anyway. That daughter got mad and left. I didn't see her again." She touched my hand.

And for the longest minute, I could only stand there and look at her. Frozen in her hazel stare. How long had it been since I felt her skin? Finally, I pulled away. "It's going to rain. We have to get to the car."

Lightning split the sky over Grassy Bald.

"Why am I in this chair?" She stood. "This was your idea." She shot me a mean look. "I'm feeble in the head, not in the body." Mama pointed her stare at Randal. "Look at that boy. He's turned out to be good. I hurt him by not being there, but I made my time count when I was. It's not the first time I wasn't there for a child. I hurt my daughters, too."

The bone-breaking sorrow swept over me again. The air turned hot and another streak of lightning cut across the black sky.

"I hope the service was suitable." Pastor Watkins stood at my elbow.

"Yes. Thank you."

"She will be missed." His look turned sad.

Randal was left staring at the grave.

"Could you excuse me? I need to check on Randal. Please help my mother to the car?"

"I can walk just fine, Paul. I don't know why she keeps calling me her mama. I only have one daughter and that was Velvet. Do you remember her?"

Pastor Watkins tenderly took her arm. "Come along, Dar."

"I'm sorry to be such a mess. I don't remember things right."

"You are fine the way you are." His voice was soft and kind.

"You've always been so sweet to me." Mama leaned into the good pastor.

"I need to talk with you, Izzie." Stuart appeared at my side.

"Not today, Stuart. We've had all we can take for one day."

"I need you to stay in town. We have to talk."

All my energy washed out through my feet. "I'm just supposed to stay here? Grassy Bald is probably a mess, filthy. There's no hotels around here. "

"Betty Sams turned that big old house by the river into a bed and breakfast. She probably has a couple of rooms. I need to talk with you. When can we?"

My head began to throb as bad as it did when Scott humiliated me with the new pastor on Saturday. "No way. I'm not staying there. Mrs. Sams was the biggest gossip in town. I'm sure that hasn't changed." I pressed the palm of my hand to my forehead to ward off the migraine I was sure to get. "I'll see you tomorrow morning. I don't know where I will be tonight. You can't insist I stay in town. You're only the fire chief."

"I'll meet you here in the morning around eleven. I know you don't want to discuss Velvet's death, but it has to be done." Stuart sure had changed from that namby-pamby boy I knew in school.

"Fine," I snapped. "Please leave me alone right now."

He nodded and walked away.

"I have always liked that young man." Mama spoke from where she and Pastor Watkins still stood, obviously listening to every word.

"You would." I walked away toward Randal.

"Wait a minute," Mama fussed.

I kept moving. Velvet was buried, and now there was the matter of finding her murderer.

CHAPTER 9

After Randal and I took Mama back to the assisted living home, I explained to Randal we had to remain in the gorge for at least one night. "If I had my way, we'd go back right now. We could."

Randal shook his head. "We might as well stay. It's too long to run back and forth until this mess is figured out."

"Stuart, I mean Mr. Collins, said something about a bed and breakfast in town. I'm not crazy about the idea."

A frown creased his forehead. "That lady doesn't like me. Her grandson is one of the kids that gives me a hard time. I don't think we'd be welcomed." He kept his eyes straight ahead, looking through the windshield.

"Grassy Bald is probably a mess. No one's been there in God knows how long."

"The Day's Inn on 411 is the closest place."

"I have to sleep somewhere clean and safe." I cut a look at him. "There has to be some good hotels on the interstate."

"That's a long way. I might know a place." Randal sounded weary. "Velvet kind of knew the lady who owns the oldest house in the gorge. It used to be a store. The Bradfords lived there."

"Ha, Millie Bradford was the queen of this town when I was young. Yes, I know it."

"Mr. Bradford was a big-time farmer in the twenties and thirties." He half grinned. "I listened to stories when I was little. Everyone says the house is haunted. But Velvet said that was only good marketing. Ghosts always make people get off the interstate and travel into small mountain towns."

"Velvet was invited to eat dinner there once. I think she was sixteen. The old woman who lived there didn't have kids, but she had this skinny little nephew who visited in the summer. He, like most of the boys in the gorge, took a liking to Velvet. Somehow, he persuaded her to come for dinner. I can't remember his name. Anyway, Velvet was there long enough to make the boy's aunt ask her to leave. God only knows what she did to shock the woman." I shook my head. and tightened my grip on the wheel. "She had a mouth on her and no filters."

At the next stop sign, I called Scott's number. His voice mail greeted me; I hung up. Never mind him. Let him wonder where I got off to for once. "I don't have any clothes and neither do you. I can't wear the same clothes tomorrow. I need a hairbrush *and* toothbrush."

Now he looked at me. "There's a Walmart and Target in town."

"Target and Walmart. This place is moving up." I said this with a smart-alecky tone. Thunder rumbled in the distance again. "Let's find our place to stay first. Maybe the owner will know a decent place to buy clothes." Fat drops of rain hit the windshield.

Randal turned to look out the window, but he wasn't fooling me even a little bit. He was laughing at me, probably enjoying every minute, thinking he was getting under my skin. He was wrong. I could take everything he threw at me.

The Bradford House sat right where the road began to wind down into the gorge's floor, guarded by large oaks on each side. The siding was dark brown, almost black, with age. A wide porch covered the front and wrapped around the house. Chimneys jutted from the roof on both sides. The air was alive with birds from the nearby forest. The sky began to clear, the rain having fallen in a short, strong burst.

"I guess we get out." I parked the car near the front gate that opened onto the street.

Randal looked out his window at the house. "Yeah."

"There isn't a sign saying this is a bed and breakfast." A porch swing moved in the gazebo that was a newer build.

"Probably haven't gotten around to putting one up yet. It would take away from the house." He studied the front yard.

"Maybe." I opened the door and was slapped in the face with the muggy, thick air. "I'm going to find out." My heels—costing upward to three hundred dollars—click-clacked, click-clacked, click-clacked across the stone path. Still, no one appeared on the porch. I knocked on the bevel-glass double doors.

The door swung open and a waif of a girl, her face covered in connect-the-dots freckles, stood in front of me. She frowned. "Are you here for a room?" Her voice was smooth as honey.

"Yes." I looked at Randal still in the car. "We will need two."

She looked around me as Randal got out.

"How long do you need to stay?" The girl was barefooted, her toenails painted yellow. She stared at me as if I were a burden instead of a paying customer.

"I'm not sure. Are you filled? It could be a few nights." My voice had that strain in it that Scott hated so much.

The girl shrugged. "No. We don't have customers standing in line to stay here. I mean, Nantahala isn't some kind of resort, is it? Aunt Kate is in the garden out back. Come on."

The word *garden* eased the tightness in my shoulders.

Randal stood beside me now and spoke to the girl. "You have the perfect shade of brown hair."

The girl gave him a disgusted look. "You're crazy. This is the most boring color ever." Her eyes narrowed further. "Are you making fun of me?"

"I wouldn't do that. It's perfect for blond coloring or gold highlights. It's just light enough."

"And the next thing you will say is my freckles are cute, and I will have to kill you."

Randal held his hands in front of him as if to ward off a blow. "They're adorable."

The girl stormed through the house. "The last thing I want is adorable."

The two rooms she ushered us through held heavy Victorian

furniture polished to a perfect sheen. Probably came with the place.

When we entered the kitchen, my breath caught. The walls were sunny yellow, and the cabinets were cobalt blue. I fell in love before I saw the wall of windows that framed the backyard. Tulip and oak trees gave way to the forest and just beyond a creek cutting a path through the pines.

"Are you coming?" the girl asked impatiently.

"Do you have a name?" I found this child incredibly trying.

The girl went outside without answering. I followed her through the single French door. To the right was a picket fence painted a peachy color. The lush garden held rows of flowers, a couple of dogwood trees, and butterfly bushes. Pink roses as big as my fist crept along the fence. A woman, looking to be around my age, with short blondish hair, stood up from where she was weeding.

"These people want some rooms, but they don't know how long they are staying." The girl avoided looking at us.

The woman walked toward us, offering me her hand. "Wonderful. I'm Kate Tucker."

I took the long, elegant fingers in my grip. Mama would have called them piano hands. Maybe she played the baby grand in the room we passed through. "Isla Weehunt." I pointed to Randal. "This is my nephew, Randal. We would love to get a couple of rooms. I'm not sure how long I will need to stay. Maybe a few nights. Maybe just one. I have to check on my grandmother's old home and I have business in Nantahala that needs attention."

A smile lit up the woman's face. "You must stay as long as you want. This area is stunning."

"Are you from here?" She didn't look familiar.

"My husband died a little over a year ago. This house once belonged to his great-aunt." Her face transformed into a shadow for a second.

Would I feel like that if Scott died? The answer was obvious. I would be relieved not to no longer have to deal with his antics. I brushed off a shiver that moved through me.

"She left this old house to my husband a few years back. Seven, to be exact. Josh, my husband, couldn't bear to part with it. This seemed the place to come when I decided I needed a change. My only family is a brother who moved to Japan for work. Miss Lily, here," she said, looking at the girl, "is my niece. She didn't want to go with her family." She made a clicking sound. "I think it would be quite exciting to live in such an exotic place. But Lily here is in a gun club of all things and didn't want to leave it."

"Not a gun club," Lily said, frowning. She looked at Randal. "I shoot skeet."

"What do you shoot with?"

"A Browning Citori 725. But I also practice target shooting with a .22 automatic."

Randal looked impressed, leaving me to wonder just how much he knew about guns for sport.

"As far as I'm concerned," Kate interjected, "shotguns are not for such pretty girls."

Lily rolled her eyes.

"We, my husband and I, lived in North Carolina. My husband was a trial lawyer in Raleigh. I was a nurse at the local hospital." She reached out and touched Lily's hair. "So, when I decided I needed a change of pace, Lily here came along on my little adventure. Of course, I never had any children of my own. I'm still attempting to get used to this place. City life suits me so much better. Not that Raleigh is a huge city, but it was home. I so miss the country club. I know how that makes me sound, but I loved playing tennis and the pool and the people." She nodded to a small Victorian-style cottage painted peach, like the fence, and white as I cocked a brow at the flurry of information she so freely gave. "So, I've tried to make a life for myself here. Money is such a nasty subject to discuss. Josh left me in decent shape, but one never knows. I'm not working as a nurse anymore, and I do plan to live until I'm a hundred." She laughed. "I had this little house moved from a nearby farm. It was falling apart. I thought I could rent it out to someone year-round. I'll show it to you later."

"You knew my mom, Velvet Leech," Randal offered.

Kate's face softened. "I recognized you. Your mother painted the cottage inside and out for me."

Randal looked surprised. "She said she worked part time for you, but I didn't know she was painting on such a large project. I could have helped."

Kate's laugh was soft and removed as if she really wanted to say something else but thought better of it. "It was more than part-time work. It was her income. We met in town at the Piggly Wiggly after she was laid off from the casino. I paid her in cash to supplement her unemployment. She was quite an interesting person."

Randal gave me a confused glance.

"I was shocked and brokenhearted over her death." Kate took his hand and squeezed it.

Tears came into his eyes and I scowled. The boy had to learn to control his feelings. People would take advantage of him.

Kate turned her watery blue stare on me. "You have to be Velvet's sister. She told me all about you. We had a lot of time to talk when she was painting. We probably got to know each other better than either of us wanted to. And really, I would never have actually sat down to talk to her if it wasn't for her working here." Kate blushed and looked at me. "You know we traveled in different circles."

I laughed. I couldn't help it. "Sounds like you knew my sister. And I understand about circles." I was liking Kate more and more.

"Are you as talented as she was?" Kate waved her hand at what I guessed was my confused expression. "We'll talk later. Lily, let's show our special guests the bedrooms. Please plan on staying as long as you need. We have no customers right now."

"Really?" Randal spoke. "I saw a woman on the landing when we walked through. She didn't seem thrilled we were here."

A smirk formed on Lily's face.

Kate studied him. "We haven't had customers for two weeks." She followed Lily in the house.

"No, no. This was a woman with dark hair dressed in a vintage suit, maybe a Chanel." Randal looked intent.

Lily turned around. "You saw a ghost. She died years ago. That's what the old woman down the road told me. We don't know her name, only that she visited the old lady who owned this house often."

Randal shook his head. "I don't believe in ghosts. Sorry."

"Good for you," Kate said. "I love a sensible young man. But there is a ghost. Lily isn't making it up. My husband talked about seeing her when he was a little boy, visiting in the summer. One of the reasons he didn't want to live here."

To my way of seeing things, Lily didn't seem the kind of girl with enough imagination to make up ghost stories.

Lily gave Randal a stern look. "And it isn't important who she is. What is important is this ghost only comes when someone is going to die."

"Lily," Kate scolded. "That's enough trying to scare our guests."

"There's already been a death. My mom. We just have to find who killed her," Randal said, then walked up the stairs without looking back at us.

CHAPTER 10

"Sit down, Isla." Kate nodded to the breakfast table in front of the large window. "I'll make us some tea. You do like tea?"

I took the chair across from her. "Yes, and I love your garden. It's magnificent. I have herb gardens."

Kate smiled, igniting the gas flame under the kettle. "Gardening saved my life after Josh died." She looked around. "And this house, of course. Sometimes a girl just has to start her life all over again. You know, a second chance. It was the right thing to do." She took two china teacups from the cupboard. "I only have to get used to it."

"Up until I got the call about Velvet's death, I was content." I ran my fingers along the edge of the antique mahogany table. Nice piece. Not cheap. "My life has evolved into pretty much what I envisioned at the end of college. Putting this place behind me, starting a real life. I honestly never saw myself here again. As you can tell, I'm not a big fan." I didn't mention my discontent with Scott.

"Oh God, I know what you mean. Nantahala is like stepping back thirty years. It is the one drawback with this whole move. The people have *no* culture. They wouldn't know what to do with a museum if someone put them in the middle of one and handed them directions. I don't see how Emily Greene has managed to keep her art gallery afloat. Its patrons must come from outside of town, maybe Asheville. Don't you think? But there is a crowd there every time she has a show." She placed each teacup on a matching saucer and filled them with steaming dark liquid.

Kate thought like me. I never imagined meeting someone I liked in Nantahala. "Emily and I went to school together. She left the same time as me. Really, I'm quite surprised she came back here. Of course, where I live now is a small town, but we have committees worth serving on and the country club. It's quite different."

Kate looked out the window. Her face was flawless, smooth. "No one is more surprised than me I've moved to some one-horse town, but Josh loved it." A shadow crossed her face for only a second and cleared. She brought the tea to the table on a dainty white wooden tray. "Do you like Russian tea?"

"It's my favorite."

"Mine too. This is crazy, Isla." She went to the cabinets and pulled two heavy pottery plates from the shelves. "You asked me if there was a good place to buy clothes. There is the most divine dress shop on the square. You have to go there. The prices are so low, but the dresses are out of this world."

How sad I was making a new friend and wouldn't get to enjoy cultivating the relationship. Maybe Kate could come visit when Randal and I went back home.

〰〰

"Thank God Kate suggested that dress shop," I said to Randal on our way back from the square. "Who would have thought things have changed so much. I bought a nice dress without going all the way to Franklin." I kept my eyes on the curvy highway famous for car accidents in my teenage years.

"The yellow sundress you bought is perfect for your style."

My style. What did he mean by *my style?* "Tell me how to get to Walmart. We need some toiletries, and you can buy some more jeans and shirts." Even I could hear my stuffy tone.

He looked at me sideways. "Have you ever been in a Walmart?"

I didn't look at him. "Of course."

"Something you need to know, Aunt Isla. You're a horrible liar."

I cut a hateful stare at him, but he was looking at the river.

"The Nantahala is so wide here."

"Yes. My father drowned in that river. But he loved it more than life. The morning he drowned the sky was tinged with red. His last words to Mama were, '*Red sky in the morning take the warning.*' Seven months later Velvet was born. Daddy never saw his second daughter."

"Velvet said that was a bunch of hogwash. That her father died because he couldn't stand living with Granny anymore."

I studied his profile for a minute while I waited on the traffic light. "How would your mother know anything about him? Mama never talked about his death, even after her black spells got better. Not around me anyway."

He shrugged. "Granny probably talked more than you know. Or maybe it's ancestral memory. I read an article about that stuff the other day. People knowing stuff about their great-grandparents' history that they couldn't have known."

Hogwash, indeed. "Velvet was always angry about not knowing our father." I sounded snippier than before.

~~~~~

Walmart was vast and cluttered with everything that appealed to the young girl in me, and this truly shamed me. I bought two tacky bright-colored t-shirts, a pair of hiking shorts with several pockets, and two pairs of jeans, skinny of course. Even though I knew the cosmetics were cheap, I bought plenty. I couldn't go out the next day without my face. And a trip to the mall in Asheville for makeup seemed too daunting.

Randal wandered up to me holding a black crochet one-piece bathing suit. "You mentioned a membership at the country club in your town. If you dare. This is perfect for you."

"No way. It's too . . ."

"Too what?"

"I don't know. Young."

"Sexy? Real? Hot mama?" He tried to look serious.

At home I had a swimsuit like professional swimmers. I did laps ever day at the country club's Olympic size pool. Still, nothing about me was sexy, especially when I wore my bathing cap. "No." Besides, what would the women at church say?

"Oh, come on, Auntie." He laughed. "We could sunbathe by the river. Not one soul from your church will see you there," he said, reading my mind. "Think of it as a mini vacation."

How long had it been since I had taken a vacation? A church retreat in Atlanta did not count. I grabbed the swimsuit. "I will look like a tramp and sunbathing makes you look old. And I don't intend to look old."

"No, you're not, and this suit proves it. How delicious is that?"

"Did you get some clothes?"

"I'm working on it."

The suit *was* pretty. That had to mean some kind of trouble. "Be sure and get some shoes you can walk in."

He gave me a suspicious look. "Okay."

"I want to go see Grassy Bald, and I want to check on Daddy's fishing camp. Someone told me it was still around."

A slow smile spread over his face and he looked more like a child. "Go." My voice cracked.

On the way to the shoe department to take my own advice, I passed the office supplies. The stacks of spiral notebooks stirred a vague emotion in my chest. Without thinking, I threw three notebooks in the buggy with a pack of gel pens. On the next aisle I saw a row of laptops. One was pale greenish blue, like a robin's egg. Inside my head, I heard Scott laughing at me, taking up space he didn't deserve. I touched the phone in my purse. He hadn't even bothered to call. Surely he had missed us by now. I grabbed the laptop box. Why not? Why couldn't I begin to take my writing seriously again? Being Isla Weehunt was a hard job. Maybe I could write the gardening book I'd been thinking about for years. No one had to find out. It could be my secret project.

The kids cleaned up after dinner in Kate's splendid kitchen.

"Why don't we go look at my Victorian cottage?" Kate stood at the backdoor. "Let these young ones visit while they clean. God, I love that they are cleaning. I miss having help. It was one of the things I loved about my life with Josh. I just can't find anyone I feel comfortable with here. And hiring someone seems trivial."

"I know what you mean about the help. I can't get anyone to cook. No one wants to work for me." I followed her into the garden so unlike mine. The sky had cleared to a grayish blue. Kate's work was for pure pleasure, no herbs or medicinal uses for her. Flowers, every kind that bloomed in North Carolina during spring, swayed in the light wind. The whole scene provided a calm that hugged me in that moment. "Thanks for the wonderful dinner. You really shouldn't have bothered though." I spoke as two birds moved across the sky in the distance.

"It was fun. There's not many people around here I can have fun with, Isla. The neighbors are so ..." She stopped speaking.

A laugh bubbled from me. "I know."

Kate's face broke into a true smile. "I had a feeling you would understand. It's hard to find someone who likes the things I do."

"These people have been who they are for generations. My grandparents came to live here at the end of the Depression, and still the locals think I'm an intruder, not from here. I was born in this stupid gorge." I laughed. "We are outsiders."

"It's so stupid, this clan stuff." Kate walked down the stone path. "You will love the cottage." She went to the elegant stained-oak door and inserted a key. "I had this moved from twenty miles away. The owner was going to tear it down."

When the door opened, a cold chill blew across my bare arms. Central air must have been installed. There was a decent-sized sitting room to the left of the entry way. The windows were tall and bookshelves, stuffed with books, covered every inch of the walls, even around the large window.

"Wow, a lot of books." I examined the titles closest to me.

"Yes, they belonged to Josh." She gave a frown. "I couldn't bear to let them go. He loved them so much. But I don't read, not much anyway."

I loved reading, even though it was a secret passion. The women on the Junior League read little and when they did talk about books, it was against some offending title that would hurt their children. Having books removed from the school's library was a regular occurrence. So I bought my books in Atlanta when I went. Or ordered them online. I peered closer. "This is a wonderful collection of Henry James."

"Old stuffy books." Kate frowned. "I wish I could make myself like reading. I just can't be still for that long. Too much to do in the garden or the house." There was disapproval in her voice.

"It is my vice, along with having herb gardens," I said, walking to another shelf.

"Herbs. How fun." Kate closed the door. "You should stay here instead of that room in the main house. You could read anything you want. It won't bother me. I'm not quite ready to rent it yet. And, Isla, I'm in no hurry to get you on your way. You are a breath of fresh air." She walked toward the back of the house. "I have some wine. Are you interested?"

I thought of the women at home, how everyone followed the rules of the church. No spirits of any kind, not even for communion. "Yes. That sounds nice."

"Would you like to have the cottage? You could rest, relax."

"Sure. That would be wonderful. I haven't taken time to relax in forever. There's always some committee project to address and the gardens have to be planted and maintained. I like doing that myself."

"We'll get your things after our wine."

"If it is no trouble." It would be a great place to write, and the books were welcoming. "But I might not go back if I spend too much time here."

"I encourage you to stay as long as you want. I need a friend." She toasted me with her wine glass.

"Thank you." I sipped the white wine, sweet and smooth. The last time I had wine and it was cheap, I lived at home with Mama.

We talked about gardening and clothes and shoes. She told me how she tried to join the Junior League in town, but they never got back to her.

"Imagine being shunned by this place." She laughed.

"I think that says a lot about you. Good things." I sipped more wine; its buzzy pleasantness spread through my body.

"Will your husband join you on the weekend? There is plenty of room here."

My face must have shown my dislike of the subject.

"Ah, you're not so keen on him coming." Kate laughed but not in a mean way.

"I guess that's a nice way of putting it. We just have our own separate lives. Many couples do these days."

"Yes. They do." She acted as if she might speak more on the subject, but instead she finished her wine.

Before climbing in the antique bed of the small turret room, I pushed open the tall narrow window to the night. The evening was so clear I saw Grassy Bald in the distance. I fell asleep reading a hardback copy of Flannery O'Connor's letters.

The next morning, I woke with a start, quite sure someone had been calling my name, a product of a dream that included a young Velvet. A pink ribbon of sky streaked through the treetops. A large black crow cawed from the backyard near the creek. I grabbed my new laptop where I'd left it on the table the night before and began to type, describing the scene outside the window. Words flowed from me as if they were my long-lost friend waiting on me to show up after so many years. I moved my fingers across the keys, my spirit leaving the room and entering a place of balance. The way the sun filtered through the bright green leaves of the tulip trees showed up on the screen. I described the bird calls echoing in the woods. The hum from the insects was music on the wind that wove its way through the thick brush that grew on the sides of the mountain. And there was Grassy Bald, my ancestral roots. Easily, in that moment of writing, I left behind being a Weehunt. My words turned me into a painter, a visual artist bound to show every vein in a leaf and each minnow in a stream. Small wild violets, delicate and fragile, became my childhood wishes hidden away for years. A worshiping emotion unlike any I felt in church moved me into contentment. When I finally stopped, I sat in stillness, listening to the songs that continued to whistle around me, braiding together something more tangible than all my years of effort could have delivered to my soul. Why had I stopped writing? But I knew the reasons that lined up in my thoughts. I had to control those places in me that wanted to burst open and tell everything, to scream at the top of my lungs.

The smell of coffee and bacon reached me from the open window. I threw on my new lime-green t-shirt and jeans. Halfway down the stairs I realized my hair was uncombed. I ducked into the small powder room in the hall. My ponytail was still perfect, frozen on me, trained to look correct at all times. The quiet places in my mind echoed with thoughts of being fourteen, wild, mouthy, and sure of what I wanted from life. I had one simple motto back then. Get out of town before I began to believe I was the person Mama saw in me. I crossed the lawn to the kitchen door of the main house.

Randal sat at the table with Lily, who had transformed into a beautiful girl with a radiant smile. Randal's plate had at least four pancakes smothered in syrup compared to Lily's one with a pat of butter.

"Whoa, Auntie, what is going on? You didn't sleep in the house last night?" Randal taunted me. "I thought you were wearing the yellow sundress to see Mr. Collins."

"So, you find my fashion choice of interest? And you missed me? I'm flattered. It just so happens I decided not to ruin the new dress in that burned-up mess. I've had to throw too many nice clothes away since this started."

Randal stuffed his last bite of pancake in his mouth. "Well, I have to get ready."

Lily's face crinkled back into her sternness.

Poor girl. She wouldn't get anything but pain from chasing Randal in a romantic way. Or would she? Maybe Scott's sideways opinion was wrong. So what if Randal liked to cook? Emeril Lagasse had been married more than once and had a houseful of children and he could cook like nobody's business. And so what if he talked about *hair* and *fashion*? What did that mean anyway? And what did it matter? A lot if my church found out, one way or the other. But truly it wasn't my business. It wasn't *anyone's* business. And besides, there was a whole lot more to raising a teenager, even for a year. My life would change radically. Already had. It was going to be tough, especially since I had no clue what to do. As Mama used to say, everything would come out in the wash. That was exactly what I was counting on. "Where's your aunt?" I asked Lily.

"She's in the garden while the air is still cool. Out near the edge of the woods."

"Thanks for breakfast, Lily." Randal patted her hand. "And the talk."

She shrugged. "Sure."

The boy was more like a grown man than I wanted to admit in front of him. And the way *he* had looked at Lily. Maybe . . .

I piled three pancakes on my plate. At this rate, I wouldn't fit into my pants. My phone vibrated in the pocket of my jeans. Scott's number. "Excuse me." I stepped out the back door. "Hello."

"Izzie, where are you? You didn't sleep here last night." Scott sounded put out, inconvenienced.

"No, I'm not home and neither is Randal."

"Where are you?"

"Good land of the living, Scott, give it a little thought."

"Did you bury Velvet?"

"Bingo, you win."

"Why did you spend the night?"

"Things happened." Exhaustion, deep and heavy, soaked into my bones.

"So the kid is with you?"

"Yes."

"He's a decent boy. But you know what *I'm* thinking ..."

"Don't."

"I know what I'm talking about, and as usual you have stuck your head in the ground. So. Velvet is buried."

I hate you. The thought pushed through my arms and into my ribs. "Yes. A simple service."

"You didn't leave me a note," he huffed.

I bit the inside of my lip. "You don't ever tell me where you're going."

He was quiet.

"I have no idea when I will be home."

"Mama will wonder where you're at. There will be questions. Don't you have some kind of church meeting that you have to be at?"

Yes, yes, yes. The word ticked off in my head like the second hand on a clock. The excited, enthusiastic feeling I had earlier left me. "It will have to wait. This is family business. I have a lot to take care of around here. Anyway, I doubt Pastor Williams will want me there after Saturday, Scott. I'm sure your mother has heard about the fiasco by now. I'll call and explain to her where I am. "

"When did your family become so important?"

"I don't know, Scott. Maybe they've always been buried somewhere under my best intentions."

"Some woman named Emily called here looking for you last night. Said she was a reporter at some newspaper. Seriously? What is this about?"

"Is that all she said?"

"No, she asked if I knew who would want to kill Velvet. I told her that I had forgotten Velvet even existed. I told her you found a better life here and put that place behind you."

"She has no business calling the house."

Scott took a deep breath. "The subject of what went on before you left did come up."

"Shut up. You lost all rights to bring that up. I told you not to talk about it again."

"Why didn't you tell me Velvet was murdered?"

"I didn't think you would give a rat's behind. Do you? Do you even care about anything?"

Scott chuckled. "I miss your lovely attitude, Izzie."

I pressed the end button. When had I started to hate Scott Weehunt? The night we sat in the bar with his friends—back in the days I still went out with him—and spouted off how he believed that the whole moonwalk was a conspiracy staged in the desert somewhere out west. I knew that night what a terrible mistake I had made thinking I could change him into someone better, someone I wanted him to be. Scott was one of those people that could be figured out in a few minutes. Nothing was complex about him.

And he would never change.

CHAPTER 11

Somewhere a chipmunk scratched in the dead leaves left over from winter. Sun splattered across my lap, promising real heat as the day wore on. The cemetery never scared me as a child. I found the marble markers friendly, comforting. Pretty much each one told a story. The low-stacked stone wall Velvet and I built as a punishment for taking out the johnboat when I was fourteen and Velvet was ten still stood, crooked in some places. The woods turned quiet as if all of nature decided to take a nap. A soft whisper of wind moved a sheet of paper in my empty notebook. I closed it, stood, and walked the path to the river. As I maneuvered down the bank, holding a limb of a dead tree, I tried not to think about snakes or lizards. Daddy said the river and its wildlife had to be respected. What would have happened had he lived? Would Velvet be dead? And me, how would I have turned out? I had a feeling I wouldn't be married to Scott Weehunt. Maybe Mama wouldn't have gotten Alzheimer's. That was really stretching the "what ifs."

The fishing camp looked almost new, its posts and foundation still sturdy, and the wide deck, where Mama and I sat in rockers as the water flowed under us, watching for Daddy's return without admitting this out loud, had been replaced with freshly painted boards. Mama had always hated the water. "That river is nothing but one long witch's spell." And at first, I had believed her. That's what daughters do; they believe their mamas even if they know them to be liars.

"Aunt Isla." Randal stood on the bank.

I nearly jumped a foot. "Good Lord, you scared the fire out of me," I laughed.

He shrugged. "Sorry. You were deep in thought?"

"I was woolgathering."

"Granny says that a lot." He nodded at my notebook. "Taking notes?"

I handed it to him. "Once upon a time I could write. Now, I'm like a rusty chain on an old bicycle. I work a little then grab tight, shutting down the whole process."

He looked at the pages. "You really have a way with words. You're probably overthinking it or too close to the subject."

"Smart boy. Here at the river, on this property, I just feel empty, numb."

He handed back the unfilled notebook. "You should write about your dad being a river man."

"Maybe." The river moved calm and lazy, but underneath was a current strong enough to pull a girl under and never let her go. "Sometimes I wonder what Daddy felt when he drowned."

"I don't think I want to know." He smiled and extended his hand so I could climb the muddy bank without slipping. "Come see all my work in the fishing camp."

I was becoming way too attached to the boy. And because I knew the whole story, I couldn't allow this to happen. I couldn't get soft. I couldn't change. My life was what I needed it to be.

~~~~~

By the time Randal and I walked out of the woods into the cemetery, Stuart stood near his truck. The residue of visiting the fishing camp dulled my usually heightened sixth sense for trouble.

The bright red jeep was parked close to my car.

Randal frowned. "That reporter woman is here. She was at the fire."

"Dang it. We have to think about what we say. She will twist situations and make the story fit her need. I know this much about her."

"You don't have to tell me. I watch out for both of 'em."

Stuart took a step toward us. "Izzie, you're out exploring the woods?" He seemed amused.

There was a time in my life I could have outrun Stuart Collins and outdone him, for that matter. Some things didn't change. He was still full of himself.

Emily got out of her jeep with a fancy camera around her neck.

"How are you today, son?" Stuart held his hand out to Randal.

He didn't take it. "Fine."

Emily wore a black t-shirt and jeans. Her expression was almost humble.

"Why is she here?" I snapped.

Stuart gave me a long look, placing his hands in his pockets. "All that stuff was in college, Izzie, a long time ago. Emily asked to come take some photos for a story about the fire and Grassy Bald, the whole family. I told her she had to talk to you. This is your place, your family." He glanced over his shoulder. "Try to play nice. She might help this case. She's pretty good at what she does."

"Maybe in this podunk town." Rage pushed through me.

Stuart cleared his throat. "We need to talk about Velvet's murder."

Randal stiffened beside me.

"What do you know?" I kept my voice steady.

Emily came to stand with us.

"Do you mind if Emily listens in?" Stuart asked me.

He drove me slap crazy. "I don't know of any secrets." I stared Emily down. "You don't have permission to write anything discussed here today. It would be pure speculation." My voice had that bossy tone I was so good at.

Emily smiled. "Sounds like a plan."

"This fire was set by an arsonist with the intent to destroy as much as possible, maybe even murder." Stuart trained his stare on Randal and then looked at me. "This is serious stuff. We found evidence that the fire was set with a delayed detonator, giving the person or persons time to get away. The Williams family, up the road, saw a car tear down the street right after smoke and flames shot above the trees. Rudy, Velvet's boss at the casino, came by around that time."

Randal and I exchanged looks.

Stuart watched us. "What?"

I shrugged at Randal. "We know that Velvet had been laid off from the casino months before."

Emily scribbled in a notebook.

"How do you know?" Stuart questioned.

"We're staying at the Bradford House. The owner told us Velvet had worked for her all winter painting because she lost her job. How in this nosy town did someone miss this detail?"

"Rudy didn't say anything." Stuart looked at the rubble and then up at Randal. "You didn't know either."

"No." Randal frowned.

"Maybe this Rudy set the fire," I said.

"I'll talk to him. It's not like him to lie."

"Sounds like he just didn't tell," I pointed out.

"Whoever did this wanted to destroy everything, but they didn't." Stuart pulled a small velvet bag with a drawstring from his pants pocket. He shook out a ring from inside and held it out to me.

"A ring?" I turned it over in my hand. It was the real deal.

"An expensive ring. I took it to the jewelers in town just to get a rough estimate. Bob knows his stuff, but the police will do their own investigation. Look at it closely. The diamond is four carats. It's an antique from the 1920s, very valuable. Upwards of twenty thousand dollars, at least."

"Wow." I slid it onto my right ring finger. A cold chill worked over my scalp. It was a perfect fit. "Where would Velvet get something like this?" I took the ring off. "It has to be eighteen karat gold. Wouldn't it melt in a fire like that one?" There was an engraving on the inside, but I couldn't make out what it said without my jeweler's loop. I took a picture of the ring with my phone.

Stuart raised his eyebrows. "I'm impressed, Izzie. Yes, had the ring been in the house, it could have melted, especially in this fire. I found this in her car, under the seat. The smoke ruined the paint job, but the car is intact." He took the ring back. "The engraving says *Forever Mine* and is fairly recent, like in the last ten years. But it wasn't done in town."

"It is exquisite. Unusual."

Stuart turned his attention back on Randal. "You lived there, son. I was hoping you could give us a clue. Did your mom say anything about this ring? Did you see it around her room? Could it have been your grandmother's?"

Randal ran his fingers through his dark hair. If I could have gone back ten days and somehow saved Velvet, I would have, just so Randal didn't have to go through losing his mom over and over with all the questions. So he wouldn't be without her. He'd lost so much. No regrets. I wouldn't make him into a regret.

"I know it's not my mother's. She only had two things of value, her wedding ring and Daddy's. The rest was costume. Maybe it belonged to my grandmother, but I don't know how Velvet would have found it."

I looked at Randal. "Did you hear Mama talk about any jewelry that belonged to Grandmother Iris? Or maybe Velvet talked about finding some of Grandmother Iris's stuff."

"Velvet only talked about selling the land here to developers and leaving for good. She talked about that a lot over the last two months." Randal stopped a minute. "I don't think she meant it. She knew we needed the land in case Granny had to have more money. She couldn't touch Grassy Bald. It has to stay in the family, but this land was free of the will that tied up my great-grandmother's estate."

Emily kept writing. "Velvet was serious about the developers."

"How do you know?" I shot her a look.

"We spent a few evenings talking. She was ready for a change. Needed to leave here."

"I don't believe you were friends."

Emily turned her full attention on me. "Coming back here was hard, crazy in many ways. But I'm not sorry I made the move. I love the gallery, my loft, and even this silly job, but a lot happened here. I lost a lot and gained nothing until I moved. People don't forget in this town when you're an outsider. Velvet was real. She was still an artist, but one who got caught up in living a hardscrabble life of her own device." She watched me for a reaction. "I came home to the place where my parents were the happiest and faced the demons I had never looked in the eyes. I guess one could say Velvet was one of them, but we ended up talking. She was using her creativity again. I encouraged her. The act of creating art allows a soul to rest from the everyday struggles of just making a living."

"So deep, Emily." I looked away from her and gave my attention to Stuart. "So, we know Velvet hung out with Emily. She was reinventing herself. Oh, yes, talking about selling land that didn't even belong to her. And somewhere along the way she talked to these developers. And the ring. She had a ring worth twenty thousand dollars. Anything else? Makes me think my sister was in way over her head somewhere." What a horrible person I could be.

Randal cleared his throat. "Velvet owned this land, Aunt Isla."

"What are you talking about?" I turned my mean stare on him. "It's Mama's land until she dies. Then it comes to her daughters. She had it spelled out in her will. There would be no selling off any of the land, hers or Grandmother Iris's."

Randal shrugged. "Before Granny went into the home, she signed the deed over to Velvet."

My head hummed. "What did Velvet think?" My voice was high-pitched. "That she could just sell our childhood home and leave me paying for Mama's care each month like I have been since she moved in there?" The words curled out of me with a harsh edge.

Randal's cheeks turned pink. "I don't think you were around for Velvet to consult at the time. Granny had to quick-deed the land to Velvet to keep the home from taking it if we couldn't afford to keep her there for as long as needed. You were living your perfect life as a Weehunt. And, just so you know, I don't have a problem with selling this land and giving it all to the assisted living home to care for my granny. If that is what needs to be done, we'll do it." His hands shook.

I had no words. *This* Randal was disturbing, but a part of me would have been glad to see he could get angry.

Stuart placed a hand on Randal's shoulder.

Randal stepped away.

"NPD is handling this."

An irrational panic slammed in my chest. I wasn't tied in with this mess. I had a life as silly and miserable as it had turned out to be. Something told me this ring had quite a story, and that it was tied in with the fire. I didn't voice this, but I had full intention of snooping around.

"Izzie, are you okay?" Stuart moved closer. And in that vulnerable moment, tears threatened to fall. I tried to swallow them. *Let go. Just cry and scream. No one deserves it more than you. Just be human.*

Stuart looked away. "You two need to stay around for a few days. It might make things easier."

"Don't worry. I plan on finding out what happened to my sister. You couldn't *make* me leave, Stuart." The passion in my voice surprised me. "Randal can do that computer school stuff."

Randal looked settled, almost relieved.

"And don't you dare bother the barn on Grassy Bald. Family stuff is there. It all belongs to me." I sounded like a kid. "I'll be back this afternoon or tomorrow to go through boxes in storage. If I find anything of Velvet's that might help or proof the ring belonged to Grandmother Iris, I'll let you know."

"Okay." Stuart walked to his truck.

"Isla, why don't you come to my gallery tomorrow night? I have something I need to talk to you about. We can talk after the art showing. Randal, you come too. Both of you will love the artist."

Why in blue blazes did she think I would go to her gallery? We finished our talking years ago. But her expression told me there was something important she needed to say. I knew the look all too well.

"Just wear jeans. We don't do fancy. The doors open at 6:30. You won't regret coming. I promise. The gallery is near town square, not far from the river." Emily walked to her jeep, assuming I would accept.

Randal came close to me, as if I wasn't mad at him. "Are you going?"

"I guess I have to. She knows something." I felt that boy smile. "Don't think for a minute I'm not mad, Randal, or that I trust one thing you say or do."

This time he outright laughed. "No ma'am. I know you don't."

I walked to the car. "Stop being a smart aleck. You made it clear you wouldn't call me 'ma'am.'"

"Yes ma'am."

"Get in the car." I looked away. I didn't want to like him. He was dangerous. More dangerous than Velvet ever was. He was her child.

"We have to talk to Mama." I turned the SUV in the direction of the assisted living home. My sudden irrational passion to know what happened to Velvet clouded any worries I had about seeing Mama in the home. When I picked her up for the funeral, Randal had gone in and brought her to the car, but when we took her back, I went in for my first look. The guilt had overwhelmed me to the point where I didn't go back to her room.

"I wouldn't sell the land. It belongs to Granny and you. Velvet really wanted to keep Granny from signing the land away. Her mind was so bad then."

"I'm glad your heart is in the right place, Randal. My sister was another story. I can't remember her ever making a decision that didn't concern her own wellbeing."

"You really hate her, don't you?"

I took a deep breath and was silent, hoping the question would go away. "It's crazy how I feel. I am determined to find out what happened to her, why she was killed, but in the same breath—I can't lie to you—I harbor harsh feelings toward her. I wish I could say the past doesn't matter, and in a lot of ways it doesn't." I looked over at him after we rolled up to a stop sign. "But some things can't be erased. A girl has to walk through trespasses made against her, and I haven't wanted to take that stroll." I stepped on the gas and was quiet for a minute. The silence was comfortable. The river snaked beside us and then we moved in the opposite direction. I looked in the rearview mirror; it appeared the river moved away from us instead of the other way around. "There is a lot you don't know."

"Tell me something I don't know. Velvet kept your existence from me. Granny never mentioned you and wouldn't talk about my grandfather. The stuff I know I had to find out by myself. On most days I feel like a freak and an afterthought."

"Maybe it's best you don't know all the details of the family." I glanced over again. "And you're not a freak."

"You don't know enough about me, Aunt Isla. You would change your mind if you did." Randal looked out the window.

"I say live and let live. I accept you for whoever you are." Jesus help me, I was using Scott's opinion.

"I bet your church friends wouldn't feel that way if they knew where I came from, how my mother acted, how crazy my grandmother is."

As shameful as it was, I didn't want the people at church to know about Randal or Velvet or even Mama. This would change their opinion of me, and I sure didn't think I could have a real conversation with him about the topic. "The church doesn't know about my family, and they don't have to know." Even I could hear the hypocrisy in that statement. "You should know more about your grandfather. He was good." I changed course.

He gave me a disgusted look. "What makes someone good or bad in another's eyes? I'm sorry, but I think my granny was good and so was Velvet. Flawed but good. I'm proud of them."

The boy wasn't a boy at all.

〜〜〜

I parked the SUV in a visitor's spot in front of the assisted living home designed to look like a large old house in the mountains with a wraparound porch filled with inviting wicker furniture. A dock even ran out into the river. "I look terrible to go in there."

"You look like a regular person, Aunt Isla. You don't have to dress up all the time. Relax." He got out of the car. "So you decided to go to that reporter's thing tomorrow?"

"I don't want to. She's nothing but trouble."

"I got a funny feeling she knows a lot about Velvet she's not saying." He matched my steps up the walk.

"She knows something that she didn't want to say in front of Mr. Collins."

"I'm going with you." He looked at me shyly. "If that's okay."

"I don't know if you should."

"I'm sorry I was such a—well, you know. I do have a temper that shows sometimes. I would do anything for Granny."

I waved my hand through the air. "Sometimes a person has to tell the truth. No reason to apologize. I *did* walk away from the family." I pulled open the door to the facility. "Even if in my mind, it was my only choice."

He walked through. .

"Mrs. Weehunt, we get to see you again." The older nurse stood behind the desk. "Lord, just look at you, Randal. Are you okay? You've been on my mind all night."

"I'm fine, ma'am."

She came out from behind the desk and placed her arm around his shoulders. "You're brave. Too old for your age. You run rings around my sassy granddaughter. She's been a real pickle these days." She gave him a genuine, sweet smile. "Your grandmother is a piece of work. One minute she's just as happy and the next she turns as ornery as a mule. It goes along with the illness." She looked at me. "Today's an ornery day." She shook her head. "Just don't expect too much, Mrs. Weehunt. It's like she understands what happened to Velvet and then she doesn't all at once." She clicked her tongue.

"I learned a long time ago not to have any expectations at all when it comes to Mama."

The nurse patted my arm. "You're one smart gal. Us daughters have to come at our mamas that way sometimes."

"She didn't like that we got her to ride in the wheelchair for the funeral," I confessed.

The nurse laughed. "That's a good sign. She remembered she was spunky and stubborn."

As we walked down the hall, my heart fluttered in my chest. A sure sign I was eating my true feelings. Memories washed over me. Mama standing at the stove with steam fogging the windows. Mama hemming a dress by a reading lamp in the living room. Now, she couldn't even understand I was of some standing in my town, church even. I was seen as accomplished, privileged. I was everything she had wanted for me but said I would never be because of my attitude. I had proved her wrong, but at what price? A question I hadn't asked myself.

Mama sat in a recliner looking out the window that faced the river. The smell of cleaning chemicals stuck in my nose. Velvet probably had a hand in the room selection. Had she visited? It was hard for me to imagine her doing so. But Mama was all she had known. Surely, she had some connection to Mama that I didn't have, some special place in her heart that should have been partly mine.

Mama's shoulders were straight and her posture good. She'd been lost in her tangled mind for five years. The woman with black depressions and who locked herself away in the bedroom weeks upon weeks after Daddy died, the woman who once wrote a twelve-page suicide note and left it for her oldest daughter, was now content in many ways. Alzheimer's had stolen her away to a new place where there were no problems. Maybe it wasn't a disease after all.

"Is that you, girl?" Mama stared hard at both Randal and me. "Lord, child, I never thought you was coming home. Look how grown up you are." She smiled. "I missed you so much."

I looked at Randal. "Mama, you know me today." I tried to sound softer, kind, but it came out as cold and fearful, almost angry.

"I know who you are." Mama blinked and gave me a solid look. "Have you figured out the secret yet? Are you ready to talk about it?"

CHAPTER 12

Randal

His aunt was like a wound-up clock since they had met, but when he told her that he was different and when he'd taken up for Velvet and Granny, electricity sparked from her. Granny seemed to catch the current.

"Mama, we came by here to let you look at this ring we found. Have you seen it before?" Aunt Isla placed her phone in front of Granny. "See how pretty it is. I never saw it before now."

Granny frowned and watched Aunt Isla. "I don't think I've seen it either. It's pretty and if the diamond is real, it would be worth some money. Looks old." She grew quiet and seemed like she wouldn't speak again but then she did. "Your grandmother had a lot of jewelry. She was always getting it from men who were in love with her." Granny clicked her tongue. "She hated men. That was the joke. Never knew her to like any man, not even and especially not Daddy. But she was friends with one. Have you been to see that boy? The odd one? He was a strange bird but much better than what you married, girl. He knows a lot about your grandmother because his grandfather was that special friend Mother had. If the ring belonged to her, I'd bet that boy would know. Lord, Mr. Jefferson had a love for Mother as deep as that old river out there. I bet that boy could give you the answer to this question. What was his name? Mark? Yes, that was it. A simple name for such a large-thinking boy. You really messed up when you let him get away." Granny shook her head and pulled at a loose thread on her shirt.

Aunt Isla looked like a lab rat caught in a maze and part of Randal enjoyed her discomfort.

"Kenneth, she always liked you the most." Granny gave him a mean smile. "Nothing I ever did was right when you were around." She nodded at Aunt Isla. "She gave me a run for my money after you died." Granny took a long, ragged breath. "Velvet died too, Kenneth." A tear rolled down Granny's cheek. "She was too young, too crazy, and hardheaded. I guess that came from growing up without a father. I thought I could take care of things on my own. I don't think I did a very good job." Granny looked back at Aunt Isla. "Go see that boy. He can help you. Finally, you've come back. I hope that means you found your senses. Child, maybe you waited too long. My answers are jumbled on my good days. Go see the boy and talk with Crow. She was the help. I think she's still alive. She should be. I don't think she'll ever die." She giggled like a disobedient child. "You'll find her on Grassy Bald. I think. Maybe. I don't know. She's somewhere around here. You remember old Crow, don't you? She was a savior for you girls. A much better mama than me."

Aunt Isla rocked back and forth on her feet. Her face was pale. "I'll try to come back tomorrow, Mama. I have some more questions for you. First, I want to look through the stuff in the barn on Grassy Bald."

"Girl, you're here to stay. You just don't know it yet. You're here to make peace with those devils. You're nothing but a wreck but you're pretty, still very pretty. What is it Velvet always called me? A beautiful wreck. That's what I'm trying to tell you, if you'll listen. To find your answers, you have to know your sister. Don't judge until you know. There is more than one secret that girl owns, and they all go together. You know, kinda how I braided your hair when you were little, bound together. You always sat still and listened to my stories. That head of hair was like a horse's mane." Granny looked out the window, lost to the real world again, smothered in another reality from the past.

Aunt Isla stepped out the door without answering. Granny drifting in and out like this always knocked Randal off balance, too, as if he were stuck in a time warp. "I'll see you tomorrow." Randal placed his cheek on top of her soft white hair and squeezed her shoulder.

"Boy, I'm sorry I couldn't stay with you. I'm deeply sorry. You need me so bad."

"Granny, you're always right here for me."

"Tell your mama to come up here and see me. We got to talk about the mess she is planning. I know what she's going to do."

His breath caught in his throat. "Don't be worrying, Granny."

"Go on now."

Randal met Aunt Isla in the hall. A dull pain had started in the back of his head.

"I don't see how you live through these visits." She touched her ponytail. "Does she always think you're my father?"

"Most of the time, but a minute ago she knew it was me. Who is this man she wants you to see? And she's talking about Mrs. Crow, who doesn't live at Grassy Bald." He walked ahead of his aunt.

"It's silly. I don't think Marcus is even here anymore. He was a guy I knew when I was in school. We grew up together. Mrs. Crow was Grandmother Iris's maid and assistant. She helped with Velvet and me when we were young. She would be older than Mama. Probably in her late eighties, early nineties. I doubt she's still around here, but Mama had a good idea. I could begin asking around. See what Velvet was into."

"Mrs. Crow is still alive. She helped take care of me too. She lives out on Pine Log Road."

"Really. That's where Marcus's family farm is too."

"Do you want to ride out there?" The sun was nearing the tree line. What a day it had been.

"No. I have somewhere I want to go. Let's grab some burgers, and I'll take you there before it gets dark." Aunt Isla smiled.

"Okay." He kind of smiled but hesitated. "Maybe I'll just get you to drop me at the fishing camp while you go to the gallery tomorrow night and pick me up on the way back."

Aunt Isla unlocked the car. "I thought you wanted to go with me. I was getting used to the idea."

"I just need some time on the river away from people. No offense."

"Well, whatever you want to do." She huffed.

He climbed into the SUV. Aunt Isla's side profile caught him in the vulnerable moment after having just left Granny. Like Velvet, his aunt had a sharp jawline and long nose. Only the two sisters could take features that challenged others and make them warm and elegant. Aunt Isla's long hair had to be her security blanket that reflected the conservative image she wanted to portray. The real woman was just below the surface of her façade. "Let me cut your hair, Aunt Isla. We'll show that reporter a thing or two."

"No. Anyway, you're not coming so you won't get to see her reaction." She pulled out on the road.

"I'll go if you let me cut your hair. I know the perfect haircut for you. Trust me."

"Something tells me this is the stupidest deal I will ever make."

"You'll love it. I promise."

"You have to go with me."

"I will. Live on the wild side, Auntie. I mean you are wearing jeans and a t-shirt, and tomorrow you're going to see an old boyfriend."

"Understand, Randal. I've worked way too hard on who I am to ruin my image now. The haircut has to fit in with who I am in Mountain City. Understood? Nothing wild and spiky. I'm not changing. I like being Isla Weehunt." She sighed, and her shoulders slumped. "And I have no old boyfriends. You'll see. Besides, I doubt Marcus is still around."

"No worries, dear Aunt Isla." Randal said, covering his laugh by pretending to cough.

CHAPTER 13

Isla

I parked the SUV in a grassy patch on an embankment overlooking the river.

Randal seemed eager for my little adventure. "I haven't been this far down. Not ever."

I handed him the sack of burgers. "I'm eating horrible here. There's a good place to sit next to the river."

"Let's go." He opened the passenger door and jumped out.

We held on to tree saplings as we took the steep, slick path down in an attempt to not lose our footing. For a minute I thought of Velvet. A tight squeeze in my chest stopped me in my tracks.

"Are you stuck, Aunt Isla?" Randal stood at the bottom looking up at me. He wore Velvet's wisecracking look.

"No. I'm just fine. I can outdo you."

He gave a snort.

When I reached him, we both looked at the rushing water in silence. There were steep cliffs on the other side of the river. I sat on the mossy ground not far from the river's edge. The dampness seeped through my jeans, but for once, I didn't feel the need to be perfect.

"Here in this place, I am Izzie." The words surprised me. I wasn't saying this to Randal as much as to the world at large.

Randal dropped to the ground beside me and passed me a cheeseburger, smashed flat and deliciously not good for me. "This is beautiful." He had the kindness to ignore my declaration.

"This isn't what I wanted you to see but we will eat first." I pointed to the cliff. "Your mother jumped from there."

His face broke into a delightful smile. "Now, that is the Velvet I knew. I could see her screaming all the way down, never worrying she would die." A shadow fell across him.

"Yes. She was fearless compared to me. Much more the elder sister in a lot of ways. Mama always said it came from being without a father, but I don't believe that. I think she was born with some group of genes I never got. Velvet was bewitching and smart. An artist."

"I just can't figure out why she stopped drawing and painting. I thought if you're an artist, you have to work on your art or you go nuts."

"A myth or maybe not, but from the time she got her first box of crayons, the girl created. She told me once when she was nine that she saw things in pictures. You know, like a writer sees an image and knows what words to use to describe it on paper? She could see the images she wanted to draw to get others to understand who she was. Everything in shadow and light. She stopped when she was sixteen. I'm not sure why." That was a lie, but I couldn't visit the reasons. I stood and brushed at my damp backside.

"There are three burgers left."

I waved them away. "You eat them." I knew he would have no problem disposing of the food. "Can you eat and walk? I have a place I want you to see. I mean, since you love the river so much."

"Sure." He walked beside me, tall and lanky in his youth but maybe not so innocent. But in that moment, us—him and me—felt right, like we had always been around each other. Me sharing my insights about the past. Him jerking me back to the present.

I couldn't help but smile. "Now keep looking. See if you can find what I brought you to see."

He chewed and studied the view in front of us.

As we rounded a curve in the trail, the water churned faster and louder.

Randal shouted. "Wow, I've never seen the Nantahala this fast."

"Keep looking."

Just ahead, as if it had grown from the banks of the river, was an opening built of stone, a black hole, an abyss. Water rushed out at a fast clip.

"Man!"

"*Yes*," I shouted back.

"How long is the tunnel?" As he spoke, a man in a bright red kayak shot out of the mouth, landing feet away in an upright position. "Did you see *that?*"

I couldn't help but laugh at his jubilance. "Sit down."

We sat on the grass. Randal waved at the kayaker, who motioned back with his paddle.

"I want to do this." He looked at me. "Would you do it?"

"I have on two occasions."

The shock on his face told me what he thought, how he had judged me for the life I had built around me. A rich housewife with no real depth or accomplishments. But isn't that what I wanted everyone to think? And hadn't I accomplished this?

"The first time I went, I was with my father in his canoe. Mama would have died if she had found out. He swore me to silence. I had just turned four. I had the time of my life, too young to be afraid. Weeks later he drowned close to here." I was quiet a minute, reaching out with my spirit to see if Daddy was wound into the rushing water. "I was pretty young, but I remember. Daddy was half Cherokee and taught me many of the beliefs his mother taught him. That's why I don't quite fit in with my church friends." I let these words sit in the air. "I know you think you have me nailed. That I'm some stodgy Bible-thumping conservative. But I believe deeply that God is here, Randal. Right here in all of this true beauty. If we want to worship him, this is the most exquisite church in the world." I opened my arms. Poor boy probably thought I was a nut. I couldn't believe it was coming out of me. "He created this. Except for the tunnel." I laughed. "It's a tunnel from when they began cutting roads through the gorge."

"Look at that water crashing out of there. When was the second time you went through?"

I smiled, mostly to myself. "I took your mama. She was ten and I was fourteen. I told her if she passed her big math test, I'd take her on an adventure, but she couldn't tell Mama."

"Velvet and you came through that tunnel." He stared at the

opening. "Somehow—no offense, Aunt Isla—I can see Velvet in that canoe better than you."

I laughed, had to. "No offense taken. That's because you know Isla Weehunt, not fourteen-year-old Izzie Leech. Like Scott told you, I was a handful."

"What was it like?"

"If I had a canoe, we'd go so you could see for yourself." Part of me—that part from so long ago—was itching to go out on the river one more time, maybe a million more times. "It was a day that looked like it might start raining again. That whole week the rain came down in buckets and the river was just below flood stage. Your mama would not take no for an answer. She told me I promised, and we had to go. Daddy would have taken me no matter what. So, I took her. She got a ninety-eight. How could I say no?

"We put in near the fishing camp. Of course we had to sneak so Mama wouldn't catch us. Marcus Jefferson—the man Mama told me to go see—brought his canoe to us. He was the same age as me, but he drove his daddy's truck anywhere he wanted on the back roads. We all had to be home by dinner. Marcus waited on us where you and I parked today to bring us home. The water was choppier than I'd ever seen it. And the canoe rocked like crazy. I told Velvet to sit in the bottom when the tunnel mouth was in view. That girl was reading that stupid tattered book you have. She was ten, Randal. How in the world did she get writing like that? But she did."

He wore an expression just like that young girl so many years before.

"As we entered the tunnel, Velvet jumped back on her seat. We were pulled into the abyss so quickly I couldn't tell her to do otherwise. The darkness was so thick you couldn't see anything, and the water so loud it swallowed all other sound. The tunnel is only a quarter of a mile long, but I tell you that was the longest stretch of water I've ever been down. I worked that paddle back and forth, fighting to keep the canoe straight. Then we hit the drop-off and the canoe tipped violently, taking in some water, but didn't turn over. That's why that book of yours is so waterlogged. The paddle kept hitting the walls. I couldn't see or hear Velvet and was sure I'd let my baby sister fall into the water to drown." *Like Daddy.* "I remembered the air hole drilled through the top of the tunnel, by the workers, I suppose. When we reached that, I would have a split second to see if Velvet was okay, and we would almost be out.

"I began praying aloud for God to save us, promising if he did, I would never go down the river again. When we passed under the air hole a streak of light showed down. Velvet's seat was empty. It took every bit of strength inside me and out to keep that canoe upright. I had been yelling for Velvet the whole time, but the screams vanished. Then it happened." I stopped talking, thinking of how I was sure Velvet had died.

"What happened?" Randal sounded like a child hearing a scary story.

"I saw Daddy plain as day. Somehow, I had the canoe pointed straight toward the opening. A jagged rock stuck out on the right side, I had to keep the canoe to the left without hitting that wall. Daddy was sitting on the bench in front of me. 'Your sister is fine. Get this canoe out of here. Keep focused.'" I paused, remembering. "I could hear him over the water. Somehow. I did what he told me. That water pushed the canoe out like a bullet from a gun. My head spun and I was screaming, screaming Velvet's name. And then I saw something bobbing out of the tunnel. I jumped into the water, leaving the canoe and paddle to float away. I was sure she was dead. But that girl flipped over on her stomach, raised her head, and looked at me. 'Let's do this again,'" I said, mimicking her little-girl voice. "I laughed so hard tears ran down my face. Velvet pointed out the canoe was way ahead. Imagine how Marcus felt when he saw that empty canoe passing him." I laughed some more. My chest heaved with the sheer joy. Wrapped in the memory, I forgot all the restraints I'd placed on my adult self.

"You lost my mama in the tunnel, Aunt Isla?" Randal was laughing hard. "Velvet was tough."

"She had to be tough." I sobered. "Our life was hard. Mama was not a happy person. But that day, as scary as it was, showed me how much I loved my sister and it showed me Daddy was still right there with me." I sighed. "When I come here, I feel him. He's right here. Probably laughing too."

"I do want to ride through the tunnel." Randal smiled.

"Let's do it before we go back to Mountain City. I'll wear that bathing suit you picked out," I teased.

"I mean it. Let's do this crazy thing, Aunt Isla." His face was young, serious, full of life that had already passed his mother and me by.

Yes, maybe I needed something scary, crazy. "It's a deal."

~~~~~

Kate was stirring something on the stove with her back to us when we arrived from our visit to the river. "We're having the best dinner you've ever tasted. I hope you're hungry."

I gave Randal a quick look. How could we say we had eaten?

"I can't wait. I'm starving, Mrs. Tucker," my nephew lied.

Kate turned a soft, relaxed smile on him. "Thank you, Randal. You must call me Kate. Lily and you have already become great friends, so we must too."

"Whatever this mystery dinner is, it smells divine." I placed my tote on the small breakfast table. "What can I do?"

Kate smiled. "Go get cleaned up." She made a face at my T-shirt and jeans.

"Well, yes." My boots were dirty but at least I hadn't tracked the floor. What was wrong with me, walking around looking like someone who had been lost in the woods? "I'll be right back to help." I turned to Randal, who wore a frown. "Go get dressed for dinner."

"Should I wear my tux?" He left the room before I could give him a swift kick.

Kate smiled at me. "Teenagers? I'm struggling with this myself. I do understand why I never had children."

"Yes. They can flip on a dime. I'll be back." I let myself out the back door. The garden glowed luscious that time of day, and I lingered for a minute. When I approached the cottage, I saw someone standing in the window of my room. I opened the front door that wasn't locked—I never thought about doing such a thing—and bounded up the stairs, running to confront whomever, and then ran right into a person. "Lily. You scared me to death." I tried to laugh.

The stormy look on her face let me know she was completely put out with adults. "I was cleaning your room, part of my job here, and some crazy woman comes running up the stairs."

"I'm sorry." Was I really apologizing to this child? "I saw someone in my bedroom window."

"Well, I guess so. I was making your bed." She huffed.

The bed looked perfect, but I couldn't help thinking she wasn't telling the truth. Had I made it? I couldn't remember. Normally I would, but there was nothing normal about this trip to the Nantahala. "Thank you but you really don't have to do that. I'll take care of things myself."

She shrugged. "I just do what my aunt tells me."

Something told me Lily did what she wanted when she wanted. "Did you know my sister? She painted the house, right?" How would Velvet have managed the pitches on the roof?

Lily's face became more closed than ever. "I saw her around here."

"You didn't talk to her?"

She wore a glare on her face and placed her hand on her hip. "I guess I had to talk to her sometimes."

I nodded. "I just wondered what your take was on her?" What a lowlife I had become.

She crossed her arms across her chest. "She was nice enough, not like other adults. That's for sure. I liked her okay." Her face softened, and I knew that the child had spent time with Velvet. Liked her.

"The last time I saw her she was only a little older than you."

Lily nodded. "I know. She told me."

I lost my breath.

"I have to go help Aunt Kate with dinner. If you don't want me to clean your room, tell her."

"That's okay. I won't rock the boat." I said this to Lily's back as she started down the stairs.

She turned. "Yep, she likes things her way." She glared at me and left.

CHAPTER 14

The midafternoon sun streamed between the canopy of trees that lined the drive I turned the car down. My heart did a little flip. How long had it been since I had stood at the foot of Pine Log Mountain?

Randal looked out the window. "I didn't even know anyone lived over here besides Mrs. Crow."

I eased the SUV down the dirt road, not because it was rough—it was maintained—but I still wasn't sure I wanted to revisit this part of my past. "I came here a lot during high school. Marcus Jefferson and I were good friends." I shook my head at the memory. "Your grandmother wanted me to marry him so bad. We weren't like that, though. She never understood or believed a boy and girl could just be friends." I parked the car behind the old farmhouse that looked silent, empty. Did Marcus still live there? More than likely Mama twisted things again. Marcus had big plans and they didn't include Nantahala or anyone from there.

Several lines of square cloths were strung from the barn roof to a large boulder on the ground. Each string held a pattern of blue, white, red, green, and yellow cloths. They were all the same exact size. When I looked at the colors flapping in the constant wind, my shoulders relaxed. The garden still grew in the backyard. Clumps of daisies were in full bloom in each corner of the fenced in area. Lavender bushes, that would bloom in September, were healthy and large. California poppies with deep orange and yellow edges, star-shaped bunches of butterfly weed, and a raised bed of purple and white columbine. The forest edged the property and whispered with a cool moist breeze. I remembered pulling weeds in the garden with Marcus's father. I was a brooding teenager then and the rhythm of hard work calmed the thoughts racing through my mind. My love for gardening was born in this place.

"This is so amazing." Randal got out of the car.

"I spent a lot of time here." The air stirred with a refreshing coolness. The cloths flapped.

"Wow, look at all the flags." Randal pointed at them.

Why hadn't I seen them as flags?

"Yes, young man, prayer flags."

I didn't turn around, but I knew that soft, solid voice. He was still in the gorge.

"Prayer flags. Interesting." I kept my stare on the colored pieces of cloth.

"Yes, Tibetan prayer flags." He stood between Randal and me.

"I'm Randal Leech, sir."

"You look just like your grandmother and this lady here." His touch to my shoulder rippled to my neck. "It's been a long time, Izzie."

"Too long, Marcus." I finally looked into his cool blue eyes. Tall and lanky with that same mop of dirty-blond hair. His face turned into a wide, welcoming smile. All the years I hadn't seen him grew in my chest as yearning. His fingers were long and slender. Piano hands had been what Mama called them. Peace was a delicious feeling; one I wasn't used to having. One that also terrified me. "Tell me how you ended up with prayer flags. I'm sure there is an adventure behind it."

"These are Lung ta prayer flags. You can tell this because they are square. They are strung on a diagonal line from highest to lowest points on such places as temples, monasteries, and mountain passes. The colors are in order and represent the five elements: earth, water, fire, air, and space."

"Space?"

The lines around his mouth softened. "As in internal space. Sitting still in the spirit, an inner life. You used to do that when you gardened. Do you still garden?"

"Yes," I answered.

"Prayers for peace, compassion, strength, and wisdom. It is believed the prayers are blown by the wind, scattering the mantras attached to them out into the world."

The flags popped. "Amazing," Randal spoke.

"I have baby goats too. Much more interesting than a bunch of flags. Do you want to see them?" He asked this as if I hadn't been gone for seventeen years, as if I belonged on his farm.

"I do," Randal said with a laugh.

"Of course," I answered.

Marcus walked toward the barn. "As the cloth of prayer flags weather, it is believed they become part of the universe. You know, like a shooting star streaking across the sky. So the prayers become part of all things."

I stopped and looked at the white clouds against the crystal-blue sky. "I don't know what to say, Marcus."

He laughed. "Let's go feed my baby goats." He took my hand in a casual, friendly way. "Sometimes it is best just to experience the silence." He opened the gate. "Of course, as I remember it, you weren't so fond of silence." A chuckle echoed from within his chest.

"Always the freethinker," I teased.

"You do remember me."

"Look at the goats, Aunt Isla." Randal spoke with childish delight.

"I hated to hear about Velvet. I used to see her in the health food store out on the interstate every now and then. Other places here and there. We talked a little. A couple of times we had tea."

"Stuart Collins says an arsonist burned the house down. He's sure of it. I'm staying here until this mess is straightened out. I have to know who killed her. And Velvet having tea with you? That seems almost civil of her."

Marcus handed a cup of feed to Randal. "Put it on the flat palm of your hand or they'll nip you without meaning to."

Randal grinned at me.

"It's nice you decided to visit me." He watched Randal and the goats. "And yes, she was one of the most honest people I knew."

"I guess you are right about that. I don't remember her telling a lie. She just kept secrets." My tone was bitter. "I should have been in touch before now. I knew it the minute I stepped out of the car." I looked around. Breathed in and out. "I miss this place."

"Dad would have loved to hear you say that." He had a slight smile on his face.

"He died?"

"Six years ago. In the garden. I had come home to help him after his first heart attack. I just stayed. It seemed the place I needed to be. I always knew I'd be here when you came back."

"How's that? I didn't even know I was coming back."

"Of course you would. This place is in your blood, my friend. You can't stay away forever. Are you writing?"

"That was a long time ago." I looked at him fully. "I wanted to talk to you about something found in Velvet's car. It makes no sense."

"What was it?" He gave another cup of feed to Randal. "They like you, son."

Randal laughed again. "They're cute."

"Yes, and they help me keep the grass in the pasture under control. And the milk is wonderful."

"Goat's milk."

"Yes, rich. Very good for you."

"Wow."

Marcus turned back to me. "What did they find?"

"They found an antique ring that is very valuable, around twenty thousand. Where would Velvet get jewelry so expensive?"

Marcus raised his eyebrows. "I have no clue."

"I thought maybe it belonged to Grandmother Iris." I pulled out my phone and showed him the photos I took.

"It's stunning. Looks like it was part of the 1920s jewelry that's so popular now. Those pieces can be quite expensive. I could pull out Grandfather Jefferson's papers and look through them. If your grandmother owned this, he would have recorded it. That is for sure. You want to come help me look?"

Randal petted the goats while feeding them. There was a part of me that wanted to keep him on the farm, to see him have fun.

"Can I come back? Randal is going to cut my hair this afternoon, and we have a gallery show to attend this evening."

A shadow passed over Marcus's face, but only for a moment before restoring his genuine smile. "That would be Emily Greene. Never thought you two would be talking again." He gave me a curious stare.

"Seems she knows something about Velvet and wants to string it out. I'm going so I can find out about my sister."

He nodded. "I don't blame you. And it doesn't surprise me. You've always been there for her."

"Ha." I couldn't help it. "I have been gone for years, Marcus."

A patient smile was turned on me. "You don't have to be right here under her to care, to want to find out where things went wrong. Velvet was headed down when you guys had the falling out. With you leaving, she jumped down the black hole. She knew she was wrong."

"How do you know all this?"

"I was probably Velvet's only friend after you left and the news hit town. We talked a lot after Randal was born and before I left. That boy has been here so many times. But he was just a baby." He looked at Randal. "Send me that picture so I can look for a mention of the ring." He took my phone and put his number in the contacts.

Randal walked to us, wiping his hands on his jeans.

"Mr. Jefferson is going to check his grandfather's papers for mention of the ring."

"Granddad's journals and papers are in the attic. I will get them out and begin going through them this evening."

"Take your time. I have your number. I'll call you in the morning to see what you found."

"That's great. We'll have dinner here. I'll cook. You can check out the old papers too. You might find them interesting since they are about your grandmother."

The thought relaxed me. "Yes, sounds good."

"Randal, you come."

"I would love it," Randal answered.

"We have to go if you're going to cut my hair and keep your promise," I said with a smile.

"I'm going to make Aunt Isla a knockout," Randal informed Marcus.

Marcus looked at me and back to Randal. "Your aunt has always been a knockout, Randal. I'm curious to see how you can improve her."

"Now it's getting crazy here." I smiled. "When is a good time to call in the morning?"

"Anytime. I'm up before the sun." He patted his pockets and produced a card. *Marcus Jefferson, Herbalist.* "Here you go. Just in case I don't answer my cell. This is the landline."

"Really. An herbalist? I thought you had other plans."

"Ah, life does sneak up on us and change things around."

"I'll call you tomorrow."

"Good. I look forward to hearing from you. It'll be fun."

"Thank you." I didn't want to leave. Were we still friends? Really? Was there any part of the old Izzie left?

"Have fun at the show. I might come by. Not sure. Emily doesn't care for me too much."

"Really? Well, I'm thinking you and I still have a lot in common because I don't care for her too much."

"Maybe. But I have a feeling, Izzie, you care for people more than you let anyone see. And she doesn't like me because I wouldn't give her an interview about my herb garden and business. She thought I still held hard feelings about how things went for you." I matched his long stride back to the car.

"She's crazy." I climbed into the SUV. "I'll call you tomorrow morning."

"Good."

I backed the car out, then headed up the road, glancing in my rearview mirror more than I should have. Marcus watched until I couldn't see him anymore. Something told me he stood there a while longer.

"Somebody has a thing for my auntie. And what is all this stuff about 'what happened' to you?"

I turned the SUV onto a crossroad. "Don't be silly. Not Marcus Jefferson. We're friends. And the other is just old news on a beautiful day. We don't have time for it."

"I'm good at reading people, Aunt Isla. It's a gift I have. The man has a thing for you."

"Well, I'm married, and when I left this godforsaken gorge, Marcus Jefferson was planning on being a priest."

Randal wore a smug smile on his face. "What was it he said? Life has a way of sneaking up on you. My dear aunt, you're not dumb."

CHAPTER 15

Randal

The rich red of Aunt Isla's hair didn't come from a bottle. It was her shining star. He wet it in the wide deep kitchen sink at the Bradford house.

Lily sat at the breakfast table to watch. "How are you going to cut it?"

Randal guided his aunt to a chair he had placed in the middle of kitchen. "I had better scissors before the fire." He studied the pair Lily had loaned him.

"Do we need to go buy a pair?" Aunt Isla asked.

Part of him loved she was so nervous. "Naw, I'll manage. I have a new look for you, dear auntie."

She gave him one of her sharp looks. "I'm not sure new will look good on me."

"I'm going to tell you like it is. You wear your hair like all the other wealthy women, the ones who don't have enough to do. I saw your scrapbook. You guys all look the same in those black-and-white newspaper photos. Like you think the same thoughts. Scares me." He shook his head as he ran a wide-tooth comb through her long straight hair.

She shot him a warning look.

"You're a river girl at heart. I saw you yesterday. I know that look. I see it on my own face."

"Bravo." Kate stood in the back door. "Do something different, Isla. Randal, you can do mine next." He should feel sorry for Lily's aunt. First, her hair was a lifeless washed-out blond, and she looked ten years older than Aunt Isla. Second, the woman tried so hard to fit in with his aunt, who seemed to like her a lot but didn't notice how hard she worked. He couldn't really read her. She was too fuzzy and bland. That happened sometimes with dull people.

"He won't have time. He's going to Emily Greene's art gallery with me," Aunt Isla said.

"That's great. We can go together. Lily and I want to see this artist's work. It is all the talk right now. Some culture in this drab place."

Lily frowned. That girl had the prettiest face when she was smiling. Even prettier than when she smiled, which was pretty enough. He swallowed back a desire.

"If you don't mind waiting around. I have to meet with Emily after the show."

"We will roam. It's First Friday." Kate nodded. "It will be fine."

"What is First Friday?"

Randal had finished combing Aunt Isla's thick hair.

"The businesses around the square stay open late and serve cocktails and food." Lily perked up and shot a wink toward Randal. "They had a great band last month."

Randal, without giving a lot of thought to his actions, began to pull and clip Aunt Isla's hair. He measured one lock and cut several inches off.

"Good Lord. How much are you cutting?" Aunt Isla tried to look at the floor.

Randal never questioned the image that formed in his mind when he began to style. "You'll see. Relax."

"You better not make me look bad. You haven't had a bit of training."

"Sometimes a talent comes to a person naturally. I'm an artist at this. Just think about how Uncle Scott will react. Or better, that Mr. Jefferson we visited today." Randal moved the scissors and hair fell away. Lily and Kate faded out of his vision. With each section, he cut, angling, shaping, feathering. The clipping reminded him of a melody floating on the air. When the feeling seeped away, Randal focused on his creation. "I need a blow dryer," he said. "With a long cord."

Lily bounded out of the room, then returned. Minutes later,

Randal had brushed his aunt's hair into the concept he'd seen in his mind.

Lily clapped. "Wow. You have to do mine."

Aunt Isla touched her hair. "It's gone. Oh God. I feel so light, naked." She looked at the floor. "You're scaring me."

"Get the mirror off the wall in the powder room," urged Kate. "You are *gorgeous*. I don't know who this Marcus guy is, but he will flip."

Randal stepped in front and looked at Aunt Isla. He had recreated Velvet. Would Aunt Isla ever forgive him?

Lily held the mirror in front of Aunt Isla.

A slow smile spread across her face. "This is me? I don't know. It's so short." She looked at Randal, studied him, waited for him to speak.

He smiled back at her. "I found the real you. That's my talent."

She gazed into the mirror for a long minute. "It does make me look younger."

"See."

"Okay. And there is nothing special about Marcus, Kate. I'm married. I take that *very* seriously."

For a minute Kate studied her. "That's why I like you, Isla. We are so much alike."

Randal could tell Aunt Isla liked the haircut. Maybe, just maybe, things would be okay between the two of them.

Once they found out who set the fire.

〜〜〜

Randal had chosen a larger room on the second floor of the Bradford House. Not because of the size but because of the big double windows looking out on the Victorian cottage that Velvet painted. A life he knew nothing about. Aunt Isla looked so much like his mother, especially now. This woman just appeared in his life at the right time. Or maybe not. Maybe she couldn't be trusted. He didn't really know who she was any more than she knew him. Two strangers stuck together because of a murder. That might not be the best of situations.

He flopped on the bed and pulled the tin out of his backpack. The same letter he always read fell into view.

March 29, 2006

Deeply Missed:

I was meant to be a part of this crazy life, the mountains, the river, even Nantahala that is full of people that hate me. All for good reason. You predicted this would happen. I've brought it on myself. I'd like to say it's not my fault, but it would be a lie. I've chosen most of the paths I've walked down.

Sometimes I hate you. Well, let's be honest, most of the time I hate you for being my judge and jury. You and all your perfect ways. Who wouldn't hate you? Then I look at the Nantahala River and my heart cracks open. I miss you so deeply I search for you in my dreams. I don't have to search in my awake hours. I know where you are, but you won't have me. For this I hate you. When I was young, Mama told me the Cherokee belief of going to the water. Something my father believed because he was half Cherokee. That moving water is sacred and could purify.

Recently I went to the river near the family's fishing camp. I thought of Virginia Woolf and the stones shoved in her coat pockets. Her last swim in the River Ouse. Then I thought of Kenneth Leech, the man I call my father. Did he make the same choice as Ms. Woolf? Did he topple his canoe in the tunnel and allow the river to take him where it pleased, to own him as it must have wanted for so long?

I peeled off my blouse and skirt. I thought I would remove the bad things I had done. I walked out into the river as if I belonged there, as if it was part of the me and pushed forward, caught the current, and rode it like a freshwater dolphin. I sailed that river a good mile before I swam to the bank and walked back to the fishing camp in my bra and panties, taking my time, thinking. Thinking. Thinking I was a wreck, a bad mangled car wreck but I was beautiful. I was a beautiful wreck. And where are you? Do you share the chaos that twists my soul? Or are you safe, taken care of, happy?

Randal folded the letter. A small glimmer of an idea popped into his head, but he couldn't be right. No. He placed the tin back in his backpack and tucked it under his pillow. For the first time since he found the letters, he decided to leave them behind, as if he had a vision they might be destroyed, stolen, found. After all, the letters belonged to him now with Velvet dead. No longer did he carry guilt for having them. They were the only thing he had that truly was his mother's. He would leave his backpack behind for the evening.

CHAPTER 16

Isla

"Hurry, Randal. We're going to be late." I knocked on his door, then tossed my hair. It amazed me how much I liked my new cut. "I'll be downstairs, so get your butt out the door." I pulled my phone from my purse. No calls.

I wore the yellow sundress instead of the suggested jeans. Maybe I was in an adolescent frame of mind. It was stupid to go to Emily's gallery anyway. She had proven long ago she was no friend of mine.

Randal charged out of the door behind me. "Gosh, Aunt Isla, I had to look twice. I didn't know you."

"I don't want to look that different," I smarted off. "I was a river girl when I was young. I've outgrown that stuff."

His face turned serious.

"What's wrong?"

"Later I want to show you something I found."

"Are we ready?" Kate stood on the landing.

"Yes." I would ask Randal about this *something* when we returned home.

~~~~~

Kate parked near the square in front of a large bottle tree covered in red, blue, and yellow bottles. "The tree looks new."

"People still believe in ghosts becoming trapped in them," Randal said. "Don't laugh, Aunt Isla."

"I've got a living spirit I would love to capture in one of those bottles." Of course, I was thinking of Scott Weehunt and how I hadn't heard from him again. Nothing. The streets were full of people. "Nantahala isn't what I remember on a Friday night."

"You haven't been here in a long time. We've moved up in the world." Randal's sarcasm didn't go unnoticed.

A group of boys around Randal's age stood on one of the corners. At first, I thought they were staring at Lily. Her hair was wound on top of her head in a knot, and she wore an evergreen-colored dress that looked great on her. She had her arm twisted around Randal's.

One of the boys, with a football player's build, stepped away from the group. Hate spread across his face.

I stopped walking and stared at him.

"Come on, Aunt Isla," Randal whispered in my ear. "That's Trevor White. He's not worth a dime of your time." Randal, a vein popping out on his forehead, pushed past the boy, all while containing his anger.

I gave the group my nastiest look and followed Randal.

"Who was that?" Lily asked.

"Lily is home schooled and doesn't know the kids here," Kate said. "I'm beginning to believe I made the perfect choice after seeing those boys."

"Aunt Kate, you can't judge all the kids by those idiots." Lily smiled up at Randal.

"He's a jerk in more ways than one." Randal's voice held an edge. "It's me he has a problem with."

"Let's go to the gallery." Maybe Randal should have gone to the fishing camp. I tucked my arm through his free arm. He gave me a surprised smile. What had gotten into me?

The art gallery was in one of the old warehouses that used to stand empty when Emily and I were kids. Long windows flanked the huge brick building, their eyes reflecting on a road of stone pavers. People were spilling from inside onto the sidewalk.

A cold chill worked through me. "Maybe we should just skip this."

What could she want to tell me that would make a big difference in our circumstances?

"No way." Randal nudged me. "We have a deal. And everyone has to see your hot haircut."

Kate opened the door and we filed inside.

The scent of apples and cinnamon greeted us with a smile. Our small group split up, each going to a different painting. I stood in front of a tall canvas, a painting of the bend in the river with a bank covered in long grass that seemed to move in a breeze. The sun slid into the tree line and reflected on the water. I knew that capturing reflections in water on canvas was challenging. This Velvet taught me when we still liked each other. The next painting, labeled as 29 X 21 inch, sported an old black woman standing over a steaming pot. Her back was turned, and the image seemed familiar. A young boy, white with a splattering of freckles and a look of both pure glee and terror held a lobster over the boiling water, poised to drop. The wrinkles on the woman's hands amazed me, so detailed.

"Don't you love this work?" Emily stood beside me.

"I'm in awe," I whispered as the room seemed to grow quiet, and all I noticed was the brilliance of the artist's detail, a happy story, maybe, with no dark edges just out of sight.

"I didn't recognize you. Randal had to point you out." She studied me. "Wow, you look great. Who did your hair?"

"Randal."

"The whole family is creative."

My chest filled with silly pride. "Yes, it seems he is very talented."

Emily walked to the next canvas. "Look at this one." The painting featured a girl with long brownish hair about the length of Lily's. Her back was to the artist, arms flung out at her sides, face upturned to the sky, as if she were completely lost in a game of pretend. Once again, the facial features were not visible. The painting brought a quietness inside. Peace spread through me.

"This one is unbelievable."

"Yes." Emily moved around the wall.

The next canvas was the largest so far. In a yard was a boy, knees skinned, swinging in a tire swing. I looked at Emily. "I would love to meet this artist. This makes me think of the tire swing I had when I was young."

"This artist's work leaves a lot of people speechless. I'm glad you came. I'll find you when things die down in a while. I have something to talk with you about."

"The last time you said that to me, we began hating each other." I gave her a smile.

Emily returned my smile. "Help yourself to food and drinks. And for the record, I never hated you, Isla." Emily left me standing in front of another tall painting of the Nantahala River. The very place Randal and I had stood the day before. A long copperhead sunned itself on a dead log. The fishing camp looked new. A woman with red hair, almost the color of mine, wearing an emerald-colored dress, stood looking out over the water. Oblivious to the danger of the snake close to her foot.

Randal came to stand beside me.

"Randal, look at this."

"Wow."

"My thoughts exactly."

"That's the fishing camp." He took a step closer to the painting. "This is too weird. It shows the work I've done."

"I know. Someone loves it as much as us. If I didn't know better, I'd say the woman was me but younger, more modern."

"The woman in the painting does look like you, Aunt Isla."

"Am I missing something? Who would paint an old me?" I looked around the room to see if I could identify the artist lurking in a corner nearby.

There was no one.

"What will you do while I talk to Emily?" I asked Randal. Kate and Lily had joined us again. "You could come with me. I have a feeling this conversation will be something you want to hear."

He shook his head. "No, I'm actually enjoying myself, and I don't want to ruin it. Besides, I want to keep hanging out with my friend here." He grinned at Lily, which sent a wrinkle I could feel to my brow.

"I'm going over to the bookstore," Kate said. "Do you two want to tag along?"

Lily wrinkled her nose. "No. I want to get a good place to hear the band."

Randal shrugged. "She's the boss."

Lily smiled. "You got it."

"I'll see you when I'm finished here," I said. "We can meet at the square. Don't get in trouble, Randal." I was thinking of that group of boys.

"It's Nantahala, Mrs. Weehunt," Lily said with a smile.

My phone rang before I could snap a comeback. Scott's number appeared on the screen. "It's Scott. I need to take this."

Randal gave me a serious look. "Let him know about your hair and that wonderful Mr. Jefferson."

I raised the phone to my ear and shooed him away.

"Is that you, Izzie?"

"Hold on, Scott." I covered my phone after Kate pointed to the girl with her arms spread out.

"I bought that painting for the sitting room at home," she informed me.

"I'm buying one too." I pointed to the painting of the fishing camp. I put the phone back to my ear. "Scott?"

"Are you still in Nantahala?"

The crowd in the art gallery had thinned but the room was still noisy. "Yes."

"Are you in a bar?"

"Not quite. I'm at an art gallery. I've found a fascinating painting that I am buying."

"Some things never change. You're always pretending to know a lot about nothing." He sounded testier than I had heard him in a while.

"I know art, Scott. That's one thing I know. Remember, I am a writer. I grew up in a family who loved art."

He laughed. "Lordy, Izzie, I thought you were a good Christian woman who went to church every time the doors open. Trying to convince everyone you're as good and as smart as them. And mostly everyone believes the fake you. You've done a good job. But see, I know the girl from the gorge. She sure as shootin' ain't some artsy person."

"You're drunk. I'm not arguing with you," I said as Emily walked toward me. "And I'm not coming home anytime soon. Maybe not at all." I tapped the end button and turned off the phone. "I want to buy the painting of the woman in green and the one of the boy on the tire swing." I'd show Scott a thing or two. "That one is our land, the fishing camp." I nodded at the painting while a young woman hung a sold tag on a hook beside the canvas.

"Good show, Emily." The young woman studied me.

"Yes. It was the best yet." Emily touched my arm. "This is Isla Leech Weehunt."

The girl looked surprised but recovered her professional face. "So nice to meet you, Mrs. Weehunt. I'm Ruth Glover. I sometimes work with Emily setting up the shows."

"This was beautifully done."

A shy smile. "Yes, the artist is very talented. This made my work easy."

"I told Emily I wanted her to introduce me to this creative person."

"Ah, the artist made me swear to keep him or her anonymous," Emily spoke.

"If I were that good, I would plaster my name everywhere."

Emily gave a short laugh. "You're that good at writing. We both know that."

"Not these days. I haven't written more than a thank you note in years."

"Come upstairs with me. The view is unbelievable." She looked at Ruth. "Watch things for a while." Emily led me through a narrow door. "The loft is up here."

We climbed the steep wooden stairs that creaked with each step. The door opened onto a huge space with big windows that framed the river that twisted on the east side of town. A set of French doors opened to a large balcony with wrought-iron railing. Two overstuffed armchairs sat facing the square. In between was a table with a bottle of red wine and glasses.

"Sit. Let's watch the sun go down for a minute. Would you like a glass of wine?"

I was on a roll, about to break the "no alcohol" rule twice. What would the church women think? "Yes. I would love a glass." Just the thought of Scott telling me I pretended to know everything drove me crazy. He might be right but coming from him it made me sick. Besides, who was he to critique me?

The sound of the bottle being uncorked moved through me as a shudder, a shadow walking over my grave as Mama used to say. Emily poured the wine into the glasses.

I placed my legs on the comfortable ottoman. When was the last time I actually relaxed? I sipped the wine, and because I didn't drink, the tingling warmth of a high buzzed through me instantly.

"So you loved the artwork?"

"Yes." The band began to tune somewhere in the distance. "Why am I here, Emily? We didn't part best of buddies. And I really doubt we're playing catch-up. If you think you can find out some secret about Velvet from me, you're going to be disappointed. I know nothing about her as an adult."

"I didn't bring you here about the fire." The first stars began to blink.

"So why?" I took another slow sip of wine.

"I wanted you to see the show."

"Really?"

"You don't have a clue? I'm disappointed. I gave you more credit." Emily's voice held an edge.

A slice of moon hung near the horizon. "What am I supposed to know?"

"Think about the art."

The thing about Emily Greene was she made me mad with all her know-it-all stuff, always had. "It's fascinating."

Emily shook her head. "I was hoping I wouldn't have to spell it out. I was betting on you nailing the artwork."

"You're talking in circles. Just tell me."

"This is about blood, family." Sirens sounded in the distance as she swatted at a pesky insect buzzing between us. "Isla, you asked me who the artist is."

"Yes."

Emily looked out over the square, now lit up with clear lights. "The artist is Velvet, your very own sister. You bought the painting she did of you. That's why we spent so much time together. She worked the whole winter painting at the Bradford House and obviously not just walls. I'm not sure how she became friends with Kate. Her own son didn't know. She was afraid she couldn't measure up to the family legacy, to you. Kate called me to look at the paintings. I thought Velvet would throw me out. She almost did. I never thought she would agree to show them. I had to swear never to tell. Not even Randal. Kate was the only one who knew, and she seems to keep secrets very well."

"Velvet." Her name sat in the air. *Velvet.* Yes, it made sense. Hadn't the knowledge been tugging at me since I saw the first painting this evening? Of course it was Velvet. My sister was a magnificent painter.

"And Kate knew? She never let on."

Emily shrugged. "They seemed to be good friends. I did point out their differences, but Velvet said they had a lot in common."

Kate must have felt sorry for Velvet since she had lost her job, but friends? This didn't fit the woman I just met. Surely she had heard about Velvet's reputation with married men. We had to sit down and talk about Velvet and what she really knew.

"I'm sorry to interrupt." Ruth Glover stood in the French doors. "There's an emergency." She looked at me. "Mrs. Weehunt, your nephew has been rushed to the hospital. There was some kind of fight in the alley under the bridge."

Emily stood, her hand reaching toward me. "I'll take you."

I stood and my legs went to water, but my head was clear, completely clear. "I turned off my phone."

"Come on. He's young. He'll be okay." Emily touched my arm.

"Your friend, Miss Kate, said to tell you that she's following the ambulance."

My stomach flipped. Had it been the boys we'd seen earlier? Was this because they saw Randal as different? Or was it because of his mother? The fire?

Please God don't punish Randal for all the wrongs the adults in his life committed.

CHAPTER 17

"My nephew, Randal Leech, has been brought here." I gripped my purse straps like a lifeline. Emily had dropped me at the door of the emergency room while she parked.

A young woman looked up from her computer screen with a sad expression I wanted to slap off her face. "Just have a seat. The doctor will be out to talk to you in a minute."

"I need to know about Randal now. I'm his guardian. My sister—his mother—just died. He needs me," I said, pointing to my chest. "What has happened? No one can tell me this?"

"I'm sorry, Ms. Leech. I don't have any information at this time."

"No." I held up my hand, showing her my wedding ring. "I'm Isla Weehunt. Leech is my maiden name."

The young woman frowned as she stood. "Mrs. Weehunt, you're making a scene. Please have a seat. They only just arrived here with him. He's not even in the system yet."

A scene? The child hadn't experienced a scene, not yet. "I just need to know if he's okay. Could you tell me that?" My voice went into a high pitch and tears ran down my face.

A hand rested on my shoulder. "Izzie, come sit down." Lo and behold, Stuart stood behind me.

"Hi, Mr. Collins," the ninny of a girl twittered.

"Hi, Annie. If you could get us some info on Randal, we would appreciate it."

I allowed him to lead me to the far corner of the waiting room that was small but nearly full of people, all of who sat in hard dull-gray, plastic chairs. A TV mounted in a corner of one wall played a 24-hour news station with the volume turned down low. The whole place had fallen silent; all attention turned on me.

"Just give them a minute. I'll be right back." Stuart walked toward the front desk.

I nodded, not sure at all that I could sit. A silent prayer begging God to spare Randal escaped my heart once again. Me. Really praying. Not for show. Things were out of control.

Now Emily stood close by. "Isla, you look like you need to sit down."

"Quit telling me to sit. I can't." I worked the strap of my purse. "Have you seen Kate? She will know what happened. And *where* is Lily?"

"Kate is outside speaking with the police. I don't know where her niece is."

"Did you find anything out?" My breath caught in my chest like a wedged stone.

"Only that Randal is seriously hurt from a fight. That's all I could get out of anyone." She gave me a small tug on the arm. "Sit down before you fall." Her voice softened. "See, Stuart is talking to someone over there." She nodded.

I dropped into a seat. What kind of guardian leaves her seventeen-year-old nephew to roam a town with thugs who hate him?

Stuart walked over to me. "They are working on him now. It is bad, Izzie. I won't lie to you." He was quiet a minute. "He coded as soon as they got him in the room."

I stood. "Dead? He *died?*"

He touched my hand. "If it was going to happen, this was the best place for it to happen."

I didn't have the energy to pull my hand away.

"The doctor will be out as soon as he can. The police will want to talk with you."

I began to bargain with God, making promises of living a pious life until I died. I begged Him to forgive me for turning my phone off, drinking wine with my feet up when Randal needed me most. What kind of person was I? But until this fire, hadn't I been doing what good church-going Christians did day in and day out? Living a life as free of sin as I believed I could? Maybe it was more than that. Maybe I should promise to live my life as honestly and to the fullest. If only Randal could get better. I could tell him everything I knew. Explain the whole family. *Please, God, let him live.*

"Mrs. Weehunt!" Lily rushed in and over to me, bright spots of blood here and there on her dress that bore a rip near the shoulder.

"What happened to Randal?"

The child was paler than normal. "It was all my fault. I caused it. I saw him just now, his ghost."

"What are you talking about?" The crazy edge in my voice sent a look of alarm across her face.

"Do you want me to call your husband?" Stuart offered.

"No." I gave him a hateful look and turned back to Lily. "Randal's ghost? What are you talking about?"

"I'm sorry. I shouldn't have said that." She looked like she might bolt from the room.

"Are you the family of Randal Leech?" I turned toward the voice to see a doctor, his mask pulled down under his chin, his scrubs wrinkled and bloodstained.

"I am his aunt and guardian," I said stepping forward. "What has happened?"

The doctor herded us deeper into the corner of the room before speaking. "Your nephew was beaten badly. He coded once—we used the paddles on him—and we got him back. He is stable for the moment but in critical condition. The extent of his head injuries is not clear and won't be until we do some tests and he regains consciousness. He has a broken leg, broken wrist, and broken elbow. The best I can tell you now is that we have to wait. The next twenty-four hours are critical." He paused. "We'll keep him sedated until we can do a CT scan and see if he has bleeding on the brain."

There was that word critical again. "Who did this to him?"

"Ma'am, I have no idea. You'll have to talk to the police about that. If you would like to see Randal before we move him to ICU, follow me." He took a step back. "But it can only be a short visit."

Tubes of different sizes ran from Randal's arms and one large ventilator tube ran from his mouth. My hands shook. I curled my fingers into fists to still them. His face was swollen and discolored. His eyes were black and his lip split. A small amount of blood trickled down his cheek. A nurse wiped it away. I would never have known this person was Randal if I hadn't talked to the doctor.

"Like I said, we don't want him to wake up right now. We want his brain to rest, so we can see what is happening. Most doctors, including me, believe a coma patient can hear everything. You can speak with him for a minute before they move him." The doctor touched my arm lightly, then left.

Coma? Had he used the word coma? I stood beside Randal, touching his hand. The knuckles were busted and crusty with blood. Why hadn't they bandaged them? Maybe because there was so much to bandage on his body. I leaned over to bring my lips close to his ear, then brushed a bit of hair back. "You will be out of here soon. We have to visit Mama, and I need someone to help me with Grassy Bald. I have to go through the writing studio and barn." I took a breath. I didn't want to make this all about me. He needed to know . . . "They are taking you up to a room, Randal. I'll be there soon. I won't leave you until you wake up. I promise. We'll see this through together." I stepped away and allowed my shoulders to slump.

"Good job." The nurse mouthed at me.

I nodded, then left.

The lights in the hall had a sickly cast. When Daddy died, Mama brought me to this same hospital. I stood alone for the longest time in the corner of the same waiting room I'd been in earlier, trying to understand what was happening. It was the first time I had seen a dead body. At first Mama refused to allow me to see Daddy—said it wouldn't be good to remember him like that—but I begged and begged, cried aloud until she gave in out of pure grief. As we walked down the long hospital corridor, my determination dissolved. My face turned hot, and everything around me went quiet. I remembered thinking *save me,*

Mama. But hadn't I begged to see him? Still, mothers were supposed to protect their children from their wants.

He was on a gurney. I hung back. Mama took my hand, pulled me closer. His skin was pure white in places, purple in others. His mouth was a line, and his eyes were half closed. Empty. That was my thought. I had only been four. But I knew. I knew my daddy wasn't there anymore.

〜〜〜

Emily and Stuart stood in the corner of the waiting room, holding Styrofoam coffee cups in their hands.

"They will let me know when he is settled in ICU." I had to force the words from my mouth. All I wanted to do was be quiet, wait, and concentrate on willing Randal to be okay.

"Let's find a place to talk." Stuart watched as if I were a caged animal. "Emily can wait here for them to call."

"No. I'm not leaving this place until I know what room he's in." I shook my head.

"I wanted to fill you in on what I know while we have time."

Lily? Where had she gone off to? "What do you mean?" In times after a tragedy, people don't stop to think about the details, the events that don't fit. I never asked how Stuart knew Randal was hurt and where to meet me. "How would you know anything?"

"Let's have some coffee." Stuart tried to guide me toward a hallway. "Maybe a donut."

"I don't want a donut, Stuart," I snapped and held my ground.

"Don't be difficult. You need to eat. You don't know how long Randal will be like this. You need your strength."

"Stop," I shouted. "Don't say things like that. Understand?"

"Yes."

A pain stabbed me in my ribs and chest. I tried to take a deep breath, but it caught.

"Are you okay?" Stuart showed genuine concern.

I nodded. "Maybe coffee would be good."

The public cafeteria was large and crowded with tables and chairs. "Cream and sugar?" he asked.

"Yes." I dropped into the nearest chair, my legs melting beneath the table, as if I had been walking for miles. I glanced around; nurses and doctors and other medical personnel sat about, taking their breaks, eating their dinners.

Stuart placed a cup and saucer in front of me. "Here you go. I hope it's the way you like it."

I thought of Scott. I had to call him. Let him know.

Stuart held his own cup up to his lips. "Hospital Joe," he said before taking a sip. "A person doesn't much think about how it tastes."

"As soon as Randal is better, we're leaving this place. I shouldn't have come back. You can figure out what happened to Velvet. And I'm taking Mama too. I'm putting this place behind all of us. I'll sell Grassy Bald and Mama's land. I don't care what anyone says. How in the world could I have stayed in town tonight, knowing Randal had kids who didn't like him? I had seen it for myself. I didn't know they would try to kill him because they think he's—" I said as though I'd already figured the thing out. "Because he doesn't love sports or hunt or any of the things, they think makes a man a man. Well, they don't know what I know."

Stuart looked surprised.

"This place is so backward." An older couple at the next table looked at me. "We're living in the twenty-first century. Boys shouldn't be beaten up for being different. What kind of place *is* this?"

Stuart leaned forward. "Settle down, Izzie. I truly doubt you would get a better response in Mountain City. Not all the people are like this. It's the same everywhere. It won't change. Different only means 'different from me.'"

"What do you know about Randal?"

"I can tell you the whole situation is not simple, Izzie. Nothing is black or white. There is always that gray area."

The man drove me crazy with his philosophical talk. "Just get to the point if there is one."

Stuart's phone rang. He removed it from his shirt pocket and stared down at the screen. His face bore a frown. "I have to take this. It's work. Sorry. Sit there."

"No," I said standing. I hadn't bothered to touch the coffee. "I'm going back to the waiting room. You can tell me later."

Stuart started to say something, then nodded and moved away.

On the way down the hall, I dialed Kate's cell but went into voice mail. She could tell me more than Stuart. We thought alike. Plus, she would know how desperate I was to find out what happened to Randal.

CHAPTER 18

I pulled the chair close to Randal's bed and watched him, studied his beaten face. How had I gotten here? In this town? In this hospital? This room? So off the track of my life? Until Velvet died, my days might not have been fulfilling but they were safe, comfortable. Yes, I had been in a place where I could be quiet and not think. Now, this boy was shaking everything up, and I didn't want that to happen. I touched his hand, and a deep rush of emotion I had almost forgotten surged through me. Love. Real love. And that was dangerous. Randal was an innocent person caught in a crazy family. He hadn't hurt me. Why couldn't I just love him?

I watched him and watched him for what seemed like hours. In that room, I couldn't tell if the sky had gone from dark to daylight. Maybe if I kept a vigil, I could bring what the church called a complete healing his way. All my involvement in Mountain City Baptist Church hadn't done a thing for my true beliefs. The ones that are way down in a gal's chest and keep her company all the time. The person who fell in love with Scott, the young, charming Scott, didn't exist. I was empty inside; echoing words of failure floated through me.

Faith wasn't a word I batted around even for show. Not one phrase from the thousands of sermons I listened to over the years came to me. There was no peace or assurance. Instead of trust, I had questions, hard questions. God wouldn't let a young man go through this, right? He only just lost his mother.

Sitting in that room with the machines whirling, I had never felt so lost and alone. In a matter of days, the assertions I counted on—one being my strong resolve not to care—were gone. But I had to believe. I had to believe in something bigger, stronger than me. Sitting in that cold room, machines ticking off seconds, minutes, hours, I was finally still enough to realize how being in control had made me hollow. My energy was gone. What plan could I make to correct this mess? It came down to believing in something outside of me to take over the situation.

"Please get better, Randal. We have a lot to say to each other. I guess I am the one who has a lot to say." I whispered. "Young boy, live so I can tell you the truth. You deserve to know."

〜〜〜

I'm not sure how much time had passed when a tap on the window looking out into the hall got my attention. Kate stood there. She was what Mama would have called a sight for sore eyes. Had she been home to change?

I went into the hall and closed the door behind me.

"I wanted to check on Randal and you." Her face was pale. "Have you eaten?"

"The look on your face tells me I must look horrible."

She smiled. "You look pretty bad, Isla."

I touched my hair and the sudden memory of Randal cutting it flooded me. I refused to allow the tears building in me to come out. "How is Lily? She left when I went back to see Randal. I thought she would wait."

"She is at home. I don't want her talking to anyone right now, Isla. I've been interviewed by the police off and on for hours now, and I have asked them to give Lily until morning before questioning her. Maybe she will be stronger."

"I hope they have caught who did this to Randal."

"It's involved, dear. We will talk about it when you've rested, and Randal is out of danger."

"Do you know who did this to him?"

Kate's expression closed. "I don't know the answer to that question."

But something felt wrong. Our companionship was tabled. Now she was saying what "should" be said. How many times had I decided to skate around a subject rather than be involved? "Thank you for checking on me." Maybe she was lying to me about what she knew. Kate was a good woman, but good women were known to lie. Look at Mama. She was the worst kind of liar, but one could only see her as a good woman. "I know those boys attacked Randal because they think he's gay, whether he is or whether he isn't. My gosh, Kate, this is not 1960. Aren't we supposed to be in a better place? People can be who they are. I don't think anything has changed in this place. I don't think it ever will."

"Don't be so quick to blame the whole town for this. You don't know what happened, but whatever did, it was a crime committed by a person or people, not everyone. You just have a cross to bear when it comes to this place."

I took a deep breath to spout words to prove my point, but I knew she wouldn't hear me. And really, Nantahala as a whole had nothing to do with the problems with my family. Did it? "What made you a lover of Nantahala?" And I knew what I saw in the eyes of that group of boys.

She gave me a sharp look. "I'm not at all. I just know the whole story. You don't."

"Then tell me." But my voice lacked conviction.

"Have you called your husband?"

I looked away. "No."

"This isn't about you two. It's about Randal. Your husband needs to know what is happening so he can help you, Isla."

I frowned. "I guess." Scott's help would come with a high price.

Kate looked disappointed. "Just call him. I have to go home. Don't wait, Isla. Call him. Please listen to me."

Exhaustion washed over me. Why did she care about me calling Scott? She didn't know a thing about us.

"I'll see you tomorrow. I hope for good changes today." She turned and left me alone in the hall.

Scott would have to wait. I went back inside and sat in the chair next to Randal's bed.

When I woke with my head on the bed, I had no idea what time it was or how long I had been asleep. A nurse came into the room and began checking Randal's IV. "Good morning. We're backing off on the medication to see how he reacts."

"Will he wake up?"

"That's the idea, but we have to see what happens. The CT scan showed no bleeding." She looked at me. "You know that chair leans back. Get a little more sleep. Today promises to be tiring."

When she left, I took my phone out of my purse and dialed Scott's number. The time on the screen flashed 4:30 am. Scott's phone rang and rang.

"Hello." It was a woman's voice.

I pressed the end button and turned off the phone. So much for telling him what was going on. We had our separate lives. Understand, I always knew just who Scott was and what he did, but I sure didn't need to have my face rubbed in it. Somewhere along the way, his being unfaithful had ceased to drive nails through me. I leaned back in the chair and closed my eyes. When Randal was better, I would pack some bags and we would go to Atlanta. He could finish school and next year go to that college he wanted to attend so badly. If he would just get better.

〜〜〜

A nurse stood close to me with her hand on my shoulder. "Sorry to wake you, Mrs. Weehunt, but I thought you would want to know the doctor ordered the breathing tube removed and to back off considerably on the medication. He likes what he saw with the first round. He wants Randal to wake up."

"How long will it take?" I looked at the swollen blue-and-purple face of my nephew.

"It varies with patients. There's no answer to that question." Her smile was careful but bright. "We will get this tube out."

"Okay."

"Watch for eye movement. That's usually the first sign. Body movement will follow. When he wakes up, he will be disoriented and may lash out. We have to watch for this too. Don't be afraid to use the call button if you see any of these activities. It won't be a bother. Better an extra trip or two into the room than you managing alone." She gave me that smile again.

"Thank you." I watched his face. I would be afraid to go to the bathroom lest I missed something important.

Lily's face appeared in the window of the door. The nurse began removing the breathing tube. I held my breath, but this was uneventful. The nurse reassured me and left the room.

Under Lily's left eye was a bruise. I met her outside, afraid she might disturb Randal. For some reason, I didn't want her around him. A silly feeling. Probably because she said she saw his ghost.

"They are easing him off the medication. He should wake up soon. I have to be in there." My voice sounded so sure and calm, in charge.

"He looked at me when they brought him into the hospital. He knows." She sounded far away, not herself at all.

"Lily, I don't have time right now. Your aunt said she didn't want you here. We have to honor her wishes."

She looked away from Randal and flashed a fearful look at me. "When he died, he saw me standing nearby. Randal only likes the truth, Mrs. Weehunt. Somewhere in his deep sleep, he knows exactly what happened."

"What are you talking about? What happened?" I peered through the glass at Randal. He was still. His eyelids fluttered.

"Tell him I am sorry."

"Wait right here, Lily. I have to check on him." I ran back into the room and pressed the call button.

"We're on the way."

I looked to Lily, but she was gone.

"Randal, are you awake?"

Randal opened his eyes, but they were blank.

The nurse entered the room and pressed the call button. "Page the doctor. The patient in 21 has opened his eyes. He's coming out of it."

CHAPTER 19

Randal

Randal came to love his life, value it, the night he died. Talk about juxtaposition. He saw Lily standing just inside the curtains in what had to be the emergency room. She'd been with him when he got hurt. Now she bit her lip in her cute anxious way. There was something he needed to tell her. Something about what happened under the bridge. He needed to reassure her, but his mind was fuzzy. He followed her stare to the bed. Several nurses surrounded someone. It took him a moment to realize it was him. His face was so swollen, he didn't look like himself.

"We've lost him. Get the cart. Start compressions." The nurse barked loudly, but her words were calm and crisp, controlled.

A man in scrubs ran in with the machine. A nurse moved so another could rub something on Randal's chest.

"Ma'am, you can't stand here. Step out, please." A nurse touched Lily's arm. She jerked away.

"I have to be here. This is all my fault."

"I really doubt that." The nurse led her away. "Stand right here, and I will come out when I know something."

"One." A male voice yelled from the table.

Randal stood close to Lily, smelled the fragrance from Paris she tried while they had strolled through the square on the way to the concert. He studied his friend, a real friend, one who in a short time accepted him the way he was, liked him for his truthfulness. She had been hurt too. Hadn't she? But she looked okay. He was sure she had hurt bad.

A sound near his bed took his attention away for only a second but long enough to lose his footing beside Lily. He fell into a black tunnel, a rabbit hole, and a thought struck him. Aunt Isla would blame herself for what happened to him. This he knew about her. He didn't want her to worry. But most of all he wanted to live.

~~~~

When Randal opened his eyes the first time, he thought he saw Lily standing outside of a window. She looked at him for a second, as if something was wrong. His body ached in places he didn't know he had. Tubes came out of his nose and arms. There was something he was supposed to remember but the memory jumped out of reach with a sharp pain to his chest. What happened? He wanted to say this, but the words slid away. Thoughts he couldn't pin down rolled through his mind, flashing photos, spinning the room.

The second time he opened his eyes, only Aunt Isla stood beside the bed. Fear inched through him and strangled his ability to settle his surroundings. He closed his eyes and welcomed the blessed darkness.

The third time he woke up, he had learned enough to keep his eyes closed so he could balance himself. A hospital room. The antiseptic smell gave it away. Why was he there?

"Is this the kid that was nearly beat to death?" A girl's voice swished around him. Someone tugged at his arm.

"Yes." This woman's voice was quiet and firm. "He's doing well. It is a miracle." A cool cloth wiped his cheek and a fiery sting let loose on his skin.

"Ouch." This time the word left him, and it was loud.

"You're awake again," the girl said with relief.

He tried opening his eyes. The room was still. "Yes," he said, his throat dry. Scratchy. "Where's Lily?" He knew he should have asked about Aunt Isla, but Lily was his biggest concern. He wasn't at all sure why.

"Here are some ice chips. Try some. They will help your throat." The nurse held a Styrofoam cup to his lips. "I don't know who Lily is, but I can tell you that your aunt is in the cafeteria getting some food."

The nurse with the firm voice spoke. "She's been here without leaving for three days."

Randal sucked on a couple of ice chips. The relief moved down his throat. "I can't remember what happened to me. Is Lily okay?"

The nurse patted his arm. "That's very common with a head injury. What is the last thing you do remember?" Her eyes were intensely blue. He remembered blue eyes, angry blue eyes, but he kept quiet and concentrated. He kept hearing Lily say seeing the ghost meant a death and paintings, big oil paintings. A rush of rage shook his insides. "I don't know," he lied.

"Think. What did you do the day this happened? It's good to try and remember." The nurse coaxed. Her tone relaxed him.

"A lot of paintings. I don't know why I feel mad about them."

"You're remembering our trip to the art gallery." Aunt Isla's voice filled the room. What a sweet sound. He never thought he'd feel that way.

He couldn't help but smile at her. "Your hair still looks good."

She gave him a grin that transformed her stern expression. Then he remembered leaving his body in the emergency room. "I died."

Aunt Isla looked away.

The younger nurse, holding an iPad, walked up to the bed. "Yes. Your heart stopped beating." She looked at the screen. "You wouldn't remember that."

"Yes, I do." That's all he could say. The tears spread through his body, but he held them inside.

"I don't like thinking about that." Aunt Isla's voice broke.

A man with a buttoned-down shirt tucked into his jeans and a yarmulke on his head stepped through the opened door.

The nurse with the firm voice stepped in front of him. "No visitors. Sorry."

"When?"

"That will be up to Dr. Robbins." She pulled the door closed behind her as she gently guided the man away.

Aunt Isla stepped out into the hall and spoke with the other nurse but only for a minute and came back inside. "Pesky reporters."

"With a yarmulke. I don't think I know any reporters from around here who are Jewish." Exhaustion washed over him in an instant. "What happened to me, Aunt Isla? I need to know."

Aunt Isla cut a quick look at him. "I'm trying to figure that out myself, Randal. I was with Emily finding out about the art. It's Velvet's. Maybe that's why you felt mad." She let this sink in, gave him space to think.

"I didn't even know she could paint until you told me."

Aunt Isla shrugged. "I never dreamed those were her paintings. I should have known. I saw enough of her work when she was a teenager. I should have recognized her style. I didn't."

"One of them had me as a boy and Mrs. Crow. She is the old Black woman cooking. Only Velvet would know those things, especially how I looked."

"Are you keeping anything from me, Randal?"

The fuzzy ache beat in his head. "What have you kept from me, Auntie?" He closed his eyes. "Why won't you tell me what happened?"

She touched his hand. "I know that you were beaten. This is all I know. It's been crazy, and my thoughts have been on you only."

"I feel like the memory is right there, waiting, but I can't get it in sight."

"Just rest. You're going to be okay and that matters the most."

He thought of Velvet, beautiful Velvet. No man could resist her. She was his mother but even he had to admit how lovely she was, wood nymph springing in and out of the forest. He missed her so bad that he thought how easy he could just give up and die, but Aunt Isla needed him. She didn't know it. She liked to believe she was strong. The woman needed him to help get balanced and find a real life.

"Everything will work out, I promise." Her voice softened.

"I know. Things will come out in the wash. Granny used to say that. Is she okay?"

"She's fine."

But he could tell by her tone that Aunt Isla was lying. "You have to go visit her."

"Randal, I went there three days ago, remember?"

"Go see her anyway. Don't let someone else tell her about me."

"I will." She never moved her hand from his arm. The warmth calmed him, even as a truth seeped through him. Somebody had died. This he knew. Was it him or someone else or both?

CHAPTER 20

Isla

"He needs time to remember on his own." Dr. Robbins looked at the iPad screen .

"Thank you."

He frowned. "I can't keep them at bay for long, Mrs. Weehunt. As you have seen there is a policeman posted outside. Those detectives are going to have their way soon. Get this boy a lawyer."

"I will as soon as I understand exactly what has happened."

"Now, Mrs. Weehunt. Don't wait for anyone to tell you what happened." He turned off the iPad screen.

"Okay."

He nodded and left me standing there, wondering why in the world no one would tell me what took place that night. Why did they feel the need to play dumb or skirt around my questions? Kate knew what happened, so I dialed her number while Randal slept.

"Hi, Isla. How is Randal?" Her voice was normal, almost light. Maybe too light, but that was just me being suspicious.

"Is Lily okay?"

"She's with me." She was quiet for a minute. "Like I said, I don't want her around Randal and exposed to this case. She has been through too much. It's nothing against Randal. We know he's a good boy. These detectives are heartless."

"I understand and will respect this. Randal is awake and talking."

"You can't understand, Isla. No one has the guts to explain to you what has happened. And I'm overjoyed Randal is better." She sounded bothered, almost angry. "You're in a horrible place, and you don't deserve this. Can you get away from the hospital long enough to talk?

Come here to the house. I have some things to tell you."

I couldn't help but wonder why she couldn't just tell me on the phone. "Okay. I'll come. Randal can't remember what happened. I don't want anyone bothering him. He needs time."

"I will make you lunch. Just tell the nurses to let you know if anything changes." She took a breath. "Isla, you can't protect him from this forever."

"Really, Kate, that is what you're attempting with Lily. She was right in the middle of what happened and knows something, and it is bothering her. Did you know she was here again this morning?"

There was silence. "No. I thought she was in her room. I will tell you everything she knows. Then you must call your husband. He has the money and connections you will need. Your SUV is where we left it in front of the bottle tree. Do you need me to come get you so you can pick it up?"

"No, I'll get someone to give me a lift or I'll walk. It's not that far. See you soon."

"Isla," she said suddenly. "I'm glad Randal is better."

"Thank you, Kate. It's good to have someone who gets me." And I really meant this.

The nurses on duty reassured me Randal would not be allowed visitors. He was sleeping. Part of me wanted to stay close, but I knew I had to see Kate before talking to the police. I walked outside and my breath caught in the heat. The dog days of August had left a hot blanket tucked around Nantahala. I realized it was going to be quite a long walk to pick up my car, but the exercise would do me good. My phone vibrated.

"Hello, Stuart."

"How is Randal?"

Some quiet voice whispered me into a lie. "He should wake up anytime now. The doctor says he will not be allowed any visitors except me for a while."

"Do you need to pick up your car? I noticed it parked near the bottle tree."

I looked around the parking lot to see if he was watching me.

"I'm up the road at the courthouse if you would like to get your car and bring it back to the hospital," he continued.

A weird feeling that something was way off clenched my stomach.

"I'll just give you a ride," he said. "No discussing Velvet or Randal. I'm a friend trying to help."

"Were you *ever* my friend?"

"Ha, some things never change. You were so removed from the rest of us."

"Not because I wanted to be."

"Let me help you."

"No talking about Randal."

"Wait for me out front of the hospital. I'll be there in five minutes."

Still, I looked around for him. "I will." As I ended the call, my phone buzzed again. "Hello, Kate."

"Isla, I forgot to tell you not to talk to Stuart."

"I hadn't planned on it. Why?"

"We'll talk. Just don't discuss Randal with him."

I put my phone in my pocket. If I didn't know better, I would think the two were trying to mess with my head. Stuart circled through the parking lot, stopping in front of me. I ran my fingers through my short hair. Lordy, I needed a shower.

Stuart reached over the seat and opened the door. "You look terrible."

I swallowed the hateful response that almost made it out of my mouth. "Thanks."

We rode in silence to my SUV.

I opened the door. "Thanks for giving me a ride."

"What can I do for you?" He gave me a quick smile.

I wanted to scream *Tell me what is going on. What exactly has happened?* "Nothing, but thanks for asking."

"Izzie."

I held my breath.

"Just for the record, I'm on Randal's side. No matter what happens." His voice turned soft.

"Everyone should be. He was wronged."

He nodded.

I shut the door.

He pulled away.

I made sure he wasn't in sight when I left. A plan. I needed a plan. My stomach clenched.

Then Grassy Bald clearly formed in my mind. Why not? I could stay at Grassy Bald, be on our land. Maybe I could sort through all the thoughts rolling through my head. "Yes," I said out loud. "Time to go home."

CHAPTER 21

K ate met me on the front porch of her house. "You took forever. I was getting worried."

"Sorry. I've decided to take the paintings I bought from Emily to Grassy Bald."

"They arrived this morning. We can take them over. Why do you want them there? You can put them in the cottage. I want you to stay there." She opened the front door and held it for me. "You're still welcome, Isla. I'm sorry if I sounded too cross. All this stuff with Randal will work its way out."

I walked into the front hall. "No, it's not that. I'm thinking of staying there until I can go back to Mountain City."

"You need a decent place to stay. The cottage is clean." Kate closed the front door and walked toward the kitchen.

"No. I need to be somewhere so I can think, Kate. I'm going home to Grassy Bald. I want to go through the things there. See if I can find anything to help with the fire. You know Stuart found an antique ring worth quite a bit of money in Velvet's car. It is a 1920's piece. One figure that has been put out there by Stuart is twenty thousand. I have a friend doing some research to see if it belonged to my grandmother or who owned it. I think whoever set the fire might have been after the ring."

She stopped and turned around. A look of shock flashed across Kate's face, but she recovered. "Really? I had no idea. A ring. Where would Velvet get it? I mean, she was a struggling artist of sorts. Josh and I were in good shape, could do what we wanted, but we couldn't afford a piece of jewelry worth that kind of money."

"If it was my grandmother's, Velvet would have found it at Grassy

Bald. I need to look through everything there."

"What did it look like?" Kate asked.

"I have a picture." I showed her the photo on my phone. "The state police have the ring now, but they are supposed to return it soon if they decide it had nothing to do with the fire. This is a place to begin. Anyway, I need to be at Grassy Bald. It's my safe place, always was."

Kate took a step back. "Okay. I just thought since you hadn't been here in so long your attachments were limited. I guess I was wrong." She walked toward the kitchen. "Let's talk about Randal. Then I will help you take the paintings over. We will have lunch there and you can show me around."

The smell of freshly baked brownies filled the air. My stomach rumbled. "Let's talk when we get to Grassy Bald. If that's okay?" The urgency to be on Grassy Bald rushed through me. The want pulled at me in a desperate way.

"I'll pack the lunch and you get your stuff. We will meet in the foyer. I feel like we are on the run." Kate laughed lightly.

"I guess I sound like I'm in a hurry. I just want to go in there. I haven't been there since I left home."

"Then Grassy Bald, here you come." Kate didn't look at me as she packed our lunch.

I got my belongings from the cottage, then went to Randal's room. I gathered his new things in the shopping bags in one hand and the ratty backpack in the other. I moved a pillow on the bed to see if he had left anything and something hard fell to the floor. It was an old blue tin. I pried the lid off and inside was a stack of letters. I knew the handwriting instantly. Velvet. I took one from the top.

May 3, 2012

Deeply Missed:

I slept in the writing studio on Grassy Bald last night. I couldn't take Mama's mess anymore. It was my night off from the casino. Mama started talking about my father. Alzheimer's seems to have opened her up. This is such an oxymoron. When a person loses her ability to remember how to brush her teeth and hair, I would have thought she would retreat inside of herself. Not Mama. The problem with all her stories is what is true and what is her imagination? Of course they are her truths, but do they pertain to me? Do they belong to this family? Can they be trusted?

When she began to tell this story about my father, there was no sign of kindness, sadness, or happiness. Anger filled every word that came out of her mouth. She talked about the months before he drowned. The whole story has me wondering if this undying love between them ever existed. The whole telling wrapped around me as if I were wearing a winter coat in the middle of July. I left. I could hear her talking, as if I was still there. I walked away from the yard into the woods. I didn't stop until I reached the studio.

The sun balanced on the trees and stretched across the overgrown lawn. Deep shadows hovered at the edge of the forest, waiting for dark. I sat on the porch of the studio and thought about the screwups I have made. How can I dislike Mama for her mistakes when I've made choices much, much worse? Who do I think I am? Sitting there on the brick pavers, leaning against the door, I thought about making a change. Can you believe it? Maybe it is time to grow up. Live a real life. What is it I want? To paint, to really lose myself in art. Maybe go to college. It's not too late. Find someone who loves me. I mean grownup love, deep down gut-wrenching love. A special man that I can't wait to see, that I think of when I'm not with him. I have been shallow, always filling time but holding the man I happen to be with at arm's length. Who knows the real Velvet? Not me. Mama did once upon a time. Even now she seems to look deep inside of me.

When it got dark, I went inside and curled up in the window seat, turned on the lamp, and read the old copy of Flannery O'Connor's Complete Stories. *I'm not sure how it ever came to be in the writing studio. The discovery was like finding an old friend. I took the collection home with me the next morning. Reading that book gave me a simple joy. The night was so peaceful. Sometime during the night I woke up to someone calling my name. I think it was you because I had been dreaming of you. Things were good between us. It was before I screwed with your life and you left me forever. I never thought you would. I need substance in my life. Change is on the horizon. Things would go smoother if you were here. That's why I write these letters I'll never send.*

My heart clenched. Velvet wrote letters. Randal hadn't told me this. Why should he? I made it clear that I hated her. I hugged the tin to me. Poor Randal, reading his mother's private thoughts must have been confusing and sad, but maybe comforting in an odd way. For the first time since I left Nantahala, I allowed myself to wish I could see Velvet. That chance had come and gone. Whom had she been writing to? Probably some man. I would read all the letters, allow myself to feel whatever came, and when Randal was better, I would confess.

"So . . . you're going to stay here?" Kate looked at the cabin. "Seems a little too outdated."

I carried Randal's backpack in my hand and inserted keys into the locks. One in a newer deadbolt and the other into an old keyhole original to the door. These keys had hung on my ring since I left the gorge. Amazing that Mama never changed the locks, but maybe not, considering no one really cared about the place. "I have to do a lot of cleaning." I opened the door. Calm slid over me despite the cobwebs hanging here and there from the ceiling. The furniture in the living room was draped in what was once white dust cloths, now dull with dirt and age. Grandmother Iris's books still rested on the shelves that flanked the fireplace, more cobwebs gathering in the corners. Across the mantel were all shapes and sizes of tarnished silver frames with sepia photos of my family long before I came to be. Why hadn't someone cared enough to take them down? Or maybe the removal would have been too painful. So much to think about. So much to do. How would I manage? My confidence in the decision to stay at Grassy Bald wavered for a moment, but I rallied when Kate walked in.

"Wow. Look at that table." Kate put the bags she carried on the antique trunk covered by a cloth.

"There's a bedroom and sitting room upstairs. Randal can have one of the apartments that are in the side wings. If he is well enough to be alone." I led Kate to the flagstone patio outside the French doors in the back. "Look at this view of the gorge." Below was a patchwork of green. "The rolling hills were farmland when Grandmother Iris lived here. She helped keep the farmers going."

Kate stood with her hands on her hips. "I'm sure your family was an asset to the gorge." There was an edge in her voice. She turned to me with a bright smile on her face. "Go get the paintings and I'll clean this long neglected, fabulous table for lunch. Then we talk, Isla."

"I'm going to open some windows and let the fresh air inside."

"Leave the French doors open. Maybe there are some old cleaning supplies under the sink. I'm afraid to look." Kate frowned.

"They used to be in the pantry. Check there. I'll be back in a minute."

Kate made an offering of sandwiches and creamy broccoli-and-cheese soup. The fixings were placed on the old oak round table, now clean. Funny how a meal brought life into a house, causing it to glow with a soft light. Maybe I was too tired from my experience with Randal and was imagining all this. Maybe I shouldn't have been on Grassy Bald. But I sat at the table with this woman who had been a stranger only days before, now my friend, and waited for her to fill in the missing pieces of the close call.

"Eat and I will talk. Then you have to call Scott."

The soup moved down my throat, soothing my aches and pains, even on a hot day. "This is good."

"My mother used to make this when I needed comfort." Kate bit into her sandwich.

"Tell me exactly what you know and don't try to protect me. I'm quite sick of people shying away on this subject."

"I can tell you don't want to call your husband, but you don't have a choice. You have to get him involved. Randal could go to prison for life or worse, be sentenced to death."

"Where do you get that idea?" Anger crept into my voice.

"Randal killed Trevor White." Kate allowed this to be absorbed.

"Randal is the one who died on his gurney. How could he kill anyone?"

"Lily saw everything. She doesn't want to talk about it to the police. She doesn't want to get Randal in trouble. That's why I've kept her closed away. It seems Trevor approached Randal and Lily under the bridge. He began taunting Randal about . . ." She shrugged one shoulder. "You know. Then he became verbally abusive and put his hands on Lily, who told him she was calling the police. He laughed and called her a name. Randal tore into him. Threw him on the sidewalk and cracked the boy's skull on the curb. Trevor's friends came along and charged after Randal after seeing Trevor. Each one of the five are denying being there or laying a hand on him. They even have alibis. That is why they are not in jail. The police got there after the boys left. Trevor's parents are painting him as a good kid, a football hero, and all-around good citizen. Everyone in the Nantahala knows Carlton White, the boy's father, and they're afraid of him. The police want to talk to Lily. I told them she has a flu bug, but they are going to demand to talk to her sooner than later." She touched my hand. "They know *someone* had to beat Randal. They are putting two and two together about the other boys." She wore an expression of pity. "They know Lily saw something. You have to get your husband to help. He is more feared in this town than Carlton White. The two are enemies."

"This is crazy. Randal would not have killed that boy. He wouldn't have raised his hand to him. And why would the people in the Nantahala be afraid of Scott? That makes no sense. How would *you* know that?"

Kate gave me a surprised look. "Isla, he owns most of the mortgages here. Didn't *you* know that?"

I shook my head.

"Your husband is the only one who can stop Carlton White."

A throbbing pain beat at the back of my head. "Randal did not kill that boy. I don't care what Lily says. She can't be right. Things happened fast. She is confused."

Kate said softly, "There was no good way to tell you."

"Lily has to tell what really happened." I slammed the flat of my hand on the table, rattling the spoons in the bowls. "I will find out. This whole incident feels like it is connected to Velvet. I won't leave here until I know what happened to my sister and nephew." The rage in my voice shocked me.

"Lily isn't lying. And why would you say such a thing about this so-called connection?" Kate folded her arms over her chest and glared at me.

"I don't know what to believe." I raked my fingers through my hair. "I'm sorry if I offended you by questioning Lily, but I *know* Randal."

Kate looked away. "I've known Lily since birth. You only met your nephew a week or so ago."

"I will find the answer," I nearly screamed. "I will know who killed my little sister, and who nearly killed my nephew." I gave her a hard look. "You don't know me, so you don't know that I don't give up easy. Stuart found that ring in Velvet's car. It means something. I find the person connected to the ring and I find the person who set the fire." I opened up the photos on my phone and showed her the ring again.

Kate gave the photo a longer look this time. "It's beautiful, expensive. The girl didn't have this kind of money. Could be something illegal involved." She looked up at me. "You had better be careful digging."

"I don't care if I expose some theft by Velvet. My friend should know by now if this belonged to my grandmother. If not, I will go door to door in this town if I have to. Someone will know this ring, remember it."

She gave me a stern look. "Be careful. Leave the investigation to the police. They will find the owner."

"And I found letters Velvet wrote." Of course I didn't say where. "I'm hoping they will tell me what happened to her in the months and weeks before her death. Maybe they will explain the ring."

Kate studied me. "Letters she wrote? Who were they to?"

"They were addressed to *Deeply Missed*."

Kate shook her head. "How mysterious. To think the girl was painting at the cottage. *Deeply Missed*. How crazy is that? Sounds like she was into something bad, Isla."

"There are plenty of people in Nantahala who know Velvet's history. Maybe someone can tell me more about her last weeks, months, maybe even years. This could go way back." I looked at the soup. I wanted to cry about having not seen my sister before she died. My new friend wouldn't understand how I could flip my opinion so quickly—so I held in my sadness. The emotion was still too new.

Kate's face relaxed. "Why not begin with asking people about Velvet in her last few days. What she was doing. Who her friends were? That might uncover something. A friend of mine back home was a detective. He said sometimes he would interview the same person three or four times before they let something out that wasn't said before. This might help. I understand you want to know who killed your sister, even if you weren't close. You two were opposites for sure." She gave me an unsettling look. "But are you sure the fire was set? You only have this Mr. Collins's opinion. What if it was an accident? Then what?" Kate shrugged. "You still need to contact Scott. This will help Randal and his situation. He needs a lawyer at the very least."

But a small voice whispered in my head not to listen, not to call Scott. "Maybe."

"Call Scott. I can't keep the police away from Lily much longer." She stood. "I will leave the food."

I walked her to the door. "Thank you for your kindness and for being my friend," I said kindly, even though I still believed she wasn't telling me the whole story. "I had better take a shower and get back to the hospital."

"Thank *you* for being *my* friend, Isla. We are a lot alike, and I will miss you being at the cottage. Let me know if I can help you or if you decide staying here is too much. You can always stay at the cottage. That's an open offer."

"Thank you, Kate."

When Kate's car was safely out of sight, I crossed the yard to the barn. According to Randal, Velvet had placed old belongings there. The ring had to have been found when she moved the items. When I was finished in the barn I would break down and call Scott.

The barn was clean and tidy for a storage area. I still wore the sundress from the night Randal was beaten, and it certainly wasn't the attire to wear while digging through boxes. I grabbed the closest box and caught the scent of honeysuckles, which made me think of Velvet because she had worn a similar fragrance when she was young. I would look through one box, but first I would call the hospital. I had been away too long.

Randal answered the phone in his room. "Hello."

"Look at you, answering the phone. I'm so glad you're getting better."

"I'm fine, Aunt Isla."

I could hear the smile in his words. "I'll be there in just a few minutes. I brought our stuff to Grassy Bald."

"Do me a favor, Aunt Isla."

"Anything you need."

"Get a bath and some clean clothes. You looked horrible." He gave a laugh. "I'll be fine until you get back. Take a bath."

"I get the message. Are you sure?"

"Yes. Take your time."

"Okay. I'll be back soon."

"Don't worry. I'm not going anywhere."

"Smart aleck." The laugh that escaped my chest felt so good. "I'll be there in a while."

"Goodbye, Aunt Isla."

The phone went dead. I took the box in the house.

<center>~~~~</center>

The box held Velvet's yearbooks and photos. I wasn't ready to see her memories displayed in front of me. After all this time of believing I didn't care, the flood of emotions nearly knocked me to my knees. Then I saw an old photo of Mrs. Crow and Mama sitting together in the living room of Mama's house. The woman was our savior. Had I ever told her thank you? Probably not. First a bath, then maybe I could go by her house before the hospital. Did she still live in the same little house close to Marcus's cabin? Maybe she could tell me something about Velvet.

CHAPTER 22

My memory placed Mrs. Crow's drive only a short distance from Marcus's farm. After passing his house I drove another quarter of a mile, and still I couldn't see her little box of a house. Randal said she was still alive, and I wanted to see her, but I needed to go back to the hospital.

Mama actually responded to Mrs. Crow's gruffness. She came to help with us when Mama was in the worst of ways. She came one night. This was a memory I never could see clearly and, honestly, I didn't try. Why dig up old pain?

The woman was no-nonsense. When she worked there, she had a way of making Velvet and me feel we were the most important people in her life. However, from the looks of things, she probably lived somewhere else by now. Just as I was about to turn around, a bright red mailbox some distance away marked a drive. There was no writing on the box, not even a house number. I turned in. The small, moss-green house I remembered sat in an overgrown yard. The paint job was fairly new, and a blue pickup truck sat close to the front door.

A figure stood in the open door.

"What do you need, girl?" Mrs. Crow looked just as I remembered her, only grayer. She was thin and lanky with tight curls against her head. "I felt you comin'."

I stepped out of my SUV. "I am Darlene Vivian's daughter, Isla."

Mrs. Crow stood tall and straight. "I know who you are. I haven't lost my mind yet. I asked you what you wanted? You've been gone so long this can't be a good sign." She gave me that long, stern stare I remembered as a kid. "You left this place instead of facing the music playing for you, girl. It's a little late now."

I tried not to smile. "I guess you are correct, Mrs. Crow. I did do just that."

"Yeah, you're Isla, all right. You married that Weehunt boy. He was meaner than a snake, and I doubt age has made him one bit more likable." She folded her arms across her chest and hiked up her breasts.

"You are exactly right, Mrs. Crow."

"I think I already proved my mind is quite intact, young lady."

"Yes, ma'am. Sharper than mine."

She nodded with satisfaction as if she had won some long-fought battle. "What you bringing yourself out here for on such a hot sunny day? Must be a hankering for old times that brings you back into Nantahala." She gave a cackle. "Or is it guilt? Have you come home to make amends to your mama?" The very thought made her throw back her head and cackle. "Come on in here, and don't stand in the yard, frowning, for all the neighbors to wonder why some fancy White woman is mad at me." She motioned me inside.

Part of me wanted to ask, *what neighbors?* Instead, I walked up the steps that looked freshly painted. The screen door still had a familiar creak that made me smile. The sitting room was flooded with natural light, a simple peaceful room.

Mrs. Crow came to stand close to me. "Now really, what brings you here after all these years or do I want to know? It can't be your mama. She's fine as frog's hair. I seen her earlier today. I suspect you got to talk to me about that mess on her place." She reached out and touched my hand and withdrew her fingers quickly, clicking her tongue and giving me a sharp look. "Girl, you're in a mess, aren't you. I sure hope you're nothing like that baby sister of yours. She was a headstrong woman and looked for trouble in every turn. She came to see me about three weeks ago. Got real mad at me."

"Why?" I stood in the middle of the sitting room.

"Well, you got manners like her. Have a seat. Don't stand there like your mama never taught you how to act when visiting your elders."

I sat in a green armchair. "Why did Velvet come here?"

"She had your granny's old deed to that land. Wanted me to say Mrs. Harris wasn't in her right mind when she had written her will or say she never wrote one. She hadn't even seen the thing. Didn't even know what it was about or why Mrs. Harris had made it so the land couldn't be sold. That girl wanted me to lie."

So Velvet did want to sell Grassy Bald. Fresh anger worked through my body. "Why did Velvet want you to say this?"

"I guess she wanted to pump old Crow's memory. See if I knew anything about the will, if I had a copy." She cackled again. "Some fancy man came into town and offered her a lot of money for your mama's place but only if he could have the Bald too."

"That's impossible. Mama always said the will stated the land has to stay in the family. Velvet couldn't sell Grassy Bald. That'd be wrong. This is family land." Of course, I'd never seen the will either. Did it even exist or had Mama just made it up in a crazy moment?

Mrs. Crow took a seat on the old floral sofa that sat under a large window, looking out at Pine Log Mountain. "Lord, girl, it's good to hear you take up for the place. I'm a little partial to the Bald myself." She eyed me. "You know I went to work for Mrs. Harris when I was no more than fourteen."

"What did you do for Grandmother Iris?" I did the math in my head. She had to be in her eighties, maybe hugging ninety.

"Everything. She hired me because, well, she felt real sorry for my mama."

"Why?" Being with Mrs. Crow was like old times, but instead of fighting the comfortable feeling, I allowed it to wash through me.

She clicked her tongue and shook her head. "My daddy went riding on his horse to find the doctor for my sister, who was right sick. Mama was afraid she was dying and since she had one child to die earlier that year, she didn't think she could live through another. But Daddy was the one who died. That mare he took was antsy and young. Threw him right off and he hit his head. Lived for a while but never woke up. That was nineteen hundred and thirty-eight."

"You must be mistaken. Grandmother Iris didn't live anywhere but Grassy Bald."

She shook her head. "Nah, her and Pastor Harris lived in that little cabin on the other side of me there for a while. It's still standing.

She never sold it. Don't look so confused. Them folks could muddle anyone."

I shook my head. "Nothing surprises me here."

"It shouldn't. You never know what new tale might come your way. But you didn't come to talk about that old place. What you dying to tell old Crow?"

"The fire Velvet died in was set on purpose."

"I did hear tell that Miss Priss died in a fire somebody started. Folks love a good story around here. I wasn't sure if it was made up or not. I wanted to come to the funeral, but it came and went without any announcement in the paper." She gave me a hard look. Once again, I had failed at being the proper lady. "That girl was doing good for about five years. She settled herself and then about a year and half ago, she started drinking heavy again. Got in over her head with someone. I know she seemed real desperate to sell the place and leave."

"So Velvet was going to sell Grassy Bald. That makes no sense."

"I guess she needed some money. But mostly that girl wanted out of here like you did, but of course there was your mama. She would have to go too. That I was worried about, seeing how she never even visited her."

"Look at this." I put my phone in front of her with the photo of the ring. "Did Grandmother Iris own this ring? You have to know."

She shook her head. "I can tell you Pastor Harris would never give her a ring like this one. He was tight with any money he made, and I can't say there was a lot of love between them two. No, that's one of them rings a man gives a woman he loves with all his heart. I never seen her with anything like that. She just wasn't a flashy person. Didn't make a big deal out of jewelry." She studied the photo on my phone. "The ring is right pretty. Looks like it might be worth some money. You got something special there with a big story." She pushed my phone away and gave me a long look. "I got me a bit of magic. Mama warned me when I predicted my daddy would die two weeks before he did. I can see things, happenings, coming. Sometimes it's just a feeling." She pointed to the phone. "The tale that goes with that ring is about love. I can feel that. But love can kill you, girl. Be careful." Mrs.

Crow bent down close to the screen and clicked her tongue again. "My oh my. It's probably a right sad love story. Most of them are. I bet your mama knows this ring."

My shoulders dropped. "Mrs. Crow, you know Mama can't tell me anything now. She acted like she had never seen it."

"Girl, you been gone a long time. Your mama has got old-timers, but she still gets a lot of things just like they were. Nobody listens 'cause they think she's just ramblin'. Try again. I bet she'll know about it the second time of looking. If not, that means she's telling the truth about not seeing it." She sat back in her chair. "Where are you staying?"

I turned off the screen. It was clear she wasn't going to say anything else, but I had a feeling she knew something. "At Grassy Bald."

She grumbled under her breath. "It's full of dust and needs some loving care. I'll come tomorrow to clean."

I opened my mouth.

She held up her hand. "I ain't listening to you. I'll be there. I got my keys. We will get you in order. There's a lot there for a girl interested in the family she left behind. If them walls could talk, they'd prob'ly tell you a story that could help you with your digging."

"How? Velvet didn't like Grassy Bald."

"There's a whole story there about that girl. Your history too."

"Can't you just tell me what you mean instead of talking in circles?" The exhaustion came out in my question.

"Naw, girl, that ain't half as fun as you finding out on your own. You might understand better than me. And besides, my memory might not be right."

"Where would I look for stories about Velvet?"

"Look in the chest at the end of Mrs. Harris's bed upstairs. That was Velvet's hiding place since she was a bitty thing." She stood. "Oh, I can tell you didn't even know she had a hiding place or a secret. See, you didn't know as much about her as you thought." She walked to the door. "The only reason I knew was I cleaned the place once a month. Caught her hiding her treasures one day. Just look." She pushed the squeaky screen door open. "I'll be at the Bald tomorrow. No need for you to be there. Go stay with that boy. He needs you. He ain't had no mothering for a long time." She paused, blocking my way out. "That can take a toll on a person. You ought to know that. And I ain't surprised at all that fire was set." She stepped through the door and held it open for me. "I'm telling you Miss Velvet was a passel of problems. Maybe it has to do with that idea she came toting in here last time."

"Thank you, Mrs. Crow." I held out my hand. She had given me a lot to think about.

She took my hand in both of hers that were scratchy from hard work. "You come on back if you need to talk, and Crow will listen. I'll be right here."

"Yes, ma'am."

She let go of me. "It's good you came home."

All the hours of watching Randal at the hospital gathered in my chest. I swallowed tears. "Thank you for welcoming me, but I'm not sure coming back was a great choice."

"Just think of the boy." She gave me a crooked but kind smile. "He is a blessing to tha' whole darn family."

"Yes." I smiled back. "He is worth the trip."

"I agree with you."

I thought of Marcus as I passed his drive. I told him I'd come back to see what he found out about the ring. Surely he heard what had happened. A glimpse of the prayer flags appeared above the trees. Maybe tomorrow. Then, instead of heading straight back to the hospital, I turned the SUV toward Mama.

≈≈≈

"Mrs. Weehunt, I'm glad you came by. I've been so worried about Randal. The newspapers said he was in critical condition. How in the world did my boy get mixed up in this? With you here, it must mean he's going to be okay." The nurse at Mama's assisted living home came out from behind the desk.

"He's doing much better. Now, we have to get this whole story straightened out."

"That boy is the best I know. I will tell anyone that. You understand? He is good."

Silly tears filled my eyes. "Thank you." What if the detectives came here too? Mama could be completely lucid at times. She shouldn't hear about Randal like that. "I need to see Mama. I know she has her clear moments, so I want to make sure no one is allowed to question her. She doesn't need to be upset." I took a deep breath. "Should I tell her about Randal?"

The nurse squeezed my shoulder. "You just let old Alice here take care of her. Ain't nobody coming in to bother that mess of a woman. Trust me. All the nurses will protect her."

I nodded. "Thank you, Alice."

"She's having a decent day. You could try to talk to her about Randal."

"Okay." The long hall was lit well and clean as could be with rooms to both left and right. Rooms that were open and airy as if part of a house, but the place closed in on me.

Mama sat in her chair with her feet up on an ottoman.

"Mrs. Leech, your daughter came to see you."

Mama looked up with a smile that faded fast. "Oh. It's you." She looked at Alice. "This woman only thinks she is my daughter. She's not. I think she might be worse off than me."

Alice smiled. "Well, she has come to talk to you about your nephew, Randal. You know who I'm talking about." Alice looked at me. "I'll check on you in a few minutes."

I nodded and sat in the other armchair.

"What's wrong with my boy?"

"He was hurt, Mama." I noticed a *Newsweek* magazine lying unopened in her lap. "He's going to be okay, but I wanted you to know."

She looked thoughtful. "Thank you. I missed him yesterday or was it the day before. Shoot, it could have been ten days ago. He always comes two times a week. That's what he tells me. I try to keep up with the days. Sometimes I do. Sometimes I don't." Mama gave me a sideways look. Her short bob was perfectly combed. She wore a bright pink button-up blouse with jean capris. If someone saw her out in public, they wouldn't know she wasn't sound of mind. "Are you still married to that horrible boy?" She shook her head. "*Are* you my daughter? Sometimes I get things backward and twisted. No, you can't be her. She would never come here and visit me. She would never come back to the gorge. She promised me that before she married that piece of trash. I tried to tell her what he did." Arthritic hands gripped the armrests, then flexed. "I was going to tell her the secret, but she didn't want to hear. Now Velvet's up and died. That's what everyone says. She died when I needed her most." Her attention went to the magazine in her lap. She opened it. Fingered through a few pages, then looked back at me. "We have a curse on us. It killed Velvet. I know it did."

"Mama, listen to me. I want to talk to you about who would kill my sister."

Mama shot me a look. "Young lady, I may not always get things right, but I know that Velvet was not a Leech. No, she wasn't." She slammed the magazine on the floor.

I took a deep breath.

"Nothing you need to worry over. This killing business." She placed her hands, fingers laced, in her lap. "I want to see my boy."

I took her hands in mine. Her skin was dry and cool. "As soon as he's better I'll bring him. I promise."

Mama huffed. "Girl, the last time you left here, you didn't come back for years. I don't trust you."

"Who is Velvet if she's not a Leech?" I asked, grabbing my chance.

A sassy look moved across her face. "My lover's child, of course. He came to me just as I thought I would kill myself. He saved my life and destroyed it at the same time."

"Who?" Was she remembering some TV show she had watched? Another man? That was impossible.

"I can't tell you that, sweetie. It's a secret."

"A lover."

"Are you shocked or ashamed of your mother? I loved him for saving me. He was good to me." Tears filled her eyes. "No, I'm not muddled. He was so good to me. Without him I would've died." She looked up and her stare met mine. "I'm glad you came home. I've wanted to tell you this for a long time." She rubbed the back of my hands with her fingers.

I studied her tissue-paper skin, the lines and creases, a map to a life before this room. And then I saw it—if a person looked at only our hands side by side, they would think we were one and the same woman.

CHAPTER 23

The next evening, I watched as Randal ate his supper of broth. His lips were still too swollen to eat anything but liquids. "Go home, Aunt Isla. You need to rest. You've been up here too much." He gave me a gentle, crooked smile. "I don't think I can stand you hovering anymore. I need to be alone and so do you."

Who was more the adult?

So, I left him and headed home to Grassy Bald. I caught a glimpse of Kate's floppy straw gardening hat as I started past her house. One had to save the skin from the sun to keep youthfulness. I pulled in front of the fence to pay her a short visit, but the little voice that guided me on most days told me to keep driving. This time I didn't listen. I didn't want to be alone with myself at the moment.

She smiled and removed her hat when she saw me standing at the back gate. "Isla, I'm so happy you're here." And she really meant it. Her face was lit up.

"I was on the way home and decided to say hello." I stepped through the gate.

"Good. We need tea. Don't you think?" She took my arm and led me to the gazebo in the backyard with a small round table and two chairs. A pitcher of tea with sliced lemons sat there with two glasses as if she knew I'd come by. "I was hoping Lily would come out and join me but she's not very happy with me these days." She poured one glass full and handed it to me. "So how was your day?"

The glass chilled my fingers, and I sipped the delicious lemony tea. "It was uneventful. This is a good thing. But odd after so much chaos."

"I would say so. Did you call Scott?" She shook her head at me. "You don't have to say a word. I can tell by the look on your face. You haven't called him. Isla, I understand how you feel, but you *have* to call him. He can help Randal."

"I really doubt that, Kate. You and your perfect marriage. How could you know?" My words were full of envy that even I could hear.

A shadow fell across Kate's face. "The best of marriages have their moments. Josh and I had our problems. The problem with one of us dying is the one left behind tends to make the relationship better than it was." She gave me a sad look. "It's easier to believe we never fought or went to bed angry. Why, the day he died, we had a huge fight before he left in his car. I didn't know I'd never see him again." Tears filled her eyes.

"I'm sorry."

"Don't. I hate the pity. This isn't about Josh and me. It is about you calling your husband so your nephew can have good legal representation."

"It's just hard to ask him for help."

"I get that, Isla, but you have to call him."

"I don't know when it got easy to ignore Scott and his unfaithfulness." When would I stop lying? Especially to myself? I knew exactly when I turned off my feelings for Scott. I knew exactly what happened. It was around the same time I decided he owed me a certain kind of lifestyle for all the grief he had caused.

"It's never easy to ignore your own pain. We just numb ourselves to the wrong being slung at us." She stopped. "Just call him, okay."

I sipped the tea. Swallowed. "I will when I get home."

Kate smiled as if she were pleased. "Look at you, calling that place home. Does this mean you're going to stay here for a while?"

"I don't know. I said I'd never come back here. How could I live here?"

"You must have been hurt badly by your family to feel that way."

"I was, and I guess all the running I've done hasn't kept me from feeling the pain."

"Running from pain is useless. It's like trying not to be mad when you are full of anger. Sometimes you just have to let the anger out." Kate poured herself another glass of tea then offered me some.

I shook my head. "I have to go. I'm exhausted. And like you said, I have to call Scott."

She stood. "Good. Come by again. I need the company."

"I will."

In the car, I thought how comforting our visit had been. We didn't really talk about Randal. Who wanted to hash over his situation? Not me. Not that night. I needed and wanted a friend. Maybe I was no longer the woman Kate liked so much when we first met. My heart had changed, torn and mended a million times since our meeting. In just under two weeks, I had found real love. Not stupid romance that wasn't worth a nickel. No, just unconditional love. And it took almost losing that boy, my nephew, to understand my heart could crack open with this singular emotion. Revealing this vulnerability, especially to myself, was the scariest risk I had truly taken. The whole experience gave me a fickle set of questions. Part of me wanted to stay by Randal's side to protect him from everyone, but the other part questioned if I was the correct person to take the job.

These jumbled thoughts crossed through my mind as I let myself into the old cabin after dark. The hairs on my arms stood up as I walked through the door. Something was out of place, wrong. The French door stood open. That's when I saw Randal's backpack emptied out on the dining room table.

"Who is in here?" My words bounced around the cabin. No one but me. Then I remembered Mrs. Crow was coming to clean. The room sparkled and the scent of lemon wax and Pine-Sol swirled around me. I should have noticed this as soon as I walked in. She probably left the door open to air the place out. But why had she turned Randal's things all over the table? That didn't seem like something she would do.

For the first time in my life, I worried about being alone on Grassy Bald. "Don't be silly." I said this out loud to whatever was spooking me.

I thought of the letters in the tin upstairs in the bedroom. One quick look and I would eat supper.

The tin was snugged under the pillow like I left it even though the sheets had been changed. The cedar chest sat in Grandmother Iris's room at the foot of the bed. When I was young, I imagined it to be a casket for a child. Mama told me I had a morbid imagination and to stay out of the cabin. Never had I opened the chest. I pulled on the lid, but it was stuck fast. Mrs. Crow had said Velvet's treasure was there. But it was locked. And for some reason, even though I had no real knowledge, I understood this fit Grandmother Iris's personality, her sense of privacy.

An old-time keyhole told me the chest was older than any of the furniture I could remember in the cabin. Maybe there were some hairpins in the old vanity for picking the lock. Busting it would ruin the piece. I opened a small drawer to the right of the large round mirror. A cold chill exploded my thoughts. Four tubes of lipstick, a small pot of face powder, and a large puff sat in perfect order, as if Grandmother Iris had put on her makeup minutes before. I turned to look at the room with a fresh view. All my life I had taken the preservation of her things for granted: clothes in the closet organized by items; skirts, dresses, coats; the bedclothes, up until I changed them, were surely the same she slept on when she was alive; now the makeup in the drawer. Imagine being so loved that your house was left undisturbed until an unruly thirty-something-year-old granddaughter came to stay. I pulled the drawer out more, hoping to see a container of hairpins. Instead, I found a small brass skeleton key. Just the size of the chest's lock. This was like something out of a badly plotted murder mystery. Too easy indeed.

The lock turned with ease. Inside were stacks of old fashioned cloth-covered books, photo books, but after a moment of shuffling, without thought to their conditions, it was obvious that they were all of Grandmother Iris's book tours and special events. The huge parties she had in her heyday of writing. Nothing to do with Velvet. Maybe Mrs. Crow was getting senile. I took the top book and opened it. The photos were old. A stern man with a full dark beard. A young woman whom I would know anywhere as Mama. Grandmother Iris was beautifully young. Her hair was cut short with lots of curls. A childish thrill spread through my arms as I closed the book. And, for a short moment, I was a kid again, searching, treasure hunting for my history, forgetting the sad circumstances that brought me to my knees in front of an antique chest. I looked one more time and a flash of reflection caught my attention. Something gold. On the bottom of the chest was a white envelope, not new but not terribly old. A brass door-sized skeleton key was tucked partway inside. Was this what Mrs. Crow was talking about? This was the item that didn't fit with Grandmother Iris's things.

My phone vibrated in my jeans pocket.

"Hello, Scott."

"I've been trying to return your call for two days, Izzie."

"Really? I haven't felt my phone vibrate."

"That was just some girl at the bar. I wasn't with her. She just grabbed my phone and answered it."

"I long ago stopped thinking about your activities on the side." I studied the neat and tiny writing on the envelope: *Velvet Leech.* Inside was a folded sheet of paper and what looked like photos.

"Don't start, Izzie."

"I have bigger problems than your infidelity." I closed the envelope with the intention of looking at its contents later. I placed the key in my pocket.

Scott was quiet.

"I will be staying here until I can resolve them."

"Is this about the woman who answered?"

"This isn't about you, Scott. Randal was hurt, almost killed. He's in ICU. One of the reasons I tried to call you. There is trouble. He is going to be physically okay, but it was touch and go for a while. His heart stopped beating when they first got him to the emergency room."

"How did he get hurt? Are you okay?"

I almost laughed at his concern. "I'm fine."

"What happened?"

"A group of boys jumped him. Beat him up. They are denying being there now."

"Why in the world did he let that happen? Randal is strong as a bull. I wouldn't mess with him."

"A friend of his, Lily, was there. I don't know all the details. I only know that a boy died, and the police think Randal killed him in a fight." I took a breath. "I think they want to charge him with murder."

"Bull. How can they do that if he was hurt so badly? *Somebody* did the damage to *him*. I'm not a complete idiot. I know you think I am. The boy is no troublemaker or killer."

A twisting knife pain shot through my chest. "I'm staying here and hoping to figure this out."

"There was a girl there, you say?"

"Yes, they're friends." Although something in the way they'd looked at each other that night told me something deeper was at play than mere friendship.

"Friends."

"I know what you think, Scott, but—I—"

"Don't you? Think that?"

I raked my fingers through the cut Scott had yet to see and that I had grown more and more fond of. "I'm not sure what I think. And I'm not so sure it matters to this story."

Scott said nothing for a moment, then, "What does she say happened?"

"Her aunt has locked her away, attempting to protect her."

"She has to know something. The police will not allow her to hide her away for long. They will talk to this girl whether the aunt wants it or not. Who is the kid that died?"

"Trevor White. A real bully."

"Oh, heck no. Not Carlton White's son. That man is nothing but a crook hiding behind family money and public office." He paused for a minute. "I know you think he sounds like me, but he's worse. He will do anything to anyone. Carlton will not stop until Randal pays dearly. I'm sending Leavitt Tollson. Where can he meet you?"

Leavitt Tollson. My husband's lawyer. How Scott met such a decent man, I wasn't sure. He was my age and liked to read, or so Scott said. "I will be back at the hospital in the morning. I'm at my grandmother's cabin. You can give him my number."

"Grassy Bald. Are you kidding?"

On more than one occasion Scott had tried to get me to sell or turn the place into a paying venue, to list it on Airbnb or Vrbo.

"What has changed? What could make you stay there again?"

"I won't stay here forever but I need to be here now. It just makes sense. I lost Velvet without ever talking to her about what happened. Mama is in the assisted living place with no clue. I can't turn my back on Randal like all the adults in his life have done. Including me. I have to see this through." I sat down, straightened my legs, and leaned my back against the chest. "They are going to charge him with murder. I know they will. This town is like you and maybe me, thinking things about him whether they're true or not. It's like stepping back into the eighties. They will punish him for what they believe is his sexual identity, fair or not." I closed my eyes. For the first time in years Scott and I were having a normal husband and wife conversation. All it had taken was two murders and an assault.

"Don't worry. And, Izzie, lock those doors on that ancient place."

I looked at the large key. "Why? It's the gorge," I mocked him. But there was the French doors downstairs.

"Your sister was burned to death on purpose."

A coldness settled in the top of my head and worked down my spine. "That was Velvet. Always getting into places she shouldn't be. No telling what she did."

"Or the whole thing could be about something else, and she just got in the way. You haven't been there in years. Be careful."

"I have to go eat. Have the lawyer call me."

"Do you need anything from me?"

A childish, rageful scream fought to get out. Really? There was a time in my life when I would have given anything to hear those words, to know he was there for me, for our marriage. Now the relationship was drowning in falsehoods, some from him, some from me. One person is never completely to blame in a bad situation. "Maybe. I'll let you know. I do need some of my clothes. I hate shopping here."

Before I went to bed, I tried the key I found in the cedar chest in the front door's old lock—sure it would fit. But, it didn't turn. The key belonged to another door.

Things were changing.

The next morning as I climbed into the SUV, my phone vibrated. An unknown but local number flashed on the console screen as I started the car. Had Randal taken a turn for the worse? "Hello."

"Mrs. Weehunt?" A professional male voice.

My stomach flipped. "Yes?"

"This is Detective John Ascher. We met a couple of days ago outside your nephew's room. I would like to speak to you about what happened on last Friday night. When could you come down to the station?"

All the words left me. I shouldn't have answered the phone. "Mr. Ascher, I cannot see you until my attorney can be with me. He's coming here today. I will let you know when he arrives."

"Attorney? You don't need an attorney, Mrs. Weehunt." He sounded tired.

"Understand this. I grew up here in the gorge. I'm aware who Carlton White is, and I know how things work here. I do need an attorney. I will contact you when he is here."

"I would really like to speak to you before we approach your nephew, but you will not keep me from talking with him or any other actions we choose to take."

"Do not threaten me, Detective Ascher."

"It's not a threat. I'm sorry you think of it as such."

"I will be in touch."

"Please do, Mrs. Weehunt."

I tapped the button to disconnect the call and sat there.

A man in a dress shirt and suit pants stood by the nurses' station. The same man as before. The one with the yarmulke. The morning nurse came out from behind the desk as soon as she saw me.

"Mrs. Weehunt," she said, keeping her voice low, "the police want to speak with your nephew. I told the detective that this wasn't possible

148

because the doctor hasn't cleared him to have visitors."

"Thank you."

The man walked in my direction. He looked a dad, a husband, a regular guy doing his job, but he saw Randal like a murderer.

"Mrs. Weehunt, we just spoke on the phone. I'm Detective Ascher."

"You must have been standing right here when you called me." I attempted to calm my churning stomach. "You can't talk to Randal until the doctor clears it. His health is most important to me. Please leave."

"But I can speak with you." He had intense brown eyes and dark hair.

"And I've explained to you I'm waiting for my attorney. Go away and stop harassing me."

Detective Ascher gave me a smirk. "Harassment? I would think you would *want* to speak with me."

A roll of anger spread through me. "Don't be a smart aleck. I am not stupid. I don't trust you or the whole police force. I know Senator White probably has all of you in his pockets. Now leave." I turned my back on the man and walked toward Randal's room.

"We will have the statement from Lily Rogers, and she will tell us what your nephew did."

I swung around. "Is she in the hospital fighting for her life? This is exactly why I don't trust the police here." I opened the door only enough for me to slip through and closed it. Randal jumped, opening his eyes. "Keep your eyes shut. There is a detective staring in the window. I want you to look as sick as you can." Randal kept still. We remained this way for a couple of minutes before I turned to find the window empty. "He's gone."

"So why is a detective here? Your temper is showing, Aunt Isla." His teasing was a pure pleasure. He was getting better each day.

I looked at my nephew, my sister's only child. The only offspring that would come from this generation. The Harris and Leech families would end if Randal did not have children.

"Are you okay?" Randal asked in a quiet voice.

My phone vibrated again from a pocket in my purse. When I

looked at the screen, I frowned. This wasn't a number I knew. "Hello."

"Mrs. Weehunt, this is Leavitt Tollson."

Ah. "Yes. Scott said you would call when you got here."

"Should I come to the hospital?"

"Yes, in the lobby."

"I'll be there in forty-five minutes. I'll call when I get there."

"I have a detective who will not take no for an answer."

"You let me handle him. What's his name?"

The air in my lungs squeezed tight. "Ascher. Call me when you get here."

"I will."

I ended the call.

"What is going on?" Randal asked.

I held up my hand. "Trevor White beat you. Do you remember?"

"No." His face closed, and again I felt he was keeping something from me.

"Randal," I said, drawing air and courage into my lungs. "He died. The police believe you killed him. That group of thugs said they weren't there, which means that Trevor did ... *this* ... to you all by himself. How in the world were you supposed to kill him is beyond me. *You* died on the table. I know I'm not telling you anything you don't know, but his father is a senator with a lot of pull. He also hates your Uncle Scott." I sighed as I crossed my arms. "You *have* to remember what you did." Then it hit me. I was doing to him what Detective Ascher wanted to do.

Randal gave me a long look. "I know I didn't kill Trevor. If I was going to kill him, I would have a long time ago. He's been torturing me—bullying me—since fifth grade. I don't remember what happened, but I do know Lily was there. He must have come out of nowhere. I can see flashes of him—or someone—beating me. I remember trying to punch. But the face is blurry." He shook his head. "Maybe I don't want to remember."

"They say you beat Trevor's head against the curb under the bridge." I didn't tell him it was Kate who said this. "Your Uncle Scott has sent his lawyer to help. When he calls me back, I'll meet him in the lobby. I'm sure he'll want to speak with you." I touched his hand. "I want you to know I don't believe you hurt Trevor. We will get this straightened out. I'm staying at Grassy Bald."

"Thank you, Aunt Isla."

"What for, Randal? There's been nothing but trouble since we met. And I haven't been much help at all."

"You believe me. I can see it in your face. That is what I need the most." He looked away. "It is enough."

"Don't be silly. It's not enough to save you from the police. We have to get Lily to talk to us without Kate."

Again, his face closed. "I don't want to upset Lily. She's fragile."

"Fragile or not, if she knows something she has to talk. You are my main concern."

〰〰〰

Leavitt stood near the vending machines when I went down to meet him. He'd grown older since the last time I'd seen him. His dark hair was sprinkled with gray and he had a few lines across his forehead, but his smile was the same. And those blue eyes still twinkled. "Mrs. Weehunt, I didn't recognize you for a minute. You look so different."

"I've cut my hair."

"You're more relaxed." He slid a dollar in the soda machine.

"It may be because I'm here in Nantahala. And I don't care so much what people think. That is a huge change for me."

"It suits you." He nodded, choosing his drink and pressing the button. The can rolled out, and he pushed the flap open to retrieve it.

"What are we going to do about Randal? He didn't kill that boy."

"I'm not here to decide that. Quite frankly, it doesn't matter. I am here to make sure he gets a fair shake. That's what I do."

How many times had he given this little speech to Scott? "No. He didn't do it. If you can't care about that, I don't want you working on the case. I'm not Scott and neither is Randal."

Leavitt looked at me. "Well, I'd have to say that this young man is lucky to have your loyalty."

"He's my nephew. My sister just died in a fire someone set. He can't take much more, and frankly I can't either."

"Mrs. Weehunt..."

"Lose the Mrs. Weehunt. I'm the same age as you, and I'm Izzie. Just plain old Izzie from the gorge."

Leavitt raised his eyebrows and his shoulders straightened. Shock or surprise? Probably a little of both. His composure returned. "You really have changed. Are you sure you're the same wife Scott had a year ago?"

"I don't know the answer to that question. What can you do to help Randal?"

He smiled. "First I have to know what happened from you and Randal. Is there somewhere good to stay? I have a feeling I will be here a few days."

"Nothing is resolved quickly in the Nantahala. There are a couple of motels near the highway but if you're up to it, you can stay at Grassy Bald. It's my grandmother's old place. I'm staying there. It has a set of rooms separate from the house. They're private and comfortable."

"I'll take you up on the offer."

He led me to the hard plastic gray chairs that were left over from when I was a girl. I took a seat beside him.

"Now, I want you to tell me what happened that night from your point of view. Leave Randal's part for him to tell." He tore open his bag of chips and opened his soda. "Don't leave anything out even if you think it's insignificant."

So we talked. I poured out the whole story beginning with the call about Velvet's death. When I finished, Leavitt slapped his knee. "Izzie, that is quite a story. Does Scott know all of this?"

"Some. We don't talk much." A rush of embarrassment heated my face.

"He's not easy to find unless he's looking for you." Leavitt stood. "Let's go check on Randal. After introductions, I'm going to ask for you to find something to do. I want to talk to him without you in the room. Is that okay?"

"I guess I need to talk to his doctor about you visiting him. He allowed Lily and Iona to come early on. Since he woke up, it's only been me. " I stood. "Let me run upstairs to the nurses' desk and see if they can get you approved, but I think it's better if I stay for the conversation." I walked to the elevator. "I'll be back."

Within fifteen minutes, the nurse had contacted the doctor and he gave his okay. "I'm glad you have a lawyer for Randal." She gave me a shy smile. "He's a good kid."

"Thank you. I think he is." I took the elevator back down.

〰〰〰

Leavitt sat in the same chair, looking at his phone. He smiled and stood when he saw me. "Are we set?"

"Yes, but I want to be with him."

"Trust me, Izzie. I promise to keep everyone away. He can talk candidly without worrying about disappointing you. You could go get food. I bet you haven't eaten."

"I'm not hungry. I'll run some errands close by, but call me if something isn't right."

"I'll call you when we finish. It could take a while." When I nodded, he said, "Okay, let's go meet Randal."

"After you talk, then what?" We walked toward the elevator.

"We wait. Probably not for long. I think your detective will be in touch soon."

CHAPTER 24

After introducing Leavitt to Randal, I left them to talk. There would have to be dinner that night, so I went to the market close by. I wandered down the pasta aisle, gathering some items for a simple dish. Leavitt would find out soon enough that I was a terrible cook. As I compared jar sauces, I noticed several women at the end of the row watching me. So … word had spread, and they knew I was involved with the murderer of Trevor White.

"Innocent until proven guilty, right?" I stared them down as they broke up and left.

The sound of one set of hands clapping made me look in the opposite direction. Marcus stood there. I released a breath I must have been holding since the accident.

"You still have your mouth and that is refreshing, Izzie."

My cheeks heated.

"I wanted to call when I heard, but I thought I'd give you some time."

"You can call anytime," I managed.

"Thank you." He blinked once. "How is Randal?"

"He is awake and better but it was scary. He died on the table," I said, keeping my voice low. "Why would those boys do this to him, Marcus? And now they want to blame him for this other boy's death. I just don't get the reasoning."

Marcus picked up a jar of pasta. "Sure you do. Fear. Hatred. And especially anger. It drives a lot of us. We both know that from being raised here." He switched the jar in my hand with his. "This is organic and much tastier."

"But what is there to fear about a seventeen-year-old boy who loves the river? Tell me that. I just don't get it."

Marcus shrugged. "Because he doesn't fit the norm around here. He's a round peg in the middle of a bunch of square holes. Izzie, look around. This place isn't very diverse. How many races live within the city limits? We're just the same old families we've always been for generations. Sure, new people move in, but they keep to themselves or befriend each other. The core of the gorge stays the same. Randal *isn't* the same. He doesn't fit in the mold constructed for him." He looked over his shoulder, then back at me. "I didn't know how far this town's strong ideas ran back in history until I began to read some of Grandfather's old letters. I'd love to say things have changed in Nantahala since he was young, that bad attitudes have dissipated, people are accepted, but what happened to Randal is proof not much has grown in the way of acceptance. Unfortunately, Randal *is* part of this place, whether he belongs here or not. So are you and I."

I laughed. "I haven't thought of myself as part of this gorge for a long time, Marcus."

"I know, Izzie, but you are. And now you are here trying to protect your nephew and find out who killed your sister." Marcus had a way of stating things as they were. Always had. "And I know when they find who killed Velvet and why, it will prove my theory of working from a place of fear and anger."

"I suppose so."

"I know you have a lot on your mind, but I wanted you to know I found some great photos of your grandmother. Also found the will. I think you will find it very interesting. It will help you understand why the land is tied up and can't be sold." He patted the back pocket of his jeans. "I wish I had them with me."

"I'd love to come by tomorrow. I did find a tin of old letters that were written by Velvet. I also visited Mrs. Crow the other day. She really couldn't help me much, but she did say Velvet was planning on selling Grassy Bald."

Marcus smiled. "Iris's will should explain a lot, but I found no mention of the ring. I don't think it belonged to your grandmother." His brow eased up. "She told my grandfather everything."

I thought for a moment before responding. Then, "You sound cryptic about the will. That's not like you."

He laughed. "Come over tomorrow and you'll see. Also, I'd love to see those letters."

"I'll be over in the morning before I go to the hospital. I have to check in on Mama first." I grew tired just thinking about it all. "And I need eggs." I laughed at this simple need.

He nodded. "It will be good to visit with you again. Tell Randal I'm thinking of him."

"I will," I answered with a smile. "He had such a good time at your far—"

"What's wrong?" Marcus asked.

"It feels like that was many weeks ago, maybe a lifetime."

He touched my shoulder. "I'm sure it does. You have to take care of yourself. Do you like tea?"

"Yes."

We wandered past the eggs and Marcus placed a dozen brown eggs in my buggy. "These are the best eggs. You need protein."

We walked down the coffee and tea aisle.

"Try some red tea. It is perfect for you." He pulled a brightly red-colored box from the shelf. "Steep it for seven minutes. Relax while you're drinking." His voice was soft, caring.

I took the box and dropped it in my buggy. "Okay. I will."

"Good. I look forward to seeing you in the morning." He paused. Smiled. "I'll make breakfast."

"I'll be there around ten."

"Perfect." He smiled as he walked away.

My phone vibrated and I answered. "Hello."

"Izzie, I'm finished talking with Randal, and we think the whole incident can be cleared up by talking with Randal's friend, Lily. This will happen on our own time, not the detectives'. If they don't like it, they can arrest him. But I don't think they have one shred of evidence. I will call your Detective Ascher and suggest he come question Randal tomorrow. The doctor stopped by and told Randal he would be moved to a regular room and the authorities would be cleared to visit tomorrow morning. I have a feeling Senator White has something in store for Scott Weehunt's nephew. I know this man. It's not the first time I've come up against him. He loves his son as much as his type can, but his actions are about him or business. He is very selfish, and, like I said, he hates Scott."

"Scott didn't have one kind thing to say either, so the feeling is mutual."

"Just remember the detectives may not want you there when they question Randal."

"I'm Randal's guardian."

"Yes, but not legally yet, and the law considers Randal an adult in these kinds of crimes."

"They *will* include me."

"We don't want to come off too touchy." He said this kindly.

"But you will be there. I'm his aunt. I should be there." I tried to keep my voice low.

"I understand. We will do our best."

"I'll be there in a minute." I moved toward the checkout counters. "I was picking up some food for supper tonight."

"Don't go to a lot of trouble."

"It'll be simple. Don't worry."

"Thank you for the offer of a place to stay."

I snagged a pack of gum from an end display and tossed it in with the rest of my purchases. "Don't thank me until you see it."

I paid for my groceries, then left the cool confines of the grocery store and stepped into the suffocating heat rising off the asphalt. Sweat instantly ran from the top of my scalp into my eyes. I started the SUV and let the windows down. The look on Marcus's face stayed in my mind. He really cared. Of course, he did. We were old pals, friends from high school. He knew everything. And when I was with him, I could be just plain old Izzie. That kind of friend was a keeper.

Randal was propped on his pillows and grinned at me lopsidedly when

I walked in the door. His face was purple and black with hints of green spilling around the bruises, but some of the swelling had gone down. "Aunt Izzie, I can't believe how hot you look with that new haircut. It shocks me every time I see you," he teased, but with a tired voice.

Stupid tears filled my eyes. "If one more person says how different I look, I'm going to deck them one."

This drew a chuckle from Randal. "A good haircut makes a new person. I hate to say—no that's a lie—I love to say I told you so."

I squeezed his hand. "I'm glad you're back to your smart-aleck self."

He pretended to look shocked. "Who, me? What would your preacher think about you calling me names?"

I gave him a hard look then sat in the nearest chair, the one angled where I could still see him. Who was that woman who worried so much about what her preacher thought? Had I really changed that much in such a short time? This seemed impossible.

His face turned serious. "What about Granny? Have you been to see her?"

"I have." I crossed my legs, then wedged my purse between my hip and the side of the chair. "We talked about you. I'm going back tomorrow morning."

He relaxed. "Good."

"She was very lucid."

"Good. It sounds like you've been busy."

Maybe it was his banged-up look that made me answer with complete honesty. Or maybe it was that I knew whatever I told my nephew would be for all the right reasons. "Randal, she told me Velvet wasn't a Leech, that she had a lover before my dad died."

Randal was silent for a minute before he spoke. "She's coming around with you. I'm glad. But you never know if what she says is real truth or just her truth. Either way, I never knew my grandfather, so it wouldn't matter to me."

My heart turned inside out. How could I ever question loving this strong young man as though he were my son? The memory of holding his infant body flashed before me and I closed my eyes.

"You should get some rest, Aunt Isla," he said, and I looked at him again. "You've been going constantly. And don't forget to go see that Mr. Jefferson. He was going to look at his grandfather's papers. He might be able to tell us something about Velvet."

"Don't worry about Mr. Jefferson. I am having breakfast with him in the morning." I smiled. "But first I have to show Leavitt Grassy Bald and fix supper. So I'll be leaving shortly."

Randal gave me a frown. "That place gives me the creeps."

"Really? It was always my safe place." I stood, walked to the bed, and squeezed his hand gently as Leavitt returned to the room.

"I see you made it."

I looked toward the door. "Everything all right out there?"

"Everything's in order."

I turned back to Randal. "I'll check on you tonight and be back in the morning after I see Mr. Jefferson."

His hand returned the same gentle squeeze. "Go see Granny too before you come."

I sighed. "Okay, boss."

He grinned.

"And, son," Leavitt said from near the door, "Remember what I told you. If the detectives show up here, call me. You have my number. Refuse to talk to them. Understand?"

"Yes sir." He looked at me. "Don't worry, Aunt Izzie. We're going to be okay. The worst has happened. We have to get to know each other after so many years apart."

I wanted to duck. Surely his confident words would send more trouble our way. But I loved this boy so much, I was scared to death.

〰〰〰

Leavitt followed me to Grassy Bald. He smiled as he got out of the rental. "What a place this is."

"I love it, always have." I walked toward the rooms where he would stay. A cold breeze—very unusual for such a hot day—embraced me. "The place may be very dusty. Mrs. Crow came and cleaned the main house but might not have cleaned these rooms."

"Don't worry," he laughed. "I'm handy. I can dust, even clean."

I turned to face him. "Heaven forbid. You're a guest."

"No, I'm your lawyer, providing a service Scott is paying for." He placed one hand on a hip and looked up and around, then readjusted the small bag he'd brought out of the car from one hand to the other. "This is a great place. I want to explore, if you don't mind? You should go rest."

I swung the door open. Bless Mrs. Crow. The rooms sparkled. "There is coffee and tea in the main cabin's kitchen. Make yourself at home. Also I'm making dinner but there is sandwich stuff Kate brought over if you need something now."

"Who is Kate?"

The smell of flowers wrapped around me, reminding me of Mama. "You might want to open the windows and air out the rooms."

"It's fine. Look at the antiques. You said this place hasn't been lived in, in a while? It's a wonder no one has stolen them." He placed a bag on the small sofa.

"I haven't been here in a long time." I ran a finger across one of the end tables. "It's off the beaten path. No one would bother us." I thought of the open French door. "Are you hungry?"

"Yes, but I can fend for myself. Don't worry about dinner."

"We have to eat. And I'm starving."

Crystal-blue eyes sparkled as he grinned. "If you insist."

"I'm not a good cook." I shrugged one shoulder. "You will probably regret agreeing."

He turned serious. "And you never answered me. Who is Kate?"

"Lily's aunt." I sighed. "We've made friends, at least until all this happened." Yes, there was a change between us. I couldn't deny it. " Come on over in an hour or so. I'll tell you more while we're eating."

"Okay, I'll change and get settled."

After returning to the car to get the groceries, I let myself into the house where a comfortable embrace of love greeted me. Grandmother Iris was happy I had come home. I looked out on the lawn. The space next to the writing studio would be perfect for a garden of herbs, and black-eyed Susans, scented geraniums with their delicate lacy blooms, and lavender. Of course I could plant rosemary and basil, some lemon verbena.

I shut the door. What was I thinking? I couldn't move back to this place. I promised myself I would never live in the gorge again.

I went into the kitchen and took out the items for my pasta dish. It would be simple. Sun-dried tomatoes, fresh basil, onions, the sauce Marcus chose and tomato paste, whole wheat pasta. The coarse homemade bread Kate brought was fresh. I slathered the slices with fresh butter—also made by Kate—sprinkled on some garlic powder and popped them in the ancient stove left over from Grandmother Iris's years there. My stomach rumbled. I set the copper kettle to heat so I could brew the red tea. The fresh tomatoes and lettuce left from the lunch Kate and I had were wrapped in plastic inside the fridge that still miraculously worked after who knew how many years. I pulled out a small pot, filled it with water, and placed three brown eggs in it for our salads.

I set the timer and settled with the tin of letters and the envelope I found in the cedar chest at the large round oak table in front of a big set of windows that flooded the room with natural light. The letters presented a paradox: the story of Velvet's years after I left and maybe a hint of why she was killed in a fire. That was a real stretch. Way too easy. My heart skipped a beat with childlike hope and anticipation for something that would solve Randal's problems.

The letters and looming disappointment seemed too daunting, too hard to read as the sun balanced on the treetops. So I chose the envelope lettered simply with Velvet's name. I placed the key to the side. Three photos fluttered out of the folded paper. One was of Mama, so stylish with a fur-collared dress coat and a smart hat angled on her head. She smiled at a young Daddy and a beautiful bright smile spread across his face. He seemed comfortable, joyful, in the embrace of Mama's arm entwined in his. In the background was a church, an old one. The next photo was of Daddy holding Mama in his arms as if he was about to take her over a threshold. A neatly lettered caption had been penned on the white edge around the photo. "After wedding. Going into our new home." I looked closely at my parents. If these younger versions of Mama and Daddy could talk to me, what would they say? What story would they tell me? They both looked as if they were the happiest couple in the world. I had wanted that so much for Scott and myself. I ran my finger over Mama. Once she had been happy and in love. This was proof.

A cool breeze from an opened window blew through the kitchen and settled on my shoulders as I picked up the third photo, which was of Mama and me, and Velvet when she was maybe three. She always acted so much older it was hard to tell. We stood in a garden, surrounded by blooming butterfly bushes. I didn't recognize the place, and the shadow of someone taking the photo loomed to the right. Who?

The whistle on the kettle caused me to jump. "Shoot." I laughed, then glanced at the photo again as I went to the stove. That photo revealed the change in Mama that took place after Daddy's death. She looked twenty years older than her age. Even though the photo was black and white, I knew Mama's once shiny dark hair was dull, unkempt. Her expression was bland, her mouth a straight line. She wanted to be anywhere but there in that garden having her picture taken with her daughters. The look she wore reminded me of the old mountain women who once lived close to Nantahala, beaten down by life. Back then husbands and wives came out of the foothills every month in beat-up rusted cars to buy the staples they didn't grow, like sugar, flour, and dried beans. Proud people who didn't like anyone offering help. When I saw them, gratitude would fill my heart because I didn't live the lives they lived. But maybe, in a way, I had led the same kind of life.

After turning off the kettle and removing the bread, I sat down to the paper inside the envelope, flipping it open. It was a birth certificate. Velvet's. Nothing special. Mama's signature was crisp and sharp. I looked hard at the space marked for the father's name and my breath caught in my ribs. The space was blank. I touched the empty place where Daddy's name should have been.

Had Mama told a real truth when she told me Velvet wasn't a Leech?

This was not a treasure Velvet had hidden away. It was a secret, a dark lie told to both of us all our lives. I doubted seriously that Mrs. Crow knew this had been added to the chest. And if Velvet really had a different father, did it mean Mama was also telling the truth when she said Daddy drowned on purpose? My mind rejected that possibility. Snapped closed, tight. Part of me ached deeply. Not because I felt less Velvet's sister. I was and would always be a full sister to her. That half-sibling crap was ridiculous. No, I hurt for the thought of Daddy knowing Mama was unfaithful, for Velvet when she found her birth certificate. Had Mama told her who her real father was? Someone Mama knew before Daddy died.

My parents weren't any different from Scott and me. The thought made me colder than the breeze had earlier. Their relationship had been what I based all my dreams on, the dreams that took me from home and never came into being. Maybe I was everything Scott said I was, especially the part of putting my head in the ground. What was I not seeing when it came to Velvet and this fire? What had I turned away from?

"What is this all about?" I spoke into the empty kitchen.

A knock on the front door made me jump. I left the certificate on the table and walked to the door. Opened it.

Leavitt stood on the other side holding a bottle of wine. "I thought you might enjoy this."

"You didn't have to," I said, stepping back.

"I ran out to the store to get some toiletries. You're cooking. I had to contribute." He read the label as though he hadn't before. "Pinot noir."

I opened the door wider. "Come on in. I have been sweeping ghosts out of the house, but supper will be ready soon. You can sit at the table and talk while I finish."

"Do you have a corkscrew?"

I couldn't help but laugh. "We'll see. There's everything else in this house. I found an egg timer earlier. One of those really old kinds you don't see anymore." I opened the first drawer I came to and, sure enough, located corkscrew in a drawer of mismatched utensils. This suggested Grandmother Iris partook of "spirits." I shoved the drawer shut with my hip. "Here you go." I found long-stem glasses in one of the cabinets, then washed them in the big farm sink and hand dried them with an old but clean dishtowel.

"This place is wonderful, Isla," Leavitt said as he waited. "I didn't know you had neighbors close by."

"I don't." I handed him the glasses.

He frowned. "I saw a woman with red hair standing on the edge of the woods as I was leaving." He poured the pinot noir into the glasses.

"Really? I've known people to have claimed seeing Grandmother Iris. She's one of the ghosts here on the bald. But I've never seen her."

"This woman looked real enough to me. And she didn't look like a grandmother." He pushed a glass of wine my way and I took it. Moving away from the person I had created back in Mountain City was becoming natural.

"Maybe it was one of the locals hiking."

"Could be. She wore shorts and a t-shirt, smeared with what looked like paint. She could have just been out reading in the woods."

"Reading?"

"She was carrying a book." He angled a brow. "And I'm not sure I believe in ghosts." He raised his glass and I paused, waiting for him to make a toast, but instead he brought the glass to his lips and sipped his wine.

"Red hair, you say." I thought of Velvet. "I'm with you. I'm too practical for ghosts. Anyway, this girl sounds of the world." I returned to the counter to chop the onions.

"She was reading, *A Good Man Is Hard to Find* by Flannery O'Connor. I'd know the cover anywhere. One of my favorites in college."

My heart pounded and I stopped chopping, then resumed. "I was looking at some things I found of Velvet's—my sister who died—in an old cedar chest upstairs. I found two interesting belongings while looking for clues about Velvet's activities before the fire, but they had nothing to do with any of that."

"Why would you think a clue would be here?" I could feel his eyes on me.

"Velvet had an antique ring worth a lot of money that Stuart Collins found in her car. I thought maybe it had something to do with Grandmother Iris and this whole fire thing. But I found nothing to indicate the ring belonged to my grandmother. I just can't figure out where Velvet would get such an expensive piece of jewelry." I gave him a half of a smile over my shoulder.

"Why would the ring have anything to do with a fire?"

"Stuart says it's valued at twenty thousand dollars. We turned it into the police, but they aren't talking. They also haven't returned the ring." I drew the onions together with the knife. "I just have a gut feeling. I've spent years pushing those kinds of feelings to the side. I've decided to honor this one and find out how Velvet came to have possession of such a ring." I placed the onions in the pan then looked fully at Leavitt. "Also, it gives me a sense of control in a situation where I have none."

He nodded. "Yes, I can see how that would work. So did you find anything useful?"

Cold prickles ran over my arms. "Yes, I did. I found a large skeleton key, but it doesn't fit this front door, three old photos, and Velvet's birth certificate." I stopped talking and emptied the sauce in the pan. "They're on the table if you want to look. At first it seemed normal, not much of a find. Then I noticed the space where my father's name should have been had been left blank. I can't help but wonder if Mama had a big secret of her own. She hinted to this in one of my recent visits. Of course, with her mind like it is, I don't take anything she says serious." I turned the stove's burner on, then picked up my glass of wine and turned to rest my hips against the counter. Leavitt was looking at the things I'd found. "Don't you find this odd? Who leaves the father's name blank? I would think a person who wants to keep the father a secret," I said, answering my own question. "But why not lie and put Daddy's name? He was dead by the time Velvet was born." I paused. Thinking. Remembering. "Maybe she was feeling too guilty to lie anymore."

"Opening family closets can expose all kinds of skeletons." He picked up the key in an almost play on words.

This time I held the glass up in toast fashion. "I have to agree with that wholeheartedly."

Leavitt watched me for a moment, then said, "I think I will go directly to the hospital in the morning and wait for the detectives to show up. You have an appointment?"

"Yes, two. One with Mama and one with Mr. Jefferson. He found my grandmother's will in his grandfather's papers. He was quite elusive about the content. He only said it would answer some questions. I'm dying to know. But he made it clear there was nothing about the ring. I worry I should be at the hospital instead of chasing these stories." My stomach twisted. "I worry something will happen to Randal, and I won't be there again."

"I'm sure that is normal after such a traumatic experience, but you can't be with him all the time." Leavitt was so practical. "I will see you when you get to the hospital. Don't worry. I'll be there handling things." He smiled as he looked toward the stove. "That sure is smelling good."

"Scott thinks I'm a terrible cook, so be careful."

I opened a cabinet and pulled out two plates.

CHAPTER 25

I pulled into the parking lot of the assisted living center at a little past nine the next morning. As I got out of the SUV, the tin of letters in my tote bumped the door, making a loud sound. I wanted Randal to know I had them before I read the rest. Our relationship had to be based on complete honesty. Actually I had decided that all my relationships had to be based on honesty going forward.

Mama sat outside on the large back deck that provided a beautiful view of Pine Log Mountain in the distance. If I hadn't known her condition, I would have thought she was her old self.

"Hello, Mama."

She looked at me. "You're back."

"Yes. You remember me."

"Of course I remember my oldest daughter," she snapped. "What have you come for this time?"

I pulled out the birth certificate. "Do you remember giving this to Velvet?" I smoothed the paper flat on her lap and placed the skeleton key on top, but held on to the photos.

She frowned. "You've been crawling around Grassy Bald again, child. There's nothing there but old ghosts. I've told you to stay away from there."

"I know, but I have to have a place to sleep while I'm here. Your house is gone." I pointed to her lap. "I looked in the chest at the foot of Grandmother Iris's bed."

Again, she frowned. "You didn't bother Mother's things, did you?"

"No, only Velvet's. I did see all the scrapbooks belonging to Grandmother Iris. I'm dying of curiosity, but I didn't open them." The truth was, I'd hardly had time. "What door does this key fit? It doesn't fit the front door at Grassy Bald." I picked up the key.

A soft smile came over her face and she rested her hand on the birth certificate. "Lord, child, there's a lot you don't know."

"Will you tell me?"

She watched me for a minute. "I don't see how it would hurt anything."

I pulled up a nearby chair, becoming an eager child looking for her mother's attention.

"When Daddy first became a pastor, he was sent to Nantahala." She paused, drifted off somewhere else, her eyes glassy. "He was a circuit rider. They'd go from town to town each Sunday preaching. That's what Daddy did, but him and Mama needed a home base. They bought a cabin at the foot of Pine Log Mountain. This key fits the door." She looked off toward the mountain. "Daddy began having his black moods. They moved to Grassy Bald. When I was born, Mama treated me like a fragile piece of antique glass. She was so afraid of losing me." Her fingers moved as though she were playing an instrument as I placed the photographs in my lap. "She gave me everything, including the most love a child could have. It didn't help. As I got older, I took after Daddy." She rolled up one sleeve of her blouse and showed me her wrist. "This is one of a pair, but it is almost gone now. It has become part of the wrinkles, blending into who I once was."

One line, a scar, on her left wrist was barely visible. I'd never noticed it before, and I would not have noticed now. I ran my finger over the mark. "Mama?" I forgot my pledge to be quiet so I wouldn't trip up her thoughts.

"Yes, dear. Your mama almost ended her life. I was in college. Would have if not for that nosy roommate. She came back to check on me." She waved her hand. "Anyway, I'm not talking about that anymore. I was sent home to stay on Grassy Bald with Mother, the best warden in the state of North Carolina. She had experience watching Daddy. I would not die on her watch. I would not die the way my father did." She looked at me. "Your sister had the same moods. The boy seems to be okay. He's his own person."

I nodded. "He is for sure."

"But people who look after us are driven crazy with the problems we cause."

I held my breath, afraid if I spoke again, I'd scream. Velvet had been suicidal? That wasn't the sister I knew. She was full of life, even if she stayed in trouble all the time. The person who created those paintings was not a person who wanted to die. Even the old letter I had read proved her love of life.

"Have you seen this ring, Mama?" I held the phone out to her and tried showing the photo to her again.

She took the phone from my hands and frowned. "This ring is of the devil. It caused nothing but trouble, nothing but trouble. It goes with the key. Both are bad."

"So it belonged to Grandmother Iris?"

Mama threw her head back and laughed in a mean way. "This ring had nothing to do with my mother, Isla. Nothing. Where do you get your ideas?"

"Then where have you seen it?"

"That is a secret like this paper." She held the birth certificate up. "I have some, you know." She rubbed her finger across the key. "But my mind plays mean tricks on me. If I could get to that river, I would heal myself. I would dip down in water and be healed. Velvet needed to be dipped in the river. Maybe if I could have straightened my mind long enough to explain this to her, we could have gone together." She pointed at the old photo of all three of us. "She went to this garden all the time. I told her to stay away but she went. I told her she would cause herself more trouble than it was worth, but she was changing. That's what she told me. Changing. Becoming a better person. That girl never listened to me one day in her life. Well, that's not true. When she wanted to give that boy up for adoption, I stopped her. She said it would be better for everyone, but he was family and I wanted to keep him." She looked at me with intention. "We did. I didn't make a scene when she showed me the ring. My mind was going in and out too much by then. I couldn't hold my grip on the story she told me—still can't—but I knew she was happy. She so much wanted to please me. You were such a rebel, Isla. You would have dug around the story she told until you found all the answers." She looked away then. "I wish you had been here. Maybe Velvet would have lived instead of dying in that fire. You know she wasn't afraid of much, but fire was her worst fear."

My phone buzzed and I sighed, not wanting this moment interrupted. But what if the police were with Randal? "Let me answer this." I stood. Looked at the phone. "Hello," I said to my husband.

"A detective called me." Scott sounded out of breath.

"Don't talk to him."

"I'm not stupid."

"Let me call you back." I hung up and looked at Mama, who extended the birth certificate and key toward me.

"Here, young lady. I think these things belong to you."

"No, they are yours."

Mama laughed, lost in her own world again. "You're so mistaken. I don't have any family, never really did. And that key doesn't fit one place I want to be. You've mixed me up with someone else."

My shoulders fell. One phone call, and Mama had lost her momentum. I nodded; I had to go see Marcus and get to the hospital anyway.

Mama searched me with her confused look. "Young lady, will you come see me again?"

I bent over her head and touched my lips to her soft white hair and delicate pink scalp. "Yes, Mama."

She touched my arm with her tissue-paper skin. "I've always loved you, girl. I knew you could make something of yourself. The other one couldn't. She didn't have the backbone. She had the blackness."

"I love you, Mama."

And those haunting words were enough to make me question why I ever left.

CHAPTER 26

As I pulled out on the main road, my phone rang again. Kate's name flashed up on the console screen. "Isla, this is Kate." She sounded a little out of breath. If I didn't know her better I'd think she was drinking.

"It's good to hear from you." And it was. I really liked her even if we were at opposite ends the last few days.

"I need to talk to you. Will you come over this morning?" There was an anxious edge to her question.

Gracious. One more thing. "Is everything okay?"

"Honestly, no. I wish I had never moved to this house. I need to go back home or start over somewhere that doesn't hold memories of my husband."

"What's happened?"

"Just come over here. You're driving. I can tell."

"Yes, but I can't come over now. I have to visit a friend and then go to the hospital."

"A friend? I thought you didn't have any friends here. I'm beginning to think I don't know you, Isla."

"I'm sorry you feel that way, Kate." A gray line of clouds sat on the horizon. Rain by the afternoon.

Kate took a long breath. "I'm out of sorts. Come see me and you will understand. Please."

"After I finish with my friend, but I can only stay a minute."

"Good, I'll see you soon." Her voice had brightened.

The air was heavy, hot and still, but the prayer flags flapped in a breeze that blew through the treetops. I sat in the idling SUV at the top of Marcus's drive. A hesitancy hung around me, reminding me that only a month ago, I would not have considered this scene an option. Marcus wouldn't have entered my mind, hadn't since I moved to Mountain City. But I was lying. This seemed to be my habit. I had opened my eyes many mornings with a wisp of an image. His younger self, of course.

Marcus still being in the gorge was a contradiction to our friendship. We had plans, life plans, that would have saved us, changed us for the better forever. But Marcus changed his while I kept mine.

The gravel crunched under the tires as I eased the car down the drive. I wasn't doing anything wrong, just going after some information he found in his grandfather's papers that would help me understand my family, maybe even help me with Velvet. Marcus was a childhood friend.

I knew this description was complete bull, mainly because I hadn't bothered to call Scott back. Marcus had never been just a friend for me. But for him, ours was pure friendship, and I went along with him so I could stay close.

Back then.

He was supposed to become a priest. Or had that been his excuse to keep from hurting my feelings?

He stood in the open back door of his house, as if he'd been watching for me, anticipating my visit. When was the last time someone waited for my return? His smile was warm. The streaks of gray running through his dirty-blond hair made him look so much like his father that my breath lodged in my chest.

Why couldn't Scott be more like Marcus? Why couldn't we have had the life I dreamed of and planned so diligently for in college? But the answer was a sharp deed sitting between us, washing away any love. There was nothing but bones, bare bones of a dream marriage. Bare bones and plenty of other women I'd chosen to ignore.

"Good morning, Izzie." Marcus held the driver's side door open.

"Good morning, Marcus." That awkward feeling that he could

read my thoughts washed over me.

"I hope you like spinach quiche with lots of cheese." He looked at the envelope in my hand. "What's that?"

"Old photos, a skeleton key, and Velvet's birth certificate. I've just come from seeing Mama." I extended the envelope.

"I'd like to see the photos." He took the envelope from me.

"We really should go through Grandmother Iris's scrapbooks then. I'm sure your grandfather is in them. These photos are not part of the scrapbooks. Mama told me—in her mixed-up way—about one of the photos. The woman can forget how to brush her teeth and comb her hair, but she knows the people in these photos."

"That's how Alzheimer's works. You must tell me everything she said." He tucked my hand in the fold of his arm.

"You won't believe it. But she was lucid at times. I think her story is true. Like I said, she's good with remembering the past. That's what Randal told me too. But I lost her before I could ask more about the birth certificate."

"Let's go in. I know you need to get to the hospital." He stopped walking, still holding my hand. "People are talking, Izzie. I want you to know so you won't get caught off guard like yesterday. They are not kind."

Marcus was such a caring person. It was hard for me to be around him and remain strong. A man like him took away the need to wear toughness as body armor and, for me, that was dangerous. When Randal and I went back to Mountain City, Marcus would be history, a memory, a warm feeling. I had to keep my guard up.

"I'm not worried about those people. Some things never change, Marcus. Part of me wishes they could but the reality of this situation says it won't happen. It's like you said yesterday, we're part of the generations this gorge created."

"It pains me to agree with you."

The old Marcus would have argued with me about people being mostly good. How disheartening to think even *he* had given up on our hometown. I should have felt validated. He'd come over to my side. What would have happened if I had stayed in Nantahala, faced the talk, become strong, and kicked Scott out of my life?

I pulled my mind away from the question. "Enough of this talk. I came to see what you have and be fed by a dear friend, who is still much like he has always been."

He placed his hand on my shoulder. "Izzie, I've changed just like you, and gladly so. Neither of us would want to be the dumb kids we were."

I stepped through the back door into the beautiful kitchen. "I love this, Marcus." The room looked lived in, loved, more than it ever did when his father was the keeper of the farm. Baskets and herbs hung from the old wooden beams in the cooking area. A large island had been added. Barstools lined one side as if he had lots of visitors. And part of me hated this, that he had made a good life, while I had a lonely pristine one. The stack of yellowing paper, belonging to Grandmother Iris along with her will, sat on the square farm table. They were held together by a large rubber band that made the sheets curl inward.

Marcus's gaze followed mine. "I'm going to let you take it because you may need a copy and it belongs to you. Grandfather never got rid of any of her papers, kept them as keepsakes, I guess."

I shook my head. "Look at the old typeset. Imagine the typewriter that he used. An old Royal, maybe. Things sure have changed."

Marcus had a wispy smile on his face. "The typewriter is upstairs in my study. And, yes, a Royal. When you read this, you will understand why the land couldn't be sold. This will belongs to you and your family."

"Thank you."

He pointed to a chair. "I'm starving."

I sat. "Me too."

"Coffee?" He held a mug in his hand.

"Yes." Scott invaded my thoughts. He always left me coffee every morning. One of those kind things husbands and wives did for each other. Up until Velvet died, it was often the only communication we had for days on end.

"We have to read one part of the will while we eat. It's especially interesting for your situation."

"Okay." The whole thing made me uncomfortable, as if I was allowing a stranger into Grandmother Iris's private thoughts, but, really, they weren't private. It was her decision on how to take care of her estate.

When we were settled at the table with food and coffee, Marcus pulled several pages from the pack. The paper crackled as he arranged them in front of him. "I thought you should hear these sections."

And he began to read:

"State of North Carolina

County of Graham

I, Iris Harris, of said State and County, do make this my Last Will and Testament, hereby revoking all wills heretofore made by me.

"Then it goes on about debt and such. But here's the next part under property.

(A) If Miss Geneva Crow is unmarried and still in my employ at the time of my death, I give to her the sum of twenty-five thousand ($25,000.00) dollars as a token of my affection and appreciation of her long and faithful service and her devotion to me. I also give her four acres, part of the land at the foot of Pine Log Mountain, so she may build a house. I don't have to tell her to use the money and land wisely, she will.

"And then there is the next section.

(B) There can be but one head of a house. Therefore, I direct that my Executor shall offer the house and surrounding land to my daughter, Darlene Vivian Harris and that she should be paid a sum of one thousand ($1,000.00) dollars a month to cover living expenses. I further direct my Executor to keep the deed to said property and include the property deed of land and small cabin at the foot of Pine Log Mountain, with exception of the four acres given to Miss Geneva Crow, in a trust. Should Darlene Vivian marry, she will not be allowed to live on Grassy Bald nor sell it. The property will be kept for her firstborn daughter to live on for as long as she would like. If this daughter decides to sell said property, she must offer it to Geneva Crow if she is still living. If Geneva Crow is deceased, she must offer it to the Executor's family because George Jefferson has been my dear friend."

The air was still. I heard this stern woman's voice in the words. I could see a young widow, Iris Harris, dictating these orders to Mr.

Jefferson. What had made her give such a mandate to her only child? Was Mama seeing my father and Grandmother Iris disapproved of him? Or was she so soured on marriage that she wanted to save her daughter? Was this Grandmother Iris's misguided way to keep Mama safe from plunging into her dark abyss again? I should have felt pity for Mama, but I couldn't because she had stood up and brushed herself off, married my father anyway, made a complete muck of her life. At least she did this on her own terms. But Mama would never again be that young girl in the photos, who seemed to love the man on her arm after marrying.

"You can see why I wanted you to hear these parts." Marcus placed the pages back in the stack and handed them to me along with another folded pack. "It's the deeds. I found them in the papers. Of course, your mother could have broken this will and sold the property at any time. This is so old, no one would have fought her."

I focused on his hands, beautifully weathered from working on the farm. This man wasn't the friend I had as a teenager. He'd grown into a respectful person with compassion. And, once again, I could learn from him just like when we were young. Lessons. When would I stop having to learn a lesson?

"And Velvet could have done the same. Right?"

"Yes, if she had the will. She could have because she was the legal guardian of your mother after she entered assisted living. Your mother signed everything over to her."

I took a deep breath. "Thank you. I wish I could talk about this but I'm speechless. I always knew Mama couldn't sell Grassy Bald, but I never thought about her not wanting to sell it."

He nodded. "I found it interesting when I read the will. Of course it wasn't my grandfather's place to agree or disagree with Iris Harris's choices. He was just a lawyer."

I took a sip of my coffee. "Mrs. Crow must know a lot more. She wanted me to find this out on my own. Her part. But it sounds like she deserved what she was given, and of course she never married. I'm not sure how we came to call her *Mrs.* Crow. Perhaps as a way to show respect. Maybe she had started it, wanting the *Mrs.* to mark her as unavailable.

"But Grandmother Iris . . . how could she do this to her only child? What mother does this?"

He looked at me. "Sometimes we just have to forgive, Izzie. Maybe you will never know the answer. Maybe you just have to live with it."

"That's easier said than done, my friend. I've never been too good at dealing with lies and disloyalty. I'm not good at forgiving or forgetting." I looked away to hide the tears attempting to reveal themselves.

"Randal has you. He will rise as strong as he wants to be. Your mother doesn't care about any of this now. I'd like to think had your grandmother lived to an old age, she would have softened and been on her daughter's side. She would have loved her grandchildren. Maybe things would have been different for your mother, maybe not. I bet Pastor Paul Watkins can tell you something of your mother's reaction to the will. He was her age, and according to Grandfather's journals, he and his father were regular visitors to Grassy Bald."

"They are close now. Mama still talks to him every day." I thought about how Pastor Watkins had looked at Mama the day of Velvet's funeral. "So you really found nothing about the ring?"

A slight tinging of red colored his cheeks. "I'm afraid not. I would tell you, Izzie. I promise. There was no mention of the ring in these papers."

"This coffee is so good."

He accepted the change of subject. "Thank you. But you need to eat healthy. Living off of coffee isn't smart. Randal is depending on you, but mostly, I have a feeling you are going through your own changes. That's why I wanted you to hear those parts of the will. You are here facing all your family's demons at once. That could be a bit much."

This time the tears appeared before I could stop them and I swiped at them. "Yes. I do feel I've bitten off more than I can chew, much less digest." I managed a laugh.

"You were going to tell me about the photos and birth certificate."

I opened the envelope and took out the photos. "Look at Mama when she married Daddy and then this one of Velvet, Mama, and me in some garden."

He examined the pictures again. "Look how young and pretty your mama was. Wow. It's a big difference. And that garden looks familiar, but I can't think of where I've seen it."

"I don't know." The silence that followed was comfortable. "Today Mama was talking about the cabin mentioned in the will. She said this key belongs to it and called it an evil place. It didn't make a lot of sense. She could have been confused because she said she needed to go into the river and heal herself. You know how she hates water." I smiled. "Do you remember when you helped Velvet and me go through the tunnel?"

"I'll never forget. I thought you two had died when that canoe came floating by me. Your mother would have killed me." He shook his head. "You were fearless."

"Ha, fearless. Was I ever fearless?" I laughed and even I could hear the ring of sadness in my voice.

He pointed to his chest. "Yes. You were to this only son, who had been coddled at home. Don't you remember how afraid of everything I was. Dad used to laugh at me. He liked you so much. It was your courage that made him like you, and he let you work in his precious garden." Marcus laughed without any malice. It seemed to be a good memory.

"You were afraid. I forgot that. I just remember how scared I was."

"Girl, I was terrified mostly of you." He stood. "More coffee?"

"Me? Yes." I held out my mug. I really had to leave.

He poured the coffee. "Yes. You could do anything, and you stood up to everyone. When kids made fun of me in grade school, you beat them up. Surely you remember?"

I'd forgotten. "Yes, it didn't take a lot to get me mad."

"That's an understatement." He sat at the table again. "When I told you I was going to be a priest, you never blinked an eyelash. You accepted me. You didn't tell me I wouldn't be happy, that a life of celibacy wouldn't work for me."

My cheeks heated. "You wouldn't have listened." The anger and sadness I felt when he told me he was leaving for seminary flooded me.

Had I hidden it that well?

"Yes, you're right. You left for college to follow your dream of writing and met Scott Weehunt. We really went our own ways."

I swallowed my emotions. "Yes, we did." My phone vibrated. It was Leavitt. "Excuse me, I have to get this." I stood and walked across the kitchen. Marcus placed the photo back in the envelope and left it on the table.

"Izzie, we have to go to the police station." Leavitt was calm but firm.

"Why?" I glanced at Marcus, who watched me.

"They have arrested Randal."

"What do you mean? He's in the hospital." My voice strained higher.

"They arrested him in his room and placed an armed guard outside the door. No one, not you, especially you, can go in right now. Only me because I'm his lawyer."

"They haven't even questioned him. You said they didn't have any evidence." I grabbed my tote and the envelope. I thought of the tin I had planned on returning to Randal.

"He wasn't arrested for killing Trevor—even though that surely will happen. This Lily girl has told the investigators she saw Randal beat Trevor's head against the curb. She also said Randal confessed to setting the fire that killed Velvet."

The floor moved under my feet, my tote hit the floor, and I gripped the edge of the counter. "Lily told them that? That is a lie. All of it. And it's hearsay."

"Yes. But people can be arrested for less. Now they have to make the case stick."

Inside my brain was an ice-cold image of Randal crossing the yard at the site of the fire, lost and worried. In shock. "I'll meet you there."

"I'm leaving your place now."

I hung up.

Marcus held out his hand. "Come on. I'm driving."

I thought of arguing but in that minute, I wanted him with me. "They've arrested Randal for Velvet's death." My voice broke.

He pushed the door open. "Where are we going?"

"The police station. They won't let me see him." My voice cracked into a million pieces.

A bright ray of sunshine caught my attention. Velvet stood at the edge of a path coming off Pine Log Mountain just over in the neighboring yard. Was it her? Was I losing my mind? She watched me, not moving. An ache ran through me. Velvet, my baby sister. Why was she there? What did she want?

Marcus pulled on my arm. "We need to go."

"Did Velvet come around here?" I got into the passenger side.

"She had a thing with that old cabin next door. That's the cabin mentioned in the will." He gave me a look as he started the engine. "The photo of you guys standing in the garden was taken there. I knew I had seen it before. You know, it still tries to bloom. Velvet thought she would fix the place up for herself. Worked really hard over there."

I cringed. "I need to see Stuart Collins. He has Velvet's ring and he knows how Randal looked the night of the fire. He knows he didn't kill his mother."

"First we go to the police station. Right?"

"Yes. Lily is saying Randal killed Trevor White and confessed to the fire that killed Velvet." I shook my head. "Randal wouldn't kill anyone."

Marcus looked out the window. "Let's take one murder at a time. Shall we? I believe you, Izzie. You've always been honest."

"Have I really? Because, Marcus, you don't even know me. You know that girl who still had a chance to make something of her life. I have been anything but honest for the last seventeen years. But I do know Randal isn't a killer."

CHAPTER 27

Lily stood on Kate's porch. A cold chill worked its way through my chest. "There's Lily," I pointed. "Randal says she is fragile, but she's told lies about him."

"Well, you don't know what she's said. I'm guessing you are going by what the police told Randal's lawyer." Marcus took the sharp curve slow as I craned my neck to watch Lily. Marcus made a startled sound and I turned around in time to see a Jeep—Emily's Jeep—coming right at us.

Marcus jerked the wheel to the right and missed her. "I wonder why she's driving so crazy?"

"Does Emily have a death wish? I'm pretty sure that's her Jeep. It was, wasn't it? But I didn't get a good look at who was driving."

Marcus flexed his fingers around the steering wheel. "I didn't get a good look at who was driving either, but it was Emily's."

"I wonder what is wrong." Something nagged at me. I wanted to turn around and follow her. " Let's just get to the station. I'll talk to her later."

~~~

"I'll wait here. You go on in." Marcus gave me a reassuring smile. "If you need me, I will be right where you left me."

Leavitt stood in the lobby. "I'm going back and find out just what they've charged him with and why. You stay here. You have to trust me, Izzie."

I nodded. "No I don't, Leavitt. I'm not good at trusting, in case you haven't figured that out. I want to hear for myself."

He smiled. "Yes, I kind of noticed. Try and relax. Let me find out what is going on."

I stood because sitting was impossible. What I wanted to do was walk, just walk as hard and as far as I could. It was what I did at home when Scott made me crazy. Instead, I took out my phone and called Kate. The phone rang and rang. When it went into voice mail, I hung up. What was I supposed to do? Leave a message that said her niece was lying? Randal was now alone in his hospital room with an armed guard outside. This had gone too far.

I called Emily next, so I must have been desperate. When I went into her voice mail, I left a message.

"You were driving crazy. What was wrong? You almost hit Marcus and me head-on. Call me. Randal has been arrested for the fire." I rattled off the words, then hung up and put the phone in my tote and touched the tin. I opened it and pulled out a letter. Just one to take my mind off what was going on. Maybe I could find an answer to straighten this whole mess out.

April 8, 2007

Atlanta, Georgia

Deeply Missed:

I have run away. Left the gorge. I'm not going back. Mama can't make me. I dreamed about you last night. You stood there hating me and disappeared. The look on your face haunted me worse than any ghost ever could. That's when I decided to call you and make you listen. I ran in the house and picked up the phone. It was one of the old rotary phones, but all the numbers were missing. The feeling I needed to chase you, persuade you to listen to me was overwhelming. I tried to remember your number and dialed blindly, not knowing if I had chosen the correct number since the printed digits were gone. The dial came off in my hand and the receiver fell apart. Sobs overtook me.

Have you ever had a dream and you knew you were dreaming? I tried to wake myself up. I didn't want to look at the phone anymore. I didn't want to try and find you. Where are you? But I know. Of course I know. You're not hidden but you are hidden from me. Before I woke up, I heard your voice calling out my name. Somehow, I knew we would never talk again. Ever. You were gone and our lives were separate.

I love you so much better than him. Don't you understand how crazy I am. How I destroy anything that means something to me. Sometimes I just want to die. I'm only nineteen and I want to die. That's crazy and wrong.

I miss you. Please come back.

My heart cracked a little at her pain. So she left home, and because she made no mention of Randal, I had to assume he was with Mama. There was no telling what she did to this person to hurt them. Probably something horrible. That's why she couldn't send the letters. She knew the person would never forgive her.

I opened one more letter.

May 20, 2015

Nantahala

Deeply Missed:

I want to tell you how much you helped me in my life. I know you think I'm this bad person, and I'll never change. Sometimes I think that about myself, maybe a lot of times. But you helped me to know I was worth something. You're the only person who ever made me feel this way. I know you will never forgive me. I won't forgive myself. Who could? I'm horrible.

Remember the tunnel and how you thought I drowned. I loved the look on your face when I popped up out of the water and was okay. I understood you would mourn me if I died. God, do you mourn me now? Are you even thinking about me? My heart aches and if I could go back and redo all the bad things I did, I would. I would fix things between you and me. But I'm a messup, plain and simple. There's no excuse. I'm grown and can't blame it on how Mama treated me. How Daddy died before I was born. You truly were my only friend and now you hate me too. That's as it should be. I miss you every day.

Do you remember how you told me that my name was special? How I was named after the most regal cloth ever made? If only I could have grown into that description. If only I could send one of these letters maybe you would see I care.

Love

Velvet

My heart pounded in my ears. God, help, the letters were written to me. I had missed that or maybe I just didn't want to know. Velvet had written *me* letters. Would they have changed how I felt if I had seen them? I was ashamed to say no, probably not. Not then. Now, maybe, after years of struggling in my marriage, of having my eyes opened to how hard it was to live a life that wasn't me, I would be more forgiving. It took her death and meeting Randal to open me enough to see who I had become, a woman who refused to forgive. A woman who couldn't really feel.

And that was all.

My phone rang, startling me. I dug it from my purse, glancing quickly at the screen before answering. "Hi, Kate." I collapsed in a chair.

"Did you call me? I thought you were coming over here." She sounded put out.

"I called to tell you I was running late. I'll be there as soon as I can manage."

A long breath. "It's important, Isla. You're disappointing me."

"I'll be there."

"Okay." She ended the call.

I looked at my phone.

"Izzie." Leavitt stood towering over me with a stern look on his face. I had been so absorbed in the call that I hadn't heard him. "We'll talk outside." He took my arm. When we stood in front of my SUV, he turned to me. "I know you want to be with Randal, but you have to keep your cool. I think you will be allowed to see him today."

I nodded.

"I mean it. You can't get mad. You're like a mama bear and that will cause us trouble."

"I don't understand why my concern for Randal will cause so much trouble, but I will trust you on this."

"Thank you. Now, tell me about Lily and Stuart Collins."

I drew a blank on Lily. "I know very little about the child. She is around Randal's age, a year younger. I think. She is homeschooled by her aunt, Kate. Her parents are in Japan. She is quiet and kind of a smart-mouth, but that, I'm told, is normal for teenagers. I went to high school with Stuart. He is the fire chief and arson investigator here."

"Tell me what you know personally about him?"

A prickly chill walked over my scalp. "He was a real pain in the rump."

"Like how?"

I crossed my arms. "He was always asking me and other girls out, following us around. It was creepy. We were way out of his league. I guess you had to give him credit for trying."

"How did he fit in? You say creepy."

I shrugged. "Maybe I'm being too hard on him. He was odd. Out of step. As if he really wasn't who he let everyone think he was. His dad died when he was ten. His mother was crazy. Everyone knew. One day she drove to the Piggly Wiggly naked, got out, and walked in the store. Bought tuna in a can. The good folks of Nantahala would die if this happened today, so just imagine their reactions back then. She was done for." The old feelings of shame washed over me. "The kids were mean to Stuart. He was teased unmercifully." I remembered the crushing fear that nearly paralyzed me at the time. Fear that Mama would pull such a stunt. I had worked so hard to keep her oddities a secret. Now, of course, as an adult, I knew these kinds of secrets were not kept quiet. "Why all the questions about him?"

"He said he heard Randal tell Velvet that he would kill her if she sold the land. The police take Mr. Collins's word as gospel."

"That's crazy. Where did he hear this said?"

"While fly-fishing near your family's fishing camp. Seems they, Randal and his mom, were yelling at each other." Leavitt paused before continuing. "I wonder if there is bad blood between him and your family."

"Not that I know of. Other than driving me crazy when I was in school, I've had no real interaction with him. Remember, Leavitt, I haven't been here for quite some time. Anything could have taken place in my absence."

"Stuart's statement—we will not talk about Lily's forthcoming one and the promise of trouble it brings—has gotten Randal arrested for the murder of his mother. There is no physical evidence and it won't stand up in court, so Randal won't be convicted. This charge of murdering his mother and setting the fire is a misuse of taxpayers' money." He patted my arm. I looked down at his hand, then back to his face. His eyes. They seemed sure. "I will see to it this goes away, Izzie."

But a shudder worked through my bones. "I'm not sure things will go so easily here."

"Trust me. I'll meet you at the hospital. We will try to get you in to see Randal." Leavitt walked to his rental.

I got into the passenger side of my SUV where Marcus remained behind in the driver's seat.

"I couldn't help but hear. I'm so sorry, Izzie." Marcus's voice was soft. "I will say again. No way Randal set that fire and killed Velvet." He said this with such conviction, I wanted to hug him.

"Thank you for caring." I held up the letters I still clutched in my hand. "Velvet wrote these letters to me. I found them in Randal's backpack. He must have carried them everywhere with him. At first, I didn't know who Velvet was writing to, but then she mentioned the tunnel, Marcus. Her voice is inside my head. I can't shake the feeling she wants me to make her death right." I took a breath and straightened my spine and shoulders. "Maybe I'm just losing my mind."

Marcus spoke just about a whisper. "I highly doubt that, Izzie."

"I need to go to the hospital. You hadn't planned on being stuck with me."

He smiled. "No worries. I have all day." He started the SUV. "I'm your friend, Izzie."

"I'm glad you are. I need one."

"Once we get there, I'll wait in the lobby for you.'

"Thank you again."

He nodded. "You can be there for me one day." It was a flippant thing, not serious, but I liked the idea of keeping Marcus in my life. I didn't care what Scott thought.

"It's a deal."

CHAPTER 28

What a difference one night made. Randal's face was better, and even though he had been arrested, even though he had every right to be deeply depressed and angry, he laughed like his old self when I came in the door, Leavitt right behind me. "I knew you would come one way or another."

It seemed he had come to trust me. "Yes, I have to make sure you're okay."

A shadow fell across his smile and he swallowed. "I'm good, Aunt Isla. Don't worry. This is all stupid. Me killing Velvet?" He shook his head. "No way, no how. I never even threatened such a thing. Velvet could make me crazy sometimes. I'm not lying—she made everyone crazy—but she accepted me the way I am—not some sports jock on the football team or avid hunter wearing camo for fashion, just me. A guy who likes to cook and cut hair." His smile wobbled. "She *always* did, and she loved me deeply. She was my best and the only friend I've ever had besides Granny." His voice broke.

I looked away. "I know you didn't hurt your mother or burn the house down. But there is a statement about you being angry over her selling the property and moving."

Leavitt gave me a dark look.

"No, I never threatened Velvet," Randal said. "She would have hit me up the side of the head with something if I had. Who said this?" He looked at Leavitt.

"That doesn't matter." I frowned at Leavitt.

"Remember what I've told you, son. You have to keep your cool," Leavitt warned.

"Yes, sir. I won't show out." His face relaxed into another grin.

"This is serious, Randal," I fussed.

He turned sober again. "I know. I'm sorry."

"You haven't done anything." Then I took a chance. "Randal, do you know of anything that would make Mr. Collins accuse you of killing Velvet?"

He shot a quick, guilty look at Leavitt.

"I've already asked him that question." Leavitt explained to me.

"There is one thing, but I don't want to talk about it. I didn't say the things Mr. Collins said he heard."

"Son, you need to tell me. Mr. Collins's statement was the only reason you were arrested." Leavitt spoke to him as if Randal was his little brother.

Randal looked at me.

"It's okay. Leavitt needs to know *every*thing. Otherwise, Randal, you're playing a dangerous game."

Randal nodded. "About three months before the fire, Mr. Collins came to the fishing camp one afternoon. Most days after school, I would go down and work on it. I'd seen him fly-fishing down the river on some evenings, but I didn't start a conversation with him."

"Why not?" Leavitt asked.

Randal shrugged his shoulders. "I don't know. I didn't know him. The other kids all think he's the best. But, I don't trust many people, and I'm not very outgoing."

This statement stabbed me in the stomach. "So, what happened?"

"He walked up to the camp and started talking. I mean, he was an okay guy. We talked about the river. He told about me his family and their connections to the Cherokee."

"I never knew that about Stuart." I looked at Leavitt.

"Yeah, well. Anyway, I just listened. He was good at talking and telling stories. He started coming to the camp every day. The truth is, I enjoyed talking to him. I mean, like I said, I didn't have any friends. And no father . . ."

My heart heaved.

"Then one evening he asked me if I wanted to come to his house for dinner." Randal gave me a funny look. "I said sure. Why not?

Velvet worked at night and I ate alone. It was nice to have a friend. But after I got there I decided to go home early."

"What happened, Randal?" Leavitt asked.

Randal looked out the window. "It's probably why Mr. Collins is trying to make me look bad. Payback and all."

"What happened?" I sounded sterner than I should have.

"He tried to get me to be more than friends. Okay?" Randal's words came out with machine-gun rapidity.

I was stunned into silence. *Stuart?*

"Well, that does change things quite a bit, Randal. Why didn't you tell me this earlier?"

He shrugged. "Who is going to believe me? Mr. Collins is well respected. You said that, Mr. Tollson. I'm just the kid everyone hates in this town." He pressed his lips together. "People think that about me anyway, right?"

I stomped my foot. "Oh, no, sir, you are not hated by everyone."

Randal half grinned. "It's good to know you care, auntie, but it's old stuff for me. I put it behind me. I left that night and walked home. I was pretty bothered. Velvet was home already. Of course, now I know she had lost her job but didn't tell me. She knew something was wrong with me and hassled me until I told her." He gave a chuckle. "She was one mad mama. The next day she called Mr. Collins to come over to our house. She told him she was going to call the police."

"What did Stuart say?" I asked.

"He didn't like it. Got really angry and told Velvet that she was a—a—well . . ." He looked at me, a slow blush rising from his neck. "A not-nice woman." I nodded. I understood what he was saying. "He said she was a drug addict, that no one would believe her over him, and no one in town would give a darn because they hated me. But what made him go ballistic was Velvet telling him he was acting like his mother, crazy on the inside but perfect on the outside. He stomped out, but before he did, he threatened to make us pay if the police found out. And, really, he didn't *do* anything. He sure didn't touch me. So, Velvet agreed to keep quiet unless Mr. Collins bothered me again. "

"Randal," I said, choosing my words carefully, "what Mr. Collins did was wrong. He is a grown man and you are underage. It is against the law." I looked at Leavitt. "Now what?"

"It's slippery. I think we pay a private visit to Mr. Collins. Let him know we found out about the incident. He may agree to recant his statement to the police, but for now, Izzie, you're out of here. I have some things to go over with Randal, and that guard outside is going to tell you to leave in a minute."

"*I* have to leave?"

"Yes, auntie dear. I could just see you causing me more trouble by going all mother on the guard." He smiled with pleasure.

"Kate wanted me to come by."

Leavitt's head jerked toward me. "I would like to be with you when you speak with her. Maybe I can get her to tell us more about that night."

"Okay. I'll find Emily and see if she knows anything more."

"Good. I'll be in touch when I'm finished." Leavitt gave me a dismissive smile.

I drew closer to Randal and slipped my hand into his. "You're going to come out of this okay."

"Since I didn't do anything, I can only hope you're right."

〜〜〜

Marcus waited for me in the lobby and stood when I got off the elevator. "How are things?"

"Well, we found out what would make Stuart Collins say the things he did, but there is still the problem of what Lily told Kate. Randal is looking more like himself each day. And he doesn't seem afraid. Even with the arrest."

"That kid has been through a lot just being himself in this town. More than I think you realize. It's going to take a lot to knock him off his feet for any length of time."

Part of me hated that Marcus knew this about Randal and I knew nothing. "I have to call Emily Greene. She might know more, and I've heard nothing from her since she left the hospital after Randal was

190

admitted. That's not like her. She is the nosy type." I pulled out my phone and dialed her number. "She's not answering." I hung up the phone. "I want to go to the paper."

"I'll drive." Marcus opened the lobby door for me.

"Marcus, I can take you home. You've been so kind."

"No. I will go with you." He grinned. "Even Sherlock had Watson."

"Thanks, but that's not necessary," I said because, really, I needed to be alone and form a plan.

"First, we go to the paper. Then you take me home." He held up his hand. "No talking about it."

Strange, having someone care.

$$\approx\approx$$

The newspaper office was something I would have imagined from the late sixties. The only difference being laptops and computers rather than typewriters at the desks. A young girl looked up from one and smiled. "Mr. Jefferson, how are you today?"

"I'm fine, Karen. How is the life of a sportswriter?"

"In this town? Boring." She pouted. "Why are you here?"

"My friend, Mrs. Weehunt, is looking for her friend Emily Greene."

A shadow fell across the girl's face at the mention of Emily's name. "Oh, she's in trouble."

A tall, lanky man came out of a side office. "She was supposed to cover a story for me, and she hasn't shown up. It's not like her. I've called her over and over, even went by her gallery and loft at lunch. No Jeep and no sign of her. If you see her, tell her she's off the story. She'll know what I mean."

I thought about her Jeep nearly running us off the road. "That seems a little harsh. Something could be wrong. I'm assuming you are her boss."

He looked thoughtful. "Yes, the editor-in-chief here, Carl Jackson. This is Nantahala. I doubt Emily's in trouble."

"That's interesting because my experience here in the past week has been much different. A *lot* happens here and so far, it hasn't been good."

191

His office phone rang and he went to answer it.

Before I left, I wrote my number on a piece of paper with a note to call me if he heard from Emily. "Pass this to Mr. Jackson." I handed the slip of paper to Karen, then Marcus and I went outside, where we stood on the sidewalk. "Now I will take you home. I'm going back to Grassy Bald and wait."

"Somehow, Izzie, I don't see you waiting on anyone," he chuckled. "If you would like some supper, I'll have plenty. Just drop in this evening. That'll be fine."

Again, I felt like some dumb high school girl about to cry. "I might do that."

"Just promise me you will *not* hunt down Stuart Collins. That will only cause you trouble."

"Between Leavitt and you, I get the message. I won't go snooping." But I wasn't sure how long I could keep myself from doing that very thing.

<hr>

When I dropped Marcus off, I decided to go to see Mrs. Crow instead of Kate. Let her be put out. Lily's comments or lies were too tough to discuss. Maybe Mrs. Crow would talk to me now that I had the brass key, the birth certificate, and letters.

She was working in a garden and wore a large-brimmed straw hat.

I got out of the SUV. The door shutting made her stand up straight. "Is that you, girl?"

"Yes, ma'am."

"Come out here. I need some help with these squash hills. Wanted to have them planted before now but we had several late frosts."

The thought of digging in the dirt relaxed me.

"At least you're dressed to help me." She gave me a half grin.

I looked down at my jeans, t-shirt, and sneakers. "Yes, ma'am, I am."

"I just don't bend over as good as I used to thirty years ago. Shoot, even a year ago." She cackled at her own humor.

"Do you want me to make the hills?" There was plenty of loose, dark dirt.

"Yes, young lady, and then you can plant the seeds. Maybe you'll bring them good luck. You being a planter yourself."

I dropped to my knees, then placed my tote at my side. The cool, moist dirt soothed my fingers, and I closed my eyes. "I love vegetable gardens. Do you plant herbs?"

"Oh yes, ma'am, I surely do. Gather them out of the woods, too. My mama was a hunter, you know."

"What do you get from the woods?"

She handed me seven flat squash seeds from a floral apron that hung loosely around her hips. "There's nothing like sassafras bark and the root. I do a lot with that. Bet you wouldn't know anything about healing with sassafras."

I looked up at her, squinting against the harsh sunlight. "You can strip the bark and make a tea. Sassafras can be used for anything from healing wounds to soothing rheumatism."

"Ha, you're smarter than I thought. You know your plants." Mrs. Crow gave me a wide grin. "Love that some young people still follow the old ways."

"I have herb gardens at my house in Mountain City. I make salves and such."

"Lordy, girl, I'm starting to like you a lot." She touched the top of my head with her fingers. "You be like your grandmother. She knew a little about everything. And she was always learning, wanted to know more. Folks here thought she was above everyone else, but that was just a show to protect herself. And if I remember right, you always had you a garden patch by her writing studio."

"Yes, ma'am, I did. Won quite a few blue ribbons at the fair."

Her smile relaxed and her chin rose a notch as her eyes settled on mine. "Did you find what I told you to look for?"

"Yes, ma'am. I think. I found these." I pulled the brass skeleton key and birth certificate out of my tote.

She nodded. Took the hidden treasures from me. "You found them, girl."

"Mrs. Crow, what is this key supposed to tell me, or for that matter Daddy's missing name on the birth certificate?" I moved over about two feet and began to form a new hill.

Mrs. Crow continued to look at the key and the envelope. "I feel your peace when digging in the dirt. Good for your soul."

Her words brought a sudden rush of tears, but I didn't let her see. I just kept working.

"Like I said, that girl was a mess, but I loved her as much as she allowed me to. You girls were a handful when you was little."

I sighed, then brushed the dirt off my hands and looked up again. "It was good when you came to keep us. It's all kind of foggy for me now."

The old woman laughed. "Lord, child, you don't remember? I guess it was easier for you to forget all that stuff. That's what happens with children sometimes. But Miss Velvet never forgot, and she was the youngest. She wore her resentment on her shoulders all her life. You left here before she got cranked up good." She shook her head like an old dog batting away the flies, then dipped into her pocket for more seeds. "I don't blame you. That mama of yours didn't help none. She was trying to make up for all her mistakes and overlooked the part of being a mama."

"What do you mean? What have I forgotten?" I pushed seeds into the new hill. I wouldn't even be around when the fat yellow squash were ready for picking. My heart squeezed at the thought of leaving, and this truly caused me to collapse into a sitting position on the ground. I was losing my mind.

"You can't know the woman your sister became without knowing what happened. You think you're going to save everyone here, make up for leaving that boy behind. But you ain't. I know you don't believe me but you ain't got one bit of saving power. That's beyond you and me."

I looked up at her. "I have to try."

"Why?" She clicked her tongue. "You can't save that boy. You can't save your mama. Especially her. You can't save that mess of a husband you married. Girl, you're old enough to know we can only save ourselves and sometimes we can't even do that. Look at this key here. That was Velvet's way of trying to save herself. A place she could go and persuade someone to love her. Young lady, did she succeed? Is she alive? Did she end up happy? No."

The questions sat on my shoulders. They made more sense than anything I had heard in a long, long time. "She was trying to do better?"

"I suppose, but she wasted it all going after the wrong things. If she would have thought about changing for herself instead of him, things might have gone a lot better for her."

"Who? There was always a him." I started forming another hill.

"Yes, girl, there was always a him with your baby sister, but this one was different. She changed. Didn't drink a drop. I didn't know much about him. Other than she saw him about once a month. Met him at the old cabin over there that was Miz Harris's." She held up the key. "That be the key to the place. The only one I ever knew existed. Them two would spend the weekend there. Never left as far as I noticed. But I'd see them in the yard." She handed more seeds to me. "She worked on that garden of your grandmother's. Mrs. Harris loved that garden when she lived there. Your mama used to bring you girls over here with her when she checked on the old cabin. She tried to take care of the garden too, but her bad spells came too often."

I thought of the photo. "So, Velvet took a man to this cabin once a month?" I paused. Pondered. "He must have been married. Doesn't sound like she changed."

"No, girl, she changed. Came over one day and brought me homemade bread. Can you see that sister of yours making bread? I don't know who the man was, but that ring showed up on her finger when she started coming to the cabin. I seen it the day she brought the bread. And she was smiling, a real happy smile, not all mean like she did before or after he disappeared. Not like she was when she came to see me about Grassy Bald."

"What happened to the man?"

"Moved on to that next hill, I guess. One day he just didn't come. I heard her crying and crying like someone had hurt her something bad. Thought about going over there, but she could be funny about her privacy, and I could understand that myself. She never came back after that. I figured something happened. Either he went back to his wife—'cause like you, I figured he was married—or he couldn't come back. Maybe he left the country."

"Or died." The words slipped from my lips before I had a chance to form them.

"I was trying to be kind, girl. But yes, the man dying did enter my mind. Of course this whole time, I was going over to sit with your mama, so I'd see Velvet leaving for work. She wore that ring for the longest after the man disappeared. She wore it when she started drinking real bad again." She looked out over the garden and shook her head. "This time the drinking was worse than it had ever been. Like that vice had been waiting on her to come back and picked up where it left off, doubling its hold on her. She never spoke to your mama, just huffed off to work every afternoon, smelling like rum. It's a wonder they didn't stop her for driving under the influence." She cleared her throat. "Then your mama tried to shoot the tax man. I thought Velvet would lose her mind. She was so upset with the police chief for threatening to take your mama to jail. Worse yet, he threatened to commit her to the state hospital. Velvet was at a breaking point. It showed in her eyes. That child couldn't take no more. She remembered what happened that night that you don't remember. She knew that her mama was unbalanced way before she turned old. Back then when Velvet and you was just little things. I think she had been trying to hide your mama's craziness all them years."

"We used to have a secret joke. We said we were the two founding members of the crazy mama club." I reached up for more seeds and she gave them.

"I heard you girls saying such things when you was in grade school. I never fussed 'cause I guessed it was just the truth, but see, you don't remember what happened when she stepped off the deep end. Velvet did. That must have been a burden."

I sighed, nearly exasperated with the game we were playing. "Are you going to tell me?"

She shook her head. "Ain't my place, child. Maybe it's meant for you not to remember. Either way, your mama has to tell that story. But just remember, no mama in her right mind gives her daughter her birth certificate with her daddy's name missing. That child was only fourteen. No telling what story your mama put along with that paper."

I took a deep breath. "Velvet never let on Mama gave her any stories about Daddy. I don't understand how I didn't know."

"Sometimes, child, we don't *want* to know."

"Why didn't I know about this cabin?" I looked in its direction. "I only found out it existed this morning when I talked to Mama and read my grandmother's will. Marcus Jefferson gave it to me from his grandfather's papers."

"I don't much know why your mama didn't talk. Could be the old story of her daddy killing himself there was too much for her."

My scalp prickled. "That's what she was trying to tell me this morning."

"Mrs. Harris talked to me about your granddaddy some. She was real torn up when he finally succeeded in killing himself. She had only left the house long enough to go pick some fresh flowers from the garden, wanted to brighten his day, wanted to make things better for him—I remember we were talking about that. She heard the gun go off. Something just spoke to her deep inside. She said he was unrecognizable. Put that gun in his mouth and pulled the trigger."

I made another hill of dirt. "Grandmother Iris must have been crazy with grief. No wonder she wrote the will the way she did."

"Mrs. Harris nearly died herself. Walked away from that cabin and left it like it was. Bought Grassy Bald. I went to work for her there."

I smiled as I squinted one eye and gazed upon her with the other. "She was lucky to have you."

"Naw, girl. I was lucky to have her. See, when my daddy died, Mama had her hands full. My pay saved my family. Just remember you can't do nothing more for that sister. Love your mama the best you can and give love to that boy. That's all you can do." She looked at me pushing the last of the seeds into the hill. "You come on back here another day and we'll talk more. I don't mind telling stories about your grandmother. She would want you to know. I got to put some cucumbers in tomorrow. Come on back."

I stood and brushed off my hands again. "I think I will. Since Randal has been arrested, I can't see him as much."

"Nonsense. That boy don't have a killing bone in his body. What are them fool police thinking? You can feel a killer in your bones. Oh, you might be getting fooled by them, but if you're still, you can sense them. They are that feeling that just doesn't fit." She looked off into the distance. "But folks aren't still no more."

I nodded. "Maybe."

"No maybes to it, girl. Now get on home and rest. Come back tomorrow."

CHAPTER 29

I had the idea to see the old cabin where Velvet met the man that changed her. I wanted to see the place she came once a month to meet this lover who gave her such an expensive ring. Where Velvet Leech began to change her life. I so hoped Mrs. Crow got that part right. A part of me wanted my sister to have *some* happiness. And that was crazy, seeing what she did to me. But I had made my share of wrong choices. One thing about age, a girl learns what is important and what isn't. And nothing is black and white. Life would be a lot nicer if that were the case. If Velvet had stood in front of me at that very moment, I would have told her those things could be discussed, moved through to the other side. In those days before I left, Velvet hated me, and I hated her. She thought she was right, and I was sure she was wrong. And we had both stood our ground.

Mrs. Crow said Velvet tried to make the cabin her own. Maybe I owed it to her to see the place, to know where she spent her happiest days. I pulled out of Mrs. Crow's drive and took the curvy road, watching for any indication of the cabin. Logically it would be in between Marcus and Mrs. Crow's but I hadn't noticed a driveway.

Then the little cabin seemed to spring from the ground between some trees, moss on its cedar shingles, as if it finally wanted to reveal itself to me. The drive was narrow and overgrown with tall grass in places. No wonder I hadn't seen the place. I had to stop a good distance from the structure because of the growth.

The grass was up to my chest in places, and I kept thinking of snakes as I trudged through. I wanted to see the garden where Grandmother Iris and Velvet had worked. Could it still be there? The closer I got to the cabin, the hairs on the back of my neck stood up. This was not a good place. A huge oak tree was uprooted, fallen, decaying. A cool touch of air brushed against my neck and I turned around. Nothing. If spirits sticking to a place were real, they would be here on these grounds.

The tree was massive even in decay. I kicked around where the base had been, thinking about Velvet working in the garden. Imagine that girl pulling weeds. Without thinking I walked in the direction of the garden spot. An old fence, newly patched in many places, appeared in the tangle of overgrown bushes and weeds. A gate hung on with one hinge to a rotten sideways post. Inside sat a stone bench. This was Grandmother Iris and Velvet's garden place.

"Velvet?" I said aloud. "Who were you here with? Does he have anything to do with the fire?" My words soaked the air. No response came. "What happened, Velvet?"

The cool air tickled my neck. I stood there for a minute longer before sitting on the bench. The cement was cool and at that vantage point I could imagine flowers blooming and Velvet working raised beds that were now a tangled mess of vines. Maybe her lover had helped. Sorrow swept over me. My taste of delirious grief when Randal was hurt was nothing to compare to this desolation.

I closed my eyes and saw Velvet's strong back as she knelt in the dirt, weeding her flowers and bushes. Her fingers working in what must have been rich dirt at the time. This garden was proof Velvet had grown up some.

A crack of a limb caused me to open my eyes. Something, or someone, stood at the window of the cabin. But when I blinked, they were gone. A creepy thought crawled up my bare arms. Was someone watching me? I stood, deciding to save the cabin for another day when my imagination wasn't so wild. I walked through the gate.

"*Izzie.*"

I turned, but no one was there. I walked fast to my SUV, my breath heaving from my chest. When I jerked open the door, I noticed something on my seat. A curl of real hair. A curl of deep red. *Velvet.* Heat moved through my fingers when I touched it. A rush of panic spread within me. I jumped in the car—the hair held tightly in my hand—and started the engine.

As I turned the SUV around, a shadow loomed large on the patio. Who was there? Was it in my mind or a real person? Maybe it was the person who put Velvet's hair on my seat.

And was this person, by chance, her killer?

The lock of hair was proof that there had been someone in that cabin, and it suggested Randal couldn't have killed Velvet. There was a person out there who had taken my sister's hair before or after he killed her. I turned toward the hospital. Leavitt had to see this. The killer—I just knew it—had placed the hair on my seat while I looked at the garden.

My phone rang. "Hello, Leavitt."

"Izzie, have you had any luck finding your reporter friend?"

"No. She's gone. Her boss is looking for her because she had a story to cover. He's not happy. But I have something to show you that is interesting. How is Randal?"

"He is reading. The doctor says he has to stay in here a few more days. That his injuries are still concerning. So he's not going anywhere."

"Can I see him?"

"Not now. They have an armed guard outside his door. He's now an inmate. You have to get permission. We'll find out when you can visit again, or if they will let you visit again while he is in the hospital."

"That's stupid. I'm his guardian."

"Yes, I know. We have a few days to get him cleared. Let's work on that."

"I'll meet you at the hospital. Tell Randal I'm working hard at finding out what is going on. I think I have something."

"What is it?"

"I'll show you and explain."

"I'll see you soon." Leavitt ended the call.

Randal had to be proven innocent on both charges.

Leavitt and I sat in a nearby diner where I'd ordered a Cobb salad and Leavitt had ordered a burger with fries. He held the lock of hair in his hand as I finished telling what had happened.

"Someone was watching you, Izzie. And that someone could be the person who set the fire. More than likely it is. Allow me to repeat myself: you *have* to be careful. Stuart had the ring found in Velvet's car, which means the police have it. I need to confirm that. They'll have to do a DNA test to see if the hair is Velvet's. And, if it is, this is enough to make the DA question whether to take Randal to trial for his mother's death." He paused. "But Trevor White's death is a different story."

"I know it is."

"I will get a copy of their interview with Lily soon. Then we'll know where we stand. It's my understanding she knows what happened."

"But is she telling the whole story? Or is she flat-out lying?"

"We have to be careful with this witness. It could work against Randal to upset her or her aunt."

"I know." I picked at my salad, then laid my fork against the bowl.

"You need to eat," Leavitt said, pointing toward my food with a French fry.

"Mmm."

"How about your friend? Any ideas where she could have taken off to?"

"No." My phone went off. I looked at the face; the number was local but unfamiliar. "Hello."

"Mrs. Weehunt, this is Carl Jackson, the editor at the paper. You wanted me to call if I found out anything about Emily."

"Yes. Did you find her?"

"No, ma'am, but the police found her Jeep abandoned."

My heart sank. "Where?"

"That's the weird thing. They found it on your mother's property where the house burned down. We're forming a search. I wanted to let you know. Do you mind? It is *your* property."

"Of course not. I'll be there to help. Search anywhere you want. I'll meet you in a few minutes."

"Okay."

I looked at Leavitt. "They've found Emily's automobile on Mama's property."

Leavitt stood with a swipe of his napkin across his lips. "Let's go."

≋≋

There were several police cars parked in Mama's yard and the Jeep was being towed. Several uniform police stood around. One walked forward. "You can't be here."

"Be careful of anything you say, Izzie." Leavitt spoke quietly.

"I will," I said, even knowing how I rambled when talking to anyone in authority.

"I'm the family's lawyer. We are concerned about what is going on on the property."

The officer looked at me. "Are you Mrs. Weehunt?"

"I am. Mr. Jackson from the newspaper called me to say they found Emily's Jeep here. I've been looking for her today. I tried getting in touch with her but my calls kept going to her voice mail." I looked around. "And now this. Something isn't right."

"We're getting ready to search the property."

"Good." I jutted my chin toward Grassy Bald. "I'm staying at the cabin on the hill. I haven't been home since early this morning and I haven't been down on this property since I met Mr. Collins here last week to discuss his investigation findings on the fire."

Leavitt gave me a long look that read "stop talking" as the police officer nodded.

"Can we please join in the search?" I asked, then looked at Leavitt. "This is Mr. Tollson—"

"Friend of the family and lawyer, like I said," Leavitt jumped in.

"That's fine," the officer said, "Since you probably know this land better than anyone. But if you see something, do *not* tamper with it."

I gave him my sweetest smile. "Of course."

The group divided and began to comb the woods surrounding the house site. When I began to span the slope to the bald with another officer, the situation hit me. We were searching for a body. They thought Emily was dead. I shook the thought away; I just couldn't take another death.

Not long after we began to descend the steep hill, someone yelled near the river. My stomach turned upside down. I ran in that direction. Leavitt, who had been looking on the right side of the property, met me and we continued forward.

"She's in trouble. I should have known this when I never heard from her. There is no telling where she is," I mumbled to Leavitt. The thought of the Jeep nearly running Marcus and me off the road sent a shiver up my spine.

Leavitt frowned. "I hope what they found isn't bad."

I turned my head to whisper, "Her Jeep nearly ran Marcus and me off the road on our way to meet you at the police station."

"Wha—" he began, but I turned away and began to walk faster.

An officer stood on the deck of the fishing camp speaking to the officer who had been with me earlier. "Someone has been in here recently."

Two officers came out of the fishing camp. "Stop," one said to me. "No one can come in here. This place is closed for investigation."

I stepped forward until Leavitt grabbed my arm, holding me back. "Is she in there? This is *my* fishing camp."

The officer shook his head.

"This is crazy. Who has been here?" My body ached like I had a fever and my voice hit a high octave.

Leavitt released my arm. "I don't like any of this, especially on your property."

"I just want to find Emily," I said.

One of the officers spoke into the radio on his shoulder. "NPD-5."

"Go ahead, 5," the staticky reply returned.

"Yeah, we need the detectives here at the Leech place. We're securing the area as a crime scene. Possible 10-64."

"What is that?" I asked Leavitt, hoping he would know.

"Not sure," he said. "If I had to guess, I'd say *crime in process*." He gave me another harsh look. "Be quiet a minute."

I huffed but understood. If we were going to learn anything, we needed to listen, not talk.

"There's evidence someone was held here against their will," one of the officers said to the one who had spoken to us earlier.

"I can't stand around, Leavitt," I said, swinging toward him. "We have to find her." For someone who drove me crazy, I sure was upset by her disappearance. But she'd helped Velvet by believing in her art. She tried to help me so many years ago, but I refused to accept her news.

Leavitt turned his back on the fish camp and the gathering of officers. "This is looking more and more like Randal will be cleared of the murder charge for his mother," he said, keeping his voice low. "But we still have to work on the pending charge. That means speaking with Lily's aunt."

"Yes."

Leavitt rested his hands on his hips and sighed. "Where do you think Emily could be?"

A helplessness washed through me. "I don't know. We weren't close friends anymore. I didn't know her habits." I looked around. "But I think she's around here somewhere. I feel it in my bones." I looked over my shoulder in the direction that I knew detectives would soon come. "We need to get the hair left on my car seat to the detectives. Should we do that now? Should we wait?"

"First things first. When we finish here, we go see Randal's friend, Lily," Leavitt said. "*And* her aunt."

CHAPTER 30

I parked the SUV out front of Kate's house and looked over at Leavitt. "She won't allow us to talk to Lily."

"I know, but I can tell a lot from body language. Let's try talking to her. You two are friends. Maybe she will relax and talk."

"Yes. She was expecting me to come by earlier today. But you being with me will put her on guard. She's trying to protect her niece. I understand this but I also know that lying about what happened isn't right."

Kate met us on the porch. She looked as stressed as I felt. "Who is this?" she asked, nodding toward Leavitt.

"Leavitt Tollson," he said, stopping and turning his face fully toward her. He wanted her to trust him, and this was Step One in securing that. "I'm Randal's attorney, Mrs.—"

"I'm Kate Tucker. And you can't see Lily," she said before I had a chance to say "boo." She looked at Leavitt. "I thought you were coming alone, Isla."

"We don't want to put Lily through anything else, ma'am," Leavitt said. "But I need to talk with you, so I insisted on coming."

Kate's shoulders relaxed and she seemed to be surprised. "Sorry, I've been fighting off the investigators. I don't know what I can tell you that I haven't already told Isla." She nodded at me and I released a pent-up breath. The warmth we had between us seem to still be there.

"Probably nothing, but I want to hear it from your mouth, not Isla's and not from the police." Leavitt smiled in such a way that I reckoned he'd practiced on many an interviewee.

Kate smiled back. "Yes, I see what you mean." She looked at me.

"Would you like some iced tea in the kitchen?"

"Thank you," Leavitt answered for us. "That would be nice."

I followed them.

"So you want me to tell you what I know?" She took glasses from the cabinet.

"If you don't mind." Leavitt sat at the table.

"And why did you need to see me so badly?" I asked, sitting. Before Kate could answer, my phone went off. Scott's number appeared. "Excuse me. I need to step out in the garden and take this. You guys talk." I went outside. "Hello?"

"Izzie, I got the strangest message on the home phone a minute ago. Are you okay?" Scott sounded sober. And genuinely concerned.

"Yes, I'm fine. What kind of call?"

He took a deep breath. "There was a woman pleading in the background. A man—I'm pretty sure, the voice was disguised—said you needed to come find your friend. That you'd been within shouting distance of her location. And to bring the letters. He said you would know what he was talking about. He said to meet him at the fishing camp at five this evening and no police. What is this about? And how did he get this number?"

My heart pounded. "He's talking about Emily. She's missing. She had our home phone number. So whoever did this used her phone for numbers."

"Don't you go meet this guy."

"I won't. And I *have* to tell the police." Not to mention that, by now, both police and the town's detectives were probably crawling all over my land.

"What letters is he talking about?"

"Velvet's." I looked around as though whoever was behind all this was somewhere close by. "That means he is watching me. I'm getting close, too close. This has to be the person who set the fire."

"I'm coming there."

"No, don't. I can handle this."

"You're my wife, Izzie, and I'm coming there."

"Leavitt is staying in one of the apartments at Grassy Bald. I'm fine. Don't come." I couldn't deal with his drinking in the middle of the events that were playing out. Scott sober was one thing, but if he decided to tie one on . . .

"I'm coming and I need to see Randal."

"Why?"

"Because I like the kid, Izzie. And I'm not a dumb person. I've put two-and-two together while you've been gone. I know you left the gorge back then for more than what Velvet did."

Over the years I had been married to Scott Weehunt, I often imagined what it would be like to have this discussion. But I never thought it would be under these circumstances. "We'll talk when you get here."

"Lock the door on that cabin and call the police about this message."

"I will if you let me off the phone." I ended the call and turned to go tell Leavitt, then gasped.

Lily stood behind me. "Aunt Kate doesn't know I'm here. You mustn't tell her."

I collected my breath enough to ask, "What is it, Lily?"

She touched my arm and I flinched. "Please tell Randal that Aunt Kate is making me tell this story. She wants me to keep the truth a secret even if Randal is found guilty. I don't want to do that to him. She says they will never believe what happened, and I'll go to jail."

"What are you talking about? What happened, Lily?"

Lily looked toward the house. "I have to go. She'll be angry if she catches me here. Please tell him."

"Lily, you have to tell the truth," I said, reaching for her arm to stop her. "Randal doesn't deserve to be punished for something he didn't do."

"I'm so sorry." She ran back across the yard, disappearing around the house.

I opened the back door.

Leavitt gave me a hard look. "What's wrong?"

"Scott is on his way. He got a message from someone who claims to have Emily. This man wants to meet me." I didn't mention the letters. "I should call the police. This is getting really crazy."

"Let's go see them." He stood. "We'll finish later." He nodded at Kate.

"My goodness," she said.

"Yes, my goodness indeed," Leavitt said as we left the room.

～～～

Leavitt held the car door open, and I got behind the wheel of the SUV. "Your friend isn't telling the truth. She's protecting her niece," he said. "Let's get to the police station quickly. We will give them the hair and tell them about the message."

"Okay."

He shut the door, then ran around the front of the car and got into the passenger's side. I pulled onto the road, then glanced toward the rearview mirror. Someone watched me from an upstairs window in Kate's house.

"Leavitt," I said, my eyes returning to the road. "Lily found me outside. She told me that Kate is forcing her to lie." I glanced his way.

His lips formed a thin line. "That's interesting," he said, then looked out the passenger's window, ending the conversation.

～～～

We made it to the police station in a flash. A blast of cold air met us when Leavitt opened the steel door leading to the department. We found the door marked NPD easily and, after we entered, Leavitt introduced us and explained to a uniformed young woman why we were there. She told us to have a seat, then picked up a phone and spoke into it.

When Detective Ascher came out to meet us, Leavitt rose, extended his hand for a shake, then said, "Detective, Mrs. Weehunt's husband has received a phone message from a man claiming to have Emily Greene. He's demanding that Mrs. Weehunt meet him."

"Come back to my office," Ascher said, and we did, finding ourselves in a room full of cluttered cubicles and desks, opened laptops

209

and secondary monitors.

"Mrs. Weehunt." Ascher turned to me once we'd made it to his desk. "Does your husband have the message on his cell phone so I can hear it?"

"It's on our landline at home. Scott is on his way here, but he told me he could hear Emily crying in the background."

"Izzie," Leavitt said quietly, letting me know I needed to get in control of myself.

Ascher waved another man over, one dressed much like himself. Black slacks. Button-down long-sleeved shirt. Another detective, I assumed. "This is Daniel McCray," Ascher said, then filled him in on why Leavitt and I were there.

"I can call and check the home messages," I told them. "I'm sure Scott didn't erase it." I retrieved my phone from my purse, dialed the number, and turned on the speaker so everyone could hear. The voice was garbled—disguised, Ascher said—but a high-pitched voice cried out in the background. "That has to be her. I know her voice."

Detective Ascher looked at his partner. "Daniel, I can't tell if the caller is male or female."

"Male," Daniel McCray answered.

"Maybe."

"It is a woman crying in the background." Daniel came closer to the phone. "Play it again."

I did. "I *have* to go meet this person," I said. "I wonder if all this is about Velvet's ring?"

Detective Ascher looked at me. "What ring?"

"The ring *you* have. Also . . ." I reached into my bag and pulled out the lock of hair. "I found this on my car seat today. It's Velvet's. I just know it is. Someone left it there while I was away from the car."

"I think it is time for the D.A. to consider dropping the charges against Randal for his mother's death." Leavitt spoke for the first time since McCray joined us.

"Not so fast." Detective Ascher frowned. "We don't even know if this is the Leech woman's hair and, if it is, who is to say where it came from. Could be one of you." He raised his brow.

"The Leech woman was my *sister*." I paused. How much to say? How much to keep close to the heart? "I'm ashamed to say I haven't seen Velvet since she was seventeen. You can ask anyone in this town. They all know the story."

The room was quiet. "I'm not sure this is tied to anything to do with the fire." Detective Ascher held the lock of hair. "We don't know if Emily Greene's disappearance has anything to do with it either."

Leavitt frowned at the detectives. "There is too much going on here. I think this is connected to the fire, and I'd be willing to believe it has something to do with Trevor White's death."

"Now you're pushing it," McCray said.

"Maybe, but I've been doing this a long time and—I just have a feeling."

"Feelings don't count in this business," Detective Ascher said.

"Sure they do." Leavitt sounded calm and confident. "What about the ring found in Ms. Leech's car. It's expensive and is obviously tied to her. What happened to the ring Mr. Collins found in Velvet's car?"

Both detectives looked as if they didn't have a clue what Leavitt was talking about.

Leavitt shook his head and grinned. "Don't tell me Mr. Collins didn't turn in the ring as evidence."

"We haven't seen a ring," Detective Ascher admitted.

"It sounds like your *very* reliable witness isn't so trustworthy," I said. "That ring was an antique valued at twenty thousand dollars. So I suggest you begin with Mr. Collins, especially since he was so quick to accuse Randal of the fire." I pressed my lips together. "Did he bother to mention that Velvet planned on outing him for what he tried to do with Randal?"

Both detectives looked dumbfounded. Ascher said, "I'm not sure what you're implying."

"Of course not. Check with him about the ring." I nodded toward Leavitt. "We're prepared to use our information in court. Tell him that." I opened my mouth to say more. To tell them about Lily and her declaration in her aunt's yard. But . . .

Leavitt touched my arm, a gentle reminder to not say more than

I should. "Your case against Randal burning the house is flimsy at best. But we need to decide how to handle this meeting and help Emily Greene. If we find her alive, we will know all the answers. I'm convinced of this." Leavitt gave me a smile.

"And if that is true, we can't allow Mrs. Weehunt to go because this person might want to kill her and Ms. Greene."

"Of course Izzie can't go. We have to come up with something better."

That is when I excused myself. "Where is your restroom? I'm feeling sick to my stomach. I just need a minute."

"Down the hall and to the right," Detective Ascher said.

I left the room and the building and got in my car. I turned the SUV toward Grassy Bald. I still had an hour to go before I met this kidnapper. Killer. Person. My intention wasn't to go to the fishing camp. That's not where this person would be. I knew that much. I also knew that catching him off guard could save Emily's life, not to mention mine.

CHAPTER 31

Randal

Randal slept a lot, even though he was healing beautifully. Or so the doctor told him. Now that he had the new room, he could tell when it was day and night by looking out his window. The police officer stationed outside of his door often leaned his chair against the glass panel and tapped it by rocking back and forth. Tap, tap, tap. The sound nearly drove Randal insane, probably another reason why he slept so much.

Didn't people with depression sleep a lot?

He tried turning on the TV to drown out the noise, but this only drove him to think of climbing out the window. This, he was pretty sure, couldn't be done without falling to his death. He needed his backpack. The tin of letters would calm him, always did. Had Aunt Isla found them, read them? If so she hadn't mentioned it. He didn't care. When this was all over, he would give them to her. After all, she was the person his mother was writing to. The knowledge of it made him happy and sad at the same time. Sad he couldn't have known his aunt all those years. Something inside told him Aunt Isla would have straightened Velvet out. But he would never know.

Tap, tap, tap.

He clinched his teeth. The doctor had told him this new reaction to noises sometimes accompanied head injuries. He closed his eyes and willed himself to drift off.

He opened his eyes because the door swished. A nurse moved out into the hall. On his table was a Styrofoam cup with lid and straw. "Thank you for the drink," he called.

She was gone without even turning around.

He sipped on the straw. Coke. He hadn't asked for anything. Maybe she was being kind. All the nurses in the ICU had made it their mission to mother him to death, even the male ones. There was a whole new set of people on this floor he hadn't gotten to know yet. He took another long drink.

The doctor said he would stay in the hospital a few more days just to make sure everything was going the way it should. The detectives hated this. At least Randal was becoming used to confinement. He laughed to himself. How weird was he, making a joke about jail? His whole life was surreal.

The window revealed a deep-blue sky. He could smell the river. Of course, that had to be in his mind. He needed a day on the river. He closed his eyes thinking about the fishing camp and fell asleep with the cup in his hand.

CHAPTER 32

Isla

The grass needed to be cut. A gutter dipped away from the eave on the cabin. These were the things I noticed as I rolled to a stop in front of Grassy Bald. A homeowner's work. Instead of feeling complete fear like a normal person would. In and out of the cabin. No one would stop me from helping Emily. When I got to the door, I realized I had forgotten to lock the deadbolt, so the door swung open with the key turned in the original old lock, as if someone was waiting.

My phone went off, but I ignored it. I knew who it was—Leavitt wanting to stop me. Leavitt and the two detectives, no doubt. But when I glanced at the screen, the number that flashed was the assisted living home where Mama stayed.

"Hello."

"Thank goodness, Mrs. Weehunt." It was Alice. "I was so afraid you wouldn't answer."

"What's wrong?"

"Well, your mama is worked up something awful. Nothing like I've seen her since she's been here. She insists that someone came into her room while she was sleeping and searched through her things. What makes this so strange is she gives a lot of details about the person. A girl with long brown hair, skinny like a dancer. She insists on this."

"A girl." Lily. It had to be Lily. What in the world would she want from Mama? "I'll come now," because Mama was more important to me, right then, than anyone.

"Thank you, Mrs. Weehunt. I think it will help her."

"Just give me a few minutes."

I shut the front door, climbed the stairs to the bedroom, and took the chest key from the vanity drawer. I placed the envelope with the photos and Velvet's birth certificate inside and locked it back, returning the key to its place. I kept the brass skeleton key in my tote.

I ran down the stairs and threw open the front door. A tall, shadowy man grabbed my shoulders, and I let out a scream, punching him in the stomach.

He doubled over and I grabbed my tote where I had dropped it and ran for the SUV.

"*Izzie.*"

The voice registered with me and I turned. "Scott."

"I know you haven't seen me in a few days, but I would assume you still remember who I am." He straightened. "They won't let me in to see Randal. I called Leavitt, and he's pretty upset at you leaving the police station. Then you punch me in the stomach. What are you up to?"

"Right now, I'm on the way to see Mama." Not a lie. "The assisted living home called me. Seems she is having an episode, thinking a young girl came in to see her." I spread my fingers, palm up. "The thing is I believe it was real. It's a long story. This whole day has been a long story." A vision of Marcus wafted dangerously close. "And no one can see Randal right now, Scott. Not even me."

"But *I* should be allowed."

"What makes you so special?"

"You know why." He gave me a stern look.

And old anger surfaced but this time it was protective of my nephew. "Now, after all these years, in the middle of a crisis, you want to do this?"

"Izzie," he said, his face growing red, "this secret of yours has always been that stone necklace hanging around my neck, weighing me down. Weighing us down. I had no idea." He took a breath. "Or maybe I knew all along."

"Thank you, Scott, for trying to put your actions and decisions off on me. I don't have any secrets. *You* are in the wrong. You nearly killed me with this, and you ruined things between my family and me. And frankly, you never cared about what was left behind here."

"That's not fair. You and Velvet were on opposite ends of the world by the time I came along." He jabbed himself in the chest. "I didn't cause anything between you two."

"You probably should shut up while you are ahead, Scott." I turned to walk to the SUV.

He grabbed my arm. "Izzie, our marriage began with a deception. Don't you think it's time to face it? You're a liar too."

Indignation rose up like a chokehold. "Who do you think you are, Scott Weehunt? Now, when I may lose Randal to prison for something he hasn't done? Now, when I have to go check on Mama? You want to hash things out *now*? When does it stop being about you?"

"Randal is my son. I know he is. You know he is. I didn't even know Velvet was pregnant. You've known it since you left here vowing never to come back." The finger now pointed at me. "You didn't even tell me he existed. Velvet never bothered. Then you come wagging the kid home, looking just like I did when I was seventeen." He stopped long enough for it to appear the air had been let out of his tire. His breath came ragged. Drawn. Then, his voice lowered as he repeated the truth I'd not wanted to repeat for seventeen years. "He is my son. I may be a two-timing drunk but I don't abandon my own flesh and blood. Tell me I have it wrong, Izzie. Tell me you didn't keep this whole birth a secret." I bit down on my lip as he continued. "You left your family just so I wouldn't find out. Most women would have hated me for what I did with Velvet. I don't have one excuse. This is who I am, and you've always known it."

My hand stung when I slapped his face, but it felt good. "Don't you dare blame this on me. No, I didn't tell you Velvet had a child. I didn't even know she was pregnant until she gave birth on Mama's living room floor that night I left the gorge for good. But I planned on leaving weeks before this happened, before I knew. I left because I couldn't stand to know that my own sister would do this to me. And *you*," I spewed. "I actually thought I could change you. Well, I sure didn't do that. Don't blame me for your bad judgment, Scott Weehunt." I walked away. "Why did you come? To *start* being a father? Because it sure wasn't your worry for me." I reached the SUV, grabbed the handle and opened the door, then looked at Scott. "I will do what I have to do to save my nephew and to save Emily. I will live here on Grassy Bald, and I will divorce you." I jumped into the SUV, started the car, and roared out of the driveway. I had the letters in my tote. But first I had to go to Mama. For the first time since I was little, I wanted Mama, needed her. And I knew that she had loved me the best way she knew how.

≋

Mama sat in her room on the edge of her bed, twisting the skirt of her dress in her hands, mumbling.

"She's been like this for a while." Alice stood in the doorway as I walked over to Mama. "You know, I'm wondering if someone got in here. She seems so sure she saw this girl. Not like her normal imagining."

I took her hands in mine. "Mama, who came to see you?"

She looked at my fingers for a minute and then moved the stare to my face. "Isla, I've lied and lied and lied. I wish I could take all them lies back."

I knelt in front of her. "I'm sorry you're so upset. What happened?"

Her grip was strong. "That girl came here. She told me what happened to my boy. She told me she was sorry that he would be hurt." She looked at me with her complete sorrow. "My boy died, Isla. The girl said he died. I've never been good at this loving stuff. Being a mother wasn't what I expected, and your father stayed on that river in his spare time. He never helped me. Then he died."

"Mama, that doesn't matter now. You were there as much as you could be, and what would have happened to Randal if you hadn't been there for him? I wasn't there. Velvet was Velvet."

She squeezed harder. "I'm not crazy. Don't you remember what happened the night you went after Paul Watkins? You went to get him so he could help. You saved us. If you hadn't been such a brave girl, we would have died. For a long time, I held that against you. When I looked at you girls, I felt dirty, bad . . . bad . . . bad."

A vacuum caught hold of the room, sucking the air out. But I held on to Mama. Held on tight, trying to figure out what Pastor Watkins had to do with any of this. "What are you talking about, Mama? You're confusing me."

"I'm not having problems with my mind, Isla. I know clearly what happened that night. I know I caused your father to die. I ruined Velvet's life, and she ruined yours. And that poor little boy has paid the price. I want a chance to make up for your pain, and for the death of your father. I'm not crazy. Listen to me."

"Mama, you didn't kill Daddy. He drowned, and I don't care what happened that night."

Her laugh was harsh, mean. "Isla, I tried to kill you and your sister with gas. You were eight and Velvet was four. I thought we'd be better off. You smelled the gas and got Velvet out. She was asleep. It was already killing her. That's when you went after Paul. He came to me. He always came when I needed him. Then Mrs. Crow started caring for you girls and watching over me. Keeping me from committing murder."

I tried to pull my hands away, but now she was the one who held on tight. "How can that be? I wouldn't forget something like that." But Mrs. Crow said I had forgotten, and Velvet remembered, held it against Mama. Of course she would. If I had remembered, I would have hated her even more for trying to kill us too.

She looked me in the eyes. "I wasn't a good mother. Some women should never become wives or mothers. I let Kenneth go to die. I had to be on Velvet's side, Isla. It was wrong and that Emily girl didn't help things by telling you what happened between that horrible boy and Velvet. But I had to be on her side. She had no one but me. I owed her because I wouldn't marry her father. I refused, and she paid by being an outsider her whole life."

"You're talking crazy," I said, but parts of her story were making too much sense.

"That girl came today. She said Randal would be punished because of his mother's actions. She said Randal would leave forever." She turned wild eyes on me. "I can't lose my boy, Isla. You have to fix this.

Save him. He is my grandson, my second chance to be a good mother."

I looked at the door where Alice stood. "Mama, I'll look after everything. Quit worrying. It's okay. *Randal* is okay."

I spoke to Alice. "I'm pretty sure she did have a visitor and I think I know who it was. She must have slipped into her room without anyone noticing. The rest of it . . . I don't know. Some truth mixed with whatever her mind tells her."

Mama stamped her foot. "Isla, listen to me. I am not mixing things up. I *killed* your father."

"Mama," I said firmly, "he died in the river when his canoe turned over."

Again the laugh. "Really Isla? Do you believe that? He killed himself because of me."

"No, Mama."

"Yes. I slept with a man and got pregnant with Velvet. I tried to make your father believe it was his child, and he did until the man came to the house."

I pulled my hands away successfully. "Mama." But somewhere deep inside I knew it was true, truer than anything I had ever known.

She raised pleading hands. "Save my boy. It's up to you. He's all we have left of Velvet. He's a good boy."

"I will, Mama." That's all I could say. I should have hated her for what she did to Daddy, but I couldn't. We all have our secrets. Each and every person. As for Mama and me, there was nothing I really knew about my mother. And she knew nothing about me. For me she had always been stern, lost, lonely, standoffish. But she had a life full of bad choices, tragic ones.

Randal needed to know the whole story. He deserved to know his father for better or worse and to know what his mother and grandmother did. And especially why I ran away and hid his existence from Scott. The truth, while bitter, was better than all the lies.

"The girl will not come back. I will find out what happened to Randal that night, and I will find out what happened the night Velvet died. I will do that for you. But mostly for Randal, Mama."

"But someone hurt Randal. The girl said so."

"It's okay," I said as emphatically as I knew how. "He's in the hospital. The police are watching him. He's safe."

When her only answer was a puff of air, I left the room.

CHAPTER 33

I drove, trying not to think about what Mama said. Should I go see Marcus? Tell him to come with me. No. It was almost time to meet this person who had Emily, and I would do this on my own. He wanted the letters. Why? The three I had read told nothing of importance, no secrets, no scandalous truths. The killer knew I would go to the police about the hair, surely, but he—it had to be Stuart—knew I would figure out where to meet him because of the lock of hair left in my car. *Stuart.* Why would he set the fire and kill Velvet? Because of what she knew about him? Maybe. People have killed for much less than a threat of exposure. He had certainly fooled me. I never saw him as a murderer. I misjudged him, but I had known something wasn't right. Felt it. Now he was luring me into a trap. And I was going willingly. But I couldn't think of any other way to save Emily. She didn't deserve to die. I knew this with my whole heart. I had hated her when she was honest and told me she had seen Scott and Velvet together on more than one occasion. I was still at college finishing off my last year. She made a special trip to Atlanta to tell me. Not one part of her wanted to hurt me, only to let me know what was taking place in my absence. I hated her for telling me. I accused her of being jealous of the life I was making for myself with Scott. Had she kept her mouth shut, I would never have known, and I would have been a part of my family. Randal would have grown up knowing me and Scott. But the lie would have revealed itself at some point. Too many people knew. Emily had tried to help me, to make me see the truth, so I would not begin a marriage buried under a lie. Here I was just now figuring her motives out.

The overgrown drive showed signs of a car having driven down it since I was there. And as I suspected, Stuart's truck sat in back of the old cabin. The place was quiet—the kind of stillness that happened before a storm hit.

I had no weapon to protect myself.

I turned on my phone and punched Scott's number instead of the police. The call went to his voice mail.

"I'm at the old cabin at the foot of Pine Log Mountain. This is property my grandmother owned. It sits off the road, but you will see the overgrown drive where I drove in. You'll have to look for it between Mrs. Crow's and Marcus Jefferson's places. Stuart Collins is here. He has to be Velvet's killer and maybe he had something to do with the stuff that happened with Randal and Trevor White. I'm going in to help Emily . . . if she isn't already dead. If something happens to me, Stuart will be the responsible person." I paused. "And Scott, I did keep Randal's birth from you, and there is no real excuse for doing it." I pressed the button to end the call.

The cabin looked sealed, as if it hadn't been open for a while. Since Velvet met her lover there. Stuart knew I was coming. I held the tin tightly in one hand, leaving the tote on the car seat. The brass skeleton key was in my jeans pocket just in case the door was locked. My phone buzzed in my pocket. I looked at the screen. It was Scott.

I ignored it. I had to help Emily.

The back door pushed open with no problem and natural light spilled into the kitchen. A dark, shadowy energy swirled in the air and surrounded me. My phone buzzed again. That time I almost answered it, but I heard a noise in another room. My steps were quiet. As I rounded the corner in what looked like the living room, I saw Emily's camera and purse. Sweat broke out on my neck and forehead. The urge to run was huge, almost too overwhelming. I began to walk down the hall and saw a small shadow move from one room to another. I stepped into a room with a single bed. On the bed was a man.

Dear God, it was Stuart. Dead. His throat cut, his eyes bulging. Blood spilled over the mattress and wall. I shoved my fist in my mouth. Who had done this? *God, help me.* He must have figured out Emily was there. Was she? She had to be.

I peeked out of the room. The hall was empty. The thought of leaving seemed the smartest idea, but I couldn't run off without Emily. One of the rooms had to be her hiding place. Maybe she was in the same shape as Stuart. Somewhere there was a killer.

Maybe watching me.

At the door of the next bedroom, I steadied myself, waiting to come face to face with the person responsible for Stuart's death, for Velvet's. The room was dark. The windows were covered with boards. In the corner I saw a pile of clothes. I blinked. Once. Twice. Hard.

Emily's red sneakers. I moved in fast. "Emily," I whispered.

She moved and there was a soft moan.

"We have to get out of here."

Her eyes were wild. She was tied at the wrists and ankles, a gag in her mouth. I removed it, then wrapped my arms around her to shush her before she began to scream.

"He'll be back," she said.

"Who?"

"I don't know," she whispered. "He came at me from behind. Hit me on the head. I think my ankle is broken. My arm." She looked over my shoulder. "We have to get out of here. I heard—someone—I think someone is dead."

I nodded as I began to pull at the tightly tied knots, managing to get the ropes around her ankles released, but unsuccessful with those that bound her wrists.

"We don't have time for that, Isla. Can you pick me up? Drag me if you have to."

Even with Emily's help I had a hard time getting her to her feet. She muffled her cry of pain and tried to stand on one foot. One ankle turned oddly. She had to be in horrible pain.

I put my arm around her midsection and pulled. We moved a few feet. I listened. Nothing. "Can you hold this?" I gave her the tin of letters, which she clutched between her hands.

I shifted and pulled her again and we made it to the door. "Just a little more. We have to get to the kitchen."

"What about the window in the other room?"

I thought of Stuart's body. I couldn't. "I can't get you through a window. We need to get to the door."

She strained to look in the small room. "Who is it? What happened?"

"We'll talk later. I have to get you out." I pulled again, not caring how loud I was. We entered the brighter living room.

And there she stood blocking the door to the kitchen.

I sighed in relief. "I don't know how you knew to come. But I'm glad you're here, my friend."

Even Emily looked relieved. "Hurry before the killer gets back."

But Kate stood there giving us a simple look, as if we weren't there at all.

"Help us, Kate," I said. "You grab Emily on this side. She has a broken ankle." I looked at Emily. "Kate used to be a nurse before she moved here."

"He should be dead by now." She looked at her delicate gold watch and reached into her pocket.

"What are you talking about?" A cold chill ran across my scalp as if my heart knew before my head. "We have to get out of here."

"You won't be leaving, Isla. I'm sorry to tell you this. And now you've caused *another* person to die." Her head dipped slightly to one side. "And I was going to let Emily live. I needed her to get you here. My original plan was to get Randal here but then that *fight* happened." Her stare turned hard and cold.

"What are you talking about?" Did I sound as hysterical to everyone else as I did to myself?

"Surely you know. You have the letters. That sister of yours never knew when to just stop, Isla. Never. I should have known this would happen. You know who I am. Why I'm doing this. The letters must be filled with the story. I just wanted to live my life out here. Be close to the place where Josh fell in love, as perverted as that sounds. What wife settles, Isla? You should know the answer to that. It's what I like about you. You settled so much with your husband. But then everything got out of control in my life." She waved her hand through the air. I saw the ring on her finger. "I hired Velvet to paint the cottage. I didn't lie about that. She came for a whole month and I liked her. Yes, she was so unconventional, but she was free. I wanted to learn how to be free like her. I encouraged her to start painting again. Gave her the cottage as a studio. Then she wore this ring one day. God help me, I almost killed her on the spot." She shook her fist. "*She wore the ring!*" Her voice was high and brittle. Crazy.

"Who does the ring belong to, Kate? I don't know. I thought it was Grandmother Iris's but there was no description even in the will. There would have been because it is valuable."

She stepped closer to me and a flash of a blade caught my eye. "Yes, that ring is worth so much money. I know *that ring*. You've read her letters. Surely the story is there."

"No. The letters didn't tell me any such thing." I took them from Emily and extended the tin to Kate. "Read them. They are written to me, but she never mailed them. They don't tell me anything about the ring." I balanced Emily against me, her weight almost dead.

Her laugh was insane. "No, no, no." She looked at the tin in her hands. "Well, I'm sorry to have to tell you this, Isla, but Randal is dead by now. He had to die . . . just like Velvet. They both had to die. And now *you* because you got too nosy. You wouldn't let the fire be an accident." Her eyes seemed to blaze. "Why wouldn't you stop? *Why?* I liked you so much. I still do. We could have been *such. Good. Friends.*"

Her words struck me then. *Randal had to die . . .* Had she— "What have you done, Kate? Why are you doing this?"

"I might as well tell you the whole story before you die," she said, as calmly as if she were about to share a cake recipe.

"*What have you done to Randal?*" I screamed, shifting Emily again. "Scott is on his way," I warned her. "He'll know it was you."

"No, he won't. He's probably at the hospital. They are all there by now trying to decide what happened to dear Randal. But that boy couldn't live. I wouldn't allow it."

A rock formed in my stomach.

"Where is Lily, Kate?" Emily whispered.

Kate's face turned into a mask of rage. "Don't speak her name. She's safe at home. Locked in. I had to. She was going to tell. She couldn't tell."

"Tell what?" I inched backward moving Emily with me. If we could get to the bedroom with Stuart, maybe I could lock the door and go out the window.

"That your nephew *didn't* kill Trevor. He wasn't the one. He was almost dead himself. Trevor attacked him when Randal pulled him off Lily. That boy hurt my niece. He was going to hurt her worse, had part of her clothes off. Randal grabbed him from behind even though he was hurt bad. Trevor White began beating Randal again in the worst kind of way." Her voice was soft, methodical, her eyes glazed over as if she were watching it happen all over again. "I came out from behind the pillar under the bridge with a brick and smashed his skull in, but not before I was sure Randal wouldn't live from the beating." She looked at me. "I thought Randal was done for and wouldn't have to be killed. I told Lily what to say." Her lips formed a frown. "But the girl just couldn't hurt Randal. The foolishness about loving him. Him loving her."

"Why is it you had to kill Randal and Velvet?" I took another two steps back.

Kate didn't seem to notice. She seemed to be in another world. "You don't know, do you?"

"Know what?" Two more steps and we were in the hall.

"You really had nothing to do with Velvet. She was not a nice girl, Isla. And she was a thief."

"She could be both of those things, but why kill her?"

"See, I really like you, Isla. You're nothing like her."

"She was my sister, Kate."

"Shut up." She pointed the knife at me. "She took my husband. Took him away from me. I know he loved her. He gave her the ring, his great-aunt's ring. I asked for that ring when the old woman died. Begged him. But he told me no." Her words were again laced with anger. Bitterness. Venom. "Said he needed to sell the ring so he could keep the house. That stupid house meant so much to him. It was the last place his mama lived. He spent every summer there." She looked at me. "I think he must have met Velvet then, back when they were teenagers. He had to. It makes the most sense. He was such a good liar.

227

When I figured out he was having an affair and confronted him, he told me it was someone in his law office downtown. I didn't question it. I was devastated that he would do such a thing. But, in the end, I got him. I took care of him." She took steps toward us. "He had a heart condition since he was a boy. I always teased him that he married me because I was a nurse. I crushed his heart medicine—too many—and put it in his coffee one morning. He drank it and ran off to work like he always did. Told me goodbye. Said we would discuss the divorce that evening. Said he would take care of me." One brow rose. "His car left the road at a great rate of speed and sliced into a tree head-on. He died on impact. Nobody was ever the wiser." Her words were dull, uncaring. "And my marriage was over. He was gone. I never had to deal with his infidelity again. Moving to his aunt's house seemed smart. A new place. You see, I thought his girlfriend—the woman he was going to leave me to marry—lived close to us. And I would have never known otherwise had Velvet not worn the ring to my house. How could I have been so dumb? She was beautiful and wild, everything I wasn't and would never be. I knew I had to kill her as soon as I saw the ring. The whole story was there."

Something deep inside of me cracked. Maybe it hadn't been Lily who'd come to see Mama. Maybe it had been Kate. "You're crazy, Kate. And as for you and me? I have *never* wanted to kill Scott's girlfriends. So you and I are nothing alike."

She stepped toward me with the knife held out. "Maybe I am crazy, but *you* will die, not me."

I took another step back, bringing Emily with me. Emily, who said nothing, and who hadn't so much as whimpered. "But why kill Randal? He had nothing to do with Velvet and your husband. I don't even think he knew him. Velvet kept Josh a complete secret. *Why kill Randal?*"

She laughed long. Mean. "You are dumb. And Randal has her blood and his father's blood. They all deserve to die."

Suddenly, I knew. I understood. "Wait. You're wrong. You're so wrong, Kate."

Kate looked at me thoughtfully. "You're the one who is crazy.

Randal is Josh and Velvet's son. I wasn't born yesterday. He's been coming here since he was a kid. You left. You didn't know about Randal."

"Kate, did you ever ask yourself why I left? Why I never wanted to come back? You are so wrong! Velvet wasn't having an affair with Josh back then. As far as I know she never knew him. I didn't either. We weren't friends with the Bradfords."

"How would you know? They had an affair. That's how she got the ring."

I nodded. "You're probably right about that, but Randal is not Josh's son. They were not having an affair. I know because Velvet was having an affair with Scott. Randal belongs to him," I screamed, not caring for that moment what she did next.

A stunned look crossed Kate's face.

"See? You may have felt the need to kill your husband and Velvet, but Randal had nothing, *nothing* to do with it. You killed a boy for no reason. You're bad. Not just crazy but *bad*."

She looked at the knife. "You might as well stop moving. I'm going to kill you. Both of you." Emily gasped and I squeezed her to my side. "I can't leave you alive. But I want you to know I'm sorry about Randal." She seemed almost apologetic. "I got that part wrong. I'm sorry."

"Why not just stop here. We'll give you a head start. " I stepped back again.

"I can't. Ever. I don't trust you, Isla. Now, it's your time to die."

"There's no reason to do that, Kate." Emily finally spoke. "We would never tell on you. Why would we? You're our friend. You were right to punish those people. Who wouldn't? We've all had our share of bad men. Look at Isla. She's married to Scott Weehunt," Emily reasoned.

I nodded, letting Emily know I understood what she was hoping to accomplish. "And I came here without the police, didn't I? I figured out what you wanted me to do. You're my friend. Why would I turn you in, Kate? Emily is okay. Let us go. You're *not* that kind of woman."

"No, you're forgetting Randal, Isla. You would never let me get away with that. I wouldn't let you get away with hurting Lily. We *are* a lot alike even if you don't want to admit it. It's nothing personal. I killed that Collins man because he had the ring. He was going to give it to the police. But most of all it was when I found out he knew Josh when he was a kid. They hung out together in the summers. He was the one person besides me who knew Josh loved Velvet. Collins was real sorry for blaming Randal for the fire. You thought it was him. You should have stayed away. Left the letters outside. I told that husband of yours for you to leave them outside on the deck of the fishing camp, along with the ring. Didn't he tell you? Then I could have let Emily go in a field or something. You could stay alive, and I would comfort you for Randal's death. You wouldn't have ever known, Isla. You could have gone back to your life with him gone. But you had to get nosy."

"You don't want to kill a Weehunt, Kate. That would be stupid. Scott will have you for lunch, and he is someone to worry about. You're way out of his league."

"Ah, he will not know. The killings will stop, and the cases will be unsolved. I'll leave here with Lily." She stepped toward us, her eyes hooded. "Let's get this over with."

"Isla, let me go and run," Emily cried.

"She's a bleeding heart. She won't do that. Maybe you're right, Isla. We're *nothing* alike." Kate came closer.

When faced with death, a million things ran through my mind but foremost regret. Regret for not having told Randal the whole story. He was dead and I would be too. Regret for not settling things with Velvet. For not standing up and saying what I thought. "You know what, Kate? Velvet was ten times the woman you are or will ever be."

Kate raised the knife and lunged, and I threw myself over Emily.

An ear-splitting noise swallowed the room. I looked up. Kate's blue-eyed stare went dull. A dark spot in the middle of her chest spread across her mint-green buttoned-down shirt. The knife tumbled through the air in what seemed to me as slow motion. Kate collapsed to the floor, and I looked beyond her to where Lily held a handgun.

"Lily," I said calmly. "Put the gun down before it goes off again."

She looked at me and placed it on the floor. "I had to save Randal, Mrs. Weehunt. He tried to save me. I couldn't let Aunt Kate hurt anyone else."

I leaned Emily against the doorjamb, crossed the room, and hugged Lily to me.

The phone in my pocket vibrated. I jerked it out and nearly shouted, "Hello."

"Where in the world are you?" Scott yelled into the phone. "I can't find that cabin and those detectives are right behind me. You've got nearly the whole police force on their way. They were with Randal."

"Randal! Scott, is he—"

"He's okay but it looks like someone put something in his drink. In the hospital."

I cupped Lily's chin. "You're going to be okay, Lily. You were a brave girl." Then I gave my attention to Scott. "We're okay now. But there are two bodies here."

"Where do I turn? Wait, there is an old Black woman by the road."

"That's Mrs. Crow. Remember, she helped Mama with us. She can show you."

"I'll be there."

I looked at Lily. "She tried to kill Randal." The phone still on so Scott could hear.

"I know. I followed Aunt Kate to the hospital and convinced the guard at Randal's door something bad had happened. Aunt Kate had dressed in one of her nurse uniforms and walked right in. I took the drink she left Randal. He drank some but, thank God, not enough to kill him. Then the guard called the detectives, and I told them the whole story. While they were asking Randal questions, I slid out the door. They didn't even notice I was gone. I knew Aunt Kate would be here. She has come here a lot since she killed Velvet. She told me Velvet owned the cabin and wanted to sell it to her." She looked up at me. "Do you think we could get in touch with my parents?"

"Yes, sweetie. We will."

Lily began to sob. "I'm sorry, Mrs. Weehunt, Ms. Greene. I'm sorry for what she did."

"Come on, Lily, let's get out of here." I looked over my shoulder at Emily leaning against the wall.

"Get her out of here. I'm fine."

"Fine, my great-aunt Martha. You have a broken arm and, from the looks of it, a broken ankle."

"Yes, but I'm alive thanks to Lily. Get her out and come back to help me."

Sirens wailed in the distance. I walked Lily out the backdoor onto the patio.

Scott was running toward us. Mrs. Crow looked comical stepping out of his big truck sitting high off the ground as the detectives' car bounded to a stop behind it.

"What happened?" Scott grabbed one of my arms.

"Lily, here, saved Emily and me. She's pretty upset."

Police cars turned into the drive behind the detectives.

Lily was paler than usual. "I need to tell them that Randal's not guilty."

"It's okay," I whispered. "They will know."

Mrs. Crow stood close to me. "Girl, what you gone and got yourself into?"

Ascher and McCray walked up sliding their shades down the length of their noses as though choreographed. Both wore frowns. "Mrs. Weehunt," Ascher began.

I looked toward the door. "Detectives, you really should get inside. There are two dead people in there."

Ascher pointed to me. "We're *not* done here," he said, but he blew out a breath and headed into the house with McCray behind him.

I turned back to Mrs. Crow. "It was the letters. Kate thought I knew a lot about Velvet that I didn't. She assumed my sister wrote about her lover, Kate's husband. She saw them as evidence that she was involved in the fire." I looked at Mrs. Crow. "She had lost her mind."

"I felt it, the evil. It hung in the air all morning. Then that sister of yours stood in my yard and spoke to me. Old Crow always listens when a haint talks. It was her that told me to go to the road and watch for this mess of a husband. Had to show him where you were." She looked at Lily. "But you was the one that saved them. You did it, child."

She took Lily's hand. "You're going to turn out good. Ain't no worries over that."

Police swarmed the house and the yard, everyone talking at once. Before I knew it, Leavitt stood by my side. "What in tarnation did you think you were doing?" Two ambulances came down the road.

"Saving Emily."

"You sure did that." He waited a minute. "They'll be dropping all charges against Randal. It's over, Izzie."

About that time, an EMT and policeman—one I recognized from the fish camp—came out with Emily on a stretcher. I walked over to her, leaving Lily with Mrs. Crow. Leavitt followed.

She reached out and took my hand with her good arm. "Thanks for coming, Isla."

"That's what friends do for each other, Emily. They try to save each other from the bad things headed their way."

A tear rolled down a dirt-smeared cheek.

"I'm sorry I blamed you for being a friend," I said, half smiling.

"Shut up, Isla."

"I have to take this one to the ambulance," the EMT said.

"Sir, will you get my camera out of the living room in there?" She spoke to Leavitt.

He smiled. "I don't think you need a camera, but I'll get it for you."

Emily was going to be okay. I was going to be okay. Randal would move on with his plans. His goals. But it was poor Lily who would live with what she did the rest of her life. No matter all the reasons, she would always know she killed her aunt.

Scott was still there watching me and I turned fully to him. "You're not coming back home, are you?"

I couldn't answer that question. He nodded slowly, then turned and walked back into the cabin.

And then I saw him, running across the field, clearing the old fence with one jump. When he was my friend, he decided to be a priest and I decided to marry the richest boy in North Georgia. A peaceful exhaustion passed through me. Maybe I was just losing my mind or having a breakdown, but I felt peace.

And, as the sun split through the thick leaves on the moss-wrapped branches arching over us, I saw her standing by the old garden gate. Velvet. She smiled at me in a sad way and I smiled back. And Marcus . . . Marcus ran right through her without even sensing her presence.

"Izzie," he said, and I blinked. "Are you okay? I heard the sirens. What happened?"

Words wouldn't form. I just went to him and hugged him.

He hugged me back.

ONE YEAR LATER

"**L**ook, Izzie, it's been raining too hard over the last few days. I'm worried about this stunt."

"Marcus, don't start being a chicken." I stand on the porch of Grassy Bald, watching the drive, waiting.

"He'll be here soon enough. Quit fretting. He probably hit rain between here and Mountain City." He smiles.

"Stop with the rain," I fuss. I always sound grouchy when I am worried.

Mrs. Crow appears in the doorway. "Girl, you'll be just fine. Don't let this worrywart spoil your afternoon. Crow knows." She takes a step outside. "That boy will be here soon, and you go have a good time. Your mama and me will be just right here entertaining each other. I got her sitting on the patio. She's telling me all about the first time she came to this house. And Pastor Watkins will stop by for his daily visit. That man's just as good as gold. Loves your mama something powerful." She chuckled. "You're lucky he does 'cause she can be right mean to him."

"I know."

"You can't be here all the time. Now go and have fun." She points at the truck coming over the hill. "There he is."

My shoulders relaxed. "I haven't seen him in four months."

"College is good for him," Marcus reminds me. "His emails show how he has learned he doesn't have to take care of everyone." He nudges me. "You could learn from him."

"Hush up. You're just as bad as me. You look after everyone." I walk out into the yard.

Randal is driving that gosh-awful truck of Scott's. And he is grinning ear to ear. "Aunt Isla," he calls from the open window, then shuts off the engine, jumps out and runs to me, picking me up. Squeezing. "I'm glad to see you." He sets me back on my feet and leans back with a grin. "Now what is my surprise? You said you would tell me when I got here." He sends one of his warm smiles to Marcus. "Hello, Mr. Jefferson."

"Hello, Randal, and can we make it 'Marcus?' You're making me feel entirely too old."

"So . . . what is my surprise?"

"Wait a minute. Do you want to bring your bags in, see your grandmother?"

"Yes. Of course." He grabs a duffel bag off the passenger seat. "But I want to know."

"How is Scott?" I ask, truly wanting to know about my ex-husband.

Randal finished out his high school living with Scott. He insisted on it. But every weekend he came to the gorge to see Mama and me and to feed those silly goats at Marcus's farm.

"The same as ever. The man drinks way too much but I can't tell him anything. He's not going to change." He squinted one eye. "I love him, though."

"How's school?"

"It's crazy good, Aunt Isla. I think I'm going to be good at this law thing." Randal has decided to become a lawyer instead of a hairdresser. And to my complete shock, I am upset. But he was adamant in his decision. He has high ideals. One can only hope he holds on to them as he grows older.

"And how is Lily?" I ask him.

"She's coming home from Japan next spring to attend Hartford U as a drama major. We're planning to meet in Atlanta. She doesn't want to come back to North Carolina. But she is good."

I smile at him, meaning it. "That's wonderful."

"So is it true? Emily Greene married Leavitt?" And when I nod, he adds, "Go figure."

I shake my head. "I sure didn't see that one coming, but I did see how he looked at her when they brought her out of that cabin. She is happy and so is he and Nantahala needed a lawyer." I wave him inside. "Come on. Go and see your grandmother for a few minutes then meet me out here in your shorts and t-shirt."

"Yes, ma'am." He laughs as he goes in the door.

"Smartie," I say loud enough for Marcus to hear.

"It's good to see him." He reaches for my hand. Squeezes.

We are taking things nice and slow. After the first life I built, I decided I needed to do what was right for me no matter how long it took.

I wish I could say that everything ended happily ever after like in a fairytale, but that's not the real world. But there's not a day goes by but what I don't thank God for Randal. His being cleared of all charges, surviving the attack.

I see his back framed by the French doors. "Hey," I call out to him, "I need a haircut while you're here. You can snip and talk to me about torts . . . or whatever."

"I know," he hollers back. "I can't believe you've let it grow that long. We *have* to find you a hairdresser, auntie."

Yes, Scott is Scott and will probably never change. Our divorce was uneventful. We still talk now and then, especially about Randal. I urge him to stop drinking. He promises he will but doesn't. I worry about him, but I never go to bed and wish I had him with me. I don't love him and probably never did. What did I know about love back then?

Mama is happy with me at Grassy Bald. I don't know for how long. She sometimes wanders down the path to the graveyard looking for Grandmother Iris and Daddy. She seems to always know who Paul Watkins is. He did tell me the story of that night when Mama tried to kill us. That *he* is Velvet's father, and how Velvet knew this before she died. As adults in pain we make stupid choices, and I can't throw stones when I live in a glass house. Mama was the best kind of mama she knew how to be. And Paul Watkins was there for all of us when we needed him.

Randal stands on the porch now dressed in shorts and a tee. "What is the big secret?"

I give him a little smile.

"It looks like rain, Izzie," Marcus warns.

"Hush, Marcus. You know where to meet us."

"Against my better judgment." He gives me a kiss on the forehead and heads for his car.

"Come along, nephew dear. Follow me." I take the path down the hill.

"We're going to the river. Right?" Randal sounds like an excited child.

"Maybe, or maybe we're going to clean the cemetery."

"No. That's not a surprise." He walks beside me, taking my hand.

Soon enough, we stand at the cemetery in front of Velvet's grave.

"You got a marker." He goes close to examine the small marble gravestone for Velvet. *Loving Daughter, Sister, and Mother.* "This is perfect, Aunt Isla."

"Yes, I thought so. I'm glad you like it."

I still have a hard time talking about Velvet. Sometimes I think her death was partly my fault because I left her. But Mrs. Crow's voice always rings in my head that I "can't save no one."

"So this is my surprise?"

"Ha. No. Follow me." I walk ahead of him.

He hoots when he sees the finished fishing camp. "*This* is my surprise. I love it."

"It's yours whenever you want."

"Can I stay there while I'm here?"

"Of course." I smile up at him. "But this *isn't* your surprise."

"Then what is it?" At that moment he sees the two kayaks on the bank. "We're going on the river."

"Yep. We're going on an adventure."

He gives me one of his sly smiles. "On the adventure I've wanted so bad."

"I think you've earned it."

He runs to one of the kayaks. "I can't believe you're not going to overprotect me and lock me in a room all week. Can I lead the way?"

"If you're man enough. And I am *not* overprotective."

"Yeah you are. You're a helicopter mom, always hovering."

"I have to look after Velvet's son."

The water is choppier than I have seen it in a while, but this doesn't scare me a bit. And when the black abyss of the tunnel opens in front of us, it is like seeing an old friend. "Just look, Daddy," I shout into the dark tunnel. "Look at us. We're still a family even after all life threw." The sound of the water absorbs the words. "We will always go to the water, Daddy. Always."

~~~~

"You have to eat dinner with us. Mrs. Crow is cooking," I say this to Marcus.

"Yeah, Marcus. We have to visit for a while. I want to hear about the goats," Randal begs.

Marcus laughs. "You twisted my arm."

"You guys go in," I tell them. "I'll be there in a minute. I need to check on something at the studio."

"Don't get caught up in your writing and forget food, Aunt Isla."

"I won't." I am writing a book about gardening. I walk up the hill to my little herb-and-flower patch. I took the cement bench from the old cabin and brought it here. I'm not sure if Velvet approves. She doesn't visit me anymore. Finally, I believe, she is at peace. Her death has been explained and her son is safe.

Sometimes when I'm deep in my writing, I look up and see Velvet's painting of the fishing camp and think of us as girls, paddling down the river in our canoe, headed to the tunnel. The trees hanging over us. The current churning away. We always went to the water to feel better. I go to the river every day now in memory of Velvet. My sister. If one will only relax in the current, the water will cradle and heal and love. I cherish my sister and have forgiven her completely.

I hope she forgives me.

I choose to hold only the memories of us at the river close. I can only hope she knows that I'm healed.

Finally, I am healed.

The End

If you enjoyed this book, you'll love ...

"Everson's love-story-through-time will appeal to every reader who cheers when love triumphs. This is Everson at her best!"
— Rachel Hauck,
New York Times bestselling author

Dust

a novel

Eva Marie Everson

Available from ShopLPC.com and your favorite retailer.